Milly Johnson is the sparkling and irrepressible author of seven bestselling novels. She is also a columnist, greetings card copywriter, poet and BBC broadcaster. Her books are about the universal issues of friendship, family, betrayal, babies, rather nice food and a little bit of that magic in life that sometimes visits the unsuspecting. Find out more at www.millyjohnson.co.uk or follow Milly on Twitter @millyjohnson

Also by Milly Johnson

The Yorkshire Pudding Club
The Birds & the Bees
A Spring Affair
A Summer Fling
Here Come the Girls
An Autumn Crush
White Wedding

milly johnson

A Winter Flame

SIMON &
SCHUSTER

London · New York · Sydney · Toronto · New Delhi

A CBS COMPANY

First published by Simon & Schuster UK Ltd 2012

1 3 5 7 9 10 8 6 4 2

Simon & Schuster UK Ltd
1st Floor
222 Gray's Inn Road
London WC1X 8HB

www.simonandschuster.co.uk

Simon & Schuster Australia, Sydney
Simon & Schuster India, New Delhi

A CIP catalogue record for this book is available from the British Library

PB ISBN: 978-1-47114-878-1
EBOOK ISBN: 978-0-85720-899-6

Typeset by Hewer Text UK Ltd, Edinburgh
Printed and bound by CPI Group (UK) Ltd, Croydon CR0 4YY

For Pete – who is my John Silkstone, my Dan Regent, my Tom Broom, my Vladimir Darq, my Captain Ocean-Sea, my Adam MacLean, my Steve Feast and my Jacques Glace all rolled into one.

DOUGLAS, Miss Evelyn Mary

*Aged 93, died peacefully in her sleep
at home 6th September.
Funeral to take place 13th September, 11 a.m.
St John the Baptist Church, Ivy Street, Barnsley.
Flowers welcome or donations in lieu of flowers to
the Maud Haworth Home for Cats.*

OCTOBER

Chapter 1

Eve sat patiently in the snug reception area of Firkin, Mead and Mead solicitors whilst the rain outside battered the window as if trying to break in to share the warmth. Winter had landed early on the heels of a very drab summer, almost squeezing out poor autumn which seemed to have come and gone in less than a fortnight. The day reflected Eve's mood perfectly: cold and depressed, as the reason for her being at Firkin, Mead and Mead was not a happy one. Her lovely great-aunt had died and left something for her; the old locket she always wore, most probably. The locket that Eve wished were still around a living Aunt Evelyn's neck.

To pass some time, Eve picked up a copy of the *Daily Trumpet*, which had to be the world's most incompetent newspaper. A snippet on page four grabbed her attention.

'The Daily Trumpet *would like to apologize to the Thompson family for the misprint which appeared in last Thursday's issue. We did of course mean to congratulate David Thompson on his new position as a consultant paediatrician at Barnsley General Hospital, not consultant paedophile. We apologize for any inconvenience this may have caused and wish Dr Thompson a speedy recovery from his injuries.'*

Another mistake – and a particularly horrible one this time. The *Trumpet* was famous for its errors. It had even reported Aunt Evelyn's funeral service as happening at 13 a.m., then in the apology printed 3 p.m. There wasn't time for a further correction and consequently just a handful of people made the service. Aunt Evelyn had deserved so much better. Her funeral had been as much of a disaster as the rest of her life.

The receptionist answered a call then waved over to Eve.

'You can go in now. Mr Mead the younger's office is up the stairs and first door on your left,' she directed.

Eve folded up the newspaper and put it back on the magazine table before going in to meet Mr Mead.

The Meads were solicitor brothers. Mr Mead the younger was so old that Mr Mead the elder must have been injected with formaldehyde to carry on working, and they were always referred to as Mr Mead the younger and Mr Mead the elder. Still, Aunt Evelyn had never used any other firm of solicitors, and it was Mr Mead the younger who had the duty of overseeing her final wishes.

Eve wondered how her aunt had ever been able to profess on oath that she was of sound mind. She was as batty as a bat hanging upside down in a Batcave dressed as Batman, but eccentric as she was, she was also a darling old lady and Eve had been incredibly sad that the ninety-three-year-old had passed away in her sleep. Women like Aunt Evelyn could have fooled you into thinking they would live for ever: robust and bright-eyed, never moaning about any health issues, always dressing immaculately with never a snow-white hair out of place and a heel to her shoe, even if those heels had got lower and thicker over the years. In the past eighteen months, Aunt Evelyn had discovered a joie de vivre she should have experienced in her youth, but alas it was all too short-lived, for four weeks ago she went to bed and never woke up again. Her home help found her in bed with a big smile on her face which the massive heart attack she'd had during the night hadn't managed to wipe off. The vicar at her funeral said, 'Evelyn Douglas died when she was healthy and happy.' Eve couldn't honestly say she found any consolation in that.

Aunt Evelyn might have been content, but she

was also quite mad. Fifteen years ago, she had combatted her customary sadness at having to take the Christmas decorations down on twelfth night by deciding not to, and leaving them up all year round. She didn't care that people said she was loop the loop; her spirits stayed continually buoyant because of that decision. She was happier than she had been for years at being continually surrounded by snowmen, boxes wrapped up as presents, and tinsel. Of course, she had to replace the real tree in the corner with a plastic one as the needles had all dropped off by mid-January, but that was a small price to pay. Her home help went insane with all the dusting of the Christmas ornaments that she collected by the bucketload from charity shops. Anything with a connection to Christmas – however cheap and rubbish – had to be bought. Then eighteen months ago, Aunt Evelyn really upped the ante. She even bought a stuffed elk from eBay. It sat in the corner of her room with baubles hanging from its antlers. She named it Gabriel.

'I needed to see you in person alone in my office,' began Mr Mead the less decrepit, after shaking Eve's hand and directing her to the chair on the other side of his huge mahogany desk, 'because your aunt specifically asked me to deliver this news to you that way.'

'Okay,' said Eve, thinking that it all sounded a

little over the top for a bit of jewellery. The old lady had nothing else of value to leave, although they were things of value to her: the ashes of her cats Fancy and Kringle that she kept in a biscuit tin, her three old broken clocks, her sepia photographs and that monstrous stuffed elk. Eve really hoped her aunt hadn't bequeathed Gabriel to her. Aunt Evelyn always said that the lovely locket would be Eve's one day. It was a beautiful large oval and had two portraits in it: those of Aunt Evelyn and the love of her life – Stanley. She had been engaged to him at sixteen but he had been killed in one of the first battles of the war. Aunt Evelyn had never married, but chose to live with her memories, which she said were enough to keep her warm. Eve knew that feeling well. But Eve was under no illusion that any money would be coming her way. Aunt Evelyn had always said that she would leave her meagre savings and the contents of her bungalow to the local cats' home.

Eve's grandmother had harrumphed and said that was a ridiculous decision; she said it summed up why Great-Aunt Evelyn should have been in a home years ago.

Eve had defended her aunt. 'It's her money, she has the right to do with it what she likes, Grandma.' Evelyn adored cats. Kringle had been her last baby, and it had nearly broken her heart when the twenty-year-old deaf white cat died last year. In fact, Eve wasn't sure she ever quite fully recovered from the shock. She had heard of lots of instances where a beloved animal died and the owner wasn't long in following.

'Your aunt left you this.' Mr Mead opened a desk drawer and pulled out a package, which he passed across to Eve. It was the lovely locket and all her late aunt's photographs. Eve smiled, sighing sadly at the same time.

'Thank you, Mr Mead.'

'And this,' the old man carried on, taking a well-stuffed envelope from the drawer. 'It's a copy of the land deed for your aunt's theme park.'

Eve laughed as her hand reached out for it, even though Mr Mead looked far too sober and professional to make jokes. Then she lifted her green eyes and looked up at his face and saw no humour there. She shook her head to dislodge whatever it was that must be stuck in her ear.

'I'm sorry, could you repeat that, Mr Mead?' she asked.

'This is a copy of the land deed,' obeyed Mr Mead, 'for your aunt's theme park.'

So, she hadn't misheard. Mr Mead really did say that.

'A theme park?'

'That's right. And here are the plans which she put in place for it.' And he handed over a great file of papers which he lifted from the floor. 'It's all immac-ulately organized and documented.'

'A theme park?' Eve said again.

'That's correct.'

'As in rides?' Eve was smiling but it was shock and confusion driving the corners of her mouth upwards. Was Mr Mead on drugs? Was he having a bit of a senior moment and getting her aunt mixed up with Richard Branson? Aunt Evelyn didn't own a theme park. She lived in a one-bedroom rented bungalow with the ashes of her old cats, roomfuls of memories and a stuffed elk.

'You don't know anything about it at all?' asked Mr Mead, scratching his ear. All those hairs in there must tickle, thought Eve.

Eve struggled to find the words to say that no, she didn't know anything about a theme park. Why would she? There wasn't one. That would be ridicu-lous. But all that came out was a shrug and more puzzled laughter.

'Well,' Mr Mead cleared his throat, 'many years ago, your aunt procured a one-hundred-and-fifty-acre plot of land adjacent to Higher Hoppleton. At the time, the landowner, Lord Rotherham, who was a client of mine, was on the brink of bankruptcy and needed to procure cash very quickly. The land was an albatross around his neck, as it could never be used for permanent residential housing, but it could be converted 'for recreational purposes'. I suggested to Evelyn that it might be a good, if very long-term, investment. She agreed so I brokered the deal and it was done. I don't believe your aunt ever intended to do anything with it, except sit on it and wait for a change in the restrictions pertaining to the land, which understandably didn't occur. Then last year, your aunt took it upon herself to have plans drawn up for Winterworld. She employed an architect, who oversaw the installation of mains services, and then she commenced the building works.'

'Aunt Evelyn?' She wondered if Mr Mead had picked up the wrong client file. Dolly Parton's for instance. 'Evelyn Mary Douglas?' Cuckoo Aunt Evelyn, with the seven-foot plastic Christmas tree in the corner of her lounge, and owner of Gabriel the elk?

Mr Mead's shaggy grey eyebrows rose so far they almost left his head. 'Your aunt may have lived frugally, but she was a woman of considerable means,' he continued.

'Frugally? That's putting it mildly,' Eve interrupted. Evelyn had a mania for Mr Kipling's French Fancies, but she would only ever buy them when they were on BOGOF.

'She was a genius on the stock exchange. She had a remarkable nose for exactly the right moment to buy and sell,' Mr Mead continued. 'I thought it was beginner's luck when she first started to dabble, and advised caution, but she was a master of financial enterprise. She could smell a shift in the market as surely as a cat can smell an injured bird.'

'You're joking.' Eve shook her head. Maybe it was she who was on drugs. Those mushrooms she had in her omelette last night did look a bit misshapen.

'I'm not joking at all, Miss Douglas,' said Mr Mead, and it was quite obvious that he wasn't either.

'You'll forgive me if I'm a bit gobsmacked, Mr Mead,' said Eve, flicking a few strands which had worked loose from her tightly tied-back, dark-brown hair, whilst thinking that Mr Mead must be getting a bit tired of her looking confounded and saying, 'You're joking.' 'It's rather a lot to take in. Old ladies don't build theme parks. Especially old ladies who live in Barnsley in one-bedroom bungalows.'

'This one did,' smiled Mr Mead, his eyebrows doing a Mexican wave now. 'I think you'll agree that your Aunt Evelyn was a woman very much made in her own unique mould.' There was a fond softness in his voice now as he talked about the old lady. He lifted another document to the side of him and started to unfold it with his large gnarled fingers.

'This is what your aunt wanted to achieve. I also have the plans proper, but they are heavily detailed and this is perhaps easier to digest, seeing as you're presently in shock.'

It was a crude plan, the words written in Aunt Evelyn's familiar scratchy handwriting, and there were illustrations simply but deftly drawn. There were log cabins amongst fir trees, a restaurant, a grotto, a reindeer enclosure . . . it all looked very festive. It was the sort of map a child would draw in a jotter.

'She was building a *Christmas* theme park?' Eve questioned. Of any theme it could have been, Eve should have known it would be a Christmas one.

'That is correct,' said Mr Mead. 'Apparently she had hundreds of Christmas trees planted there in the seventies. I wouldn't be at all surprised if she had forgotten that she had done so.'

'A Christmas theme park. *In Barnsley*?'

'Indeed. And now it's your Christmas theme park. In Barnsley.'

'Can the theme be changed?'

'Most categorically not. It is stipulated in the will.'

Oh God, anything but Christmas. There was no way on this planet that Eve could live, breathe and eat Christmas as a business. She hated Christmas – loathed it, detested it, abhorred it as much as her aunt had lived, breathed and eaten it. She couldn't think of one Christmas that hadn't been tainted by a sour memory. For the last four Christmases, she had holed herself up at home and read books as if it didn't exist.

'How long had all this been in her head?' Eve
wasn't aware she had spoken her thoughts aloud as
she stared at the plans. She was going to wake up in
a moment and find that she had dropped off at her
desk halfway through arranging a retirement party
for a Chairman with a penchant for cancan dancers.

'She acquired the land in the sixties. She started
building—' he checked his records '—in March
last year. If you peruse the files, you'll find everything you need to know in them. Mr Glace has
his copy also.'

Eve totted up in her head how many months ago
that was. Eighteen. That might explain it. Just over
nineteen months ago, Aunt Evelyn had a mini-
stroke. But rather than it grind her down, she had
bounced out of hospital like a spring chicken. Her
brush with death had totally altered her outlook on
life and sent her mentally off-kilter, if that scraggy
old elk Gabriel was anything to go by.

'She never said a word about any of this and I saw
her at least once a month.' Eve shook her head in
disbelief. Something was niggling at her brain too.
'How can you keep this sort of thing secret? You
can't. It's too big. What was she thinking of? How
come no one knew? This is crazy.' If she scratched
her head any more she'd reach bone.

Mr Mead allowed himself a little smile. 'I thought
she had told you. I rather got the impression she was

planning to when I last spoke to her. Such a shame that she was taken before she delivered her news. She was very excited about it all. Poor, dear Evelyn. You could almost say she was born in the latter years of her life.'

'So it seems,' said Eve, who didn't quite reconcile the rather batty old lady with the power magnate alter ego she obviously had. 'What if I don't want to do anything with the park?' Eve asked.

'You both have three months to either undertake the project or all rights will revert to the other. If both of you resign your rights, then ownership will pass to the Maud Haworth Home for Cats—'

'Wait a minute,' Eve interrupted, holding her hand up in a gesture of *shush*. That's what was nipping at the edge of her thoughts – that name. 'Who the heck is Mr Glass?'

'Mr Jacques Glace is the joint beneficiary.'

'Jack Glass? Who is he? I've never heard of him.'

'All I can tell you is that he is the joint beneficiary of the estate and the person to whom your aunt bequeathed the care of Fancy's and Kringle's ashes.'

Blimey, thought Eve. She must have thought a lot of this Mr Glass to leave her precious 'children's' ashes to him. But that still didn't explain who he was.

Mr Mead shrugged. He would offer no more information on the man other than that he was an associate of Evelyn's, lived in Outer Hoodley and was very tall. And he, apparently, was as gobsmacked as Eve about being left a theme park. Mr Mead had seen him that morning and given him the news. He was going to give both parties a week to study the files to decide if they wanted to take the project forward or resign their rights before meeting again in his office. Eve looked up at the ceiling to see if there were any candid cameras recording her reaction to all this.

'So, let me just get this straight in my brain,' Eve said, tapping both sides of her head simultaneously. 'My aunt Evelyn wants me – and this Jack Glass – to finish off a theme park which she started to build and then run it as a business concern.'

'Correct.'

Eve laughed. 'Well, I presume she's left us a fortune to be able to do that.'

'Yes, that's also correct.'

Eve nearly fainted.

'Subject to all the expenses being approved by you and Mr Glace and myself,' went on Mr Mead. 'Obviously you won't be able to take the monies and spend them on cruises and fine wines.'

'How much did she leave?' said Eve in a voice shocked into temporary laryngitis.

'A very considerable sum,' said Mr Mead. 'I don't have the exact figure in front of me because interest accrues at a daily rate, but I will have for our next meeting. It's quite a few million pounds.'

'A few mill . . .' Eve couldn't even finish the word. This is what lottery winners must feel like – seeing all those numbers on the screen that matched their own and yet there was a membrane as thick as a plank of wood over the part of their brain that let them absorb the information. 'Mr Mead, you cannot be serious,' she gulped, like a bustier, Yorkshire version of John McEnroe. For a moment she thought her life had been hijacked by a computer game – 'Zoo Tycoon' or the equivalent 'Christmas Park Tycoon'. People inherited jewellery and nick-nacks from old aunts, not 'quite a few million pounds' and future expenses for reindeers.

'A fifth percentage of the revenue earned by your venture will be split between your aunt's affiliated charities: The Maud Haworth Home for Cats and the Yorkshire Fund for Disabled Servicemen. Any remaining profit, of course, will be equally divided between yourself and Mr Glace.'

It was sinking in, slowly but surely, that Mr Mead was not as barmy as Aunt Evelyn. Not that it mattered. Eve had little interest in being part of such a ridiculous scheme. She was happy as she was, with a good, profitable events-organizing business, and didn't need or want to change professions and work alongside a total stranger. She was a lone wolf in business and always would be. Jack Glass, whoever he was, could have the bloody thing. It all sounded far too good to be true – and that was a sure sign that there must be catches as big as man-traps waiting for her. Little old ladies who bought stuffed elks from the internet did not know the first thing about building theme parks – how could they? She had obviously just flung her money at a ludicrous self-indulgent project – what a total waste of a fortune.

'I'll think about it, of course,' said Eve. She wasn't that daft to dismiss it all out of hand without looking through the paperwork, but really it was madness. A theme park in Barnsley wouldn't work. People would laugh their socks off at the incredulity of it. A seasonal theme park was especially dodgy – who would want to see Santa in August?

She left Mr Mead's office determined to let the mysterious 'Jack Glass' take the helm and go bankrupt after three months – because that is surely what would happen. But by the time she had got to her car, Eve Douglas's brain was fast at work and a sea change of mind had already happened.

Chapter 2

Try as she might, she could not sleep that night. As if she were in a courtroom, a defence barrister popped up in her head, in full wig and silk ensemble, and presented his case.

'If a ninety-three-year-old woman can do most of the hard graft of planning and starting off such extensive building work, I put it to you, Eve Douglas, that you could not possibly reject the challenge of finishing off what your aunt had begun and make yourself a zillionaire in the process. This is the chance of a lifetime. It is the greatest challenge of your career. Can you tell the court that you could honestly turn your back on that magic word "challenge", Miss D?'

That damned barrister knew that the word 'challenge' was like a red rag to a bull to Eve. That barrister sounded a lot like Aunt Evelyn as well. He was even accompanied by a scent of yellow French Fancies.

Eve abandoned her goose-down quilt, slid her feet into her slippers and headed for the kettle to make some strong coffee. She knew there was no way she would get a wink of sleep until she had taken those files apart and read every word. So she did. Then she checked out the competition on the internet. Then she made a note to ring her friend in the morning and borrow her secret weapon – Phoebe May Tinker.

'I didn't get you up, did I?' asked Eve, with the hint of a yawn. After all, she'd only had four hours' sleep.

'Are you joking?' returned a jolly voice. 'I'm up sorting out her ladyship's Crunchy Nut Cornflakes. You're ringing early. Are you okay?'

'Sort of,' said Eve.

'You don't sound so sure.'

'Alison. Aunt Evelyn left me her locket.' Eve thought she'd build up to this one slowly. Alison was six months pregnant and she didn't want to shock her too much.

'Aw, bless.'

'And a theme park.'

Alison laughed. 'Alton Towers or Pleasure Island?'

'Neither – Winterworld. And I'm not kidding.'

Now there was a shocked silence on the other end of the phone.

'Winterworld is a one-hundred-and-fifty-acre

plot just outside Higher Hoppleton. Aunt Evelyn bought the land in the sixties as an investment and then last year went mad and starting building log cabins on it, apparently.'

'Dear God, you aren't joking,' said Alison, half laughing, half breathless with amazement.

'Nope. That is as much as I know for now. I'll fill you in with more when I've got my brain around it all. Anyway, why I'm ringing you is because I want to borrow Phoebe to come with me to Birmingham on Saturday. There's a place called "White Christmas" that I want to check out. I thought she could help me spy.'

'I'm sure she'd be delighted,' said Alison.

'Wonderful. I'll pick her up at nine.'

'She'll be ready,' said Alison. 'Blimey, Eve. You really do know how to start my day off with a bang. I'll have to ring Rupert and tell him. It's not every day your oldest friend has news like that.'

Eve put down the phone and wished her life was more like Alison's. A smooth ride instead of a roller coaster of white-knuckle dips and rises. Especially as there had been more dips in the past five years than she cared to think about.

Chapter 3

'Auntie Eve, why is that elf smoking?' Phoebe pulled down on her honorary aunt's sleeve as she asked the question at 43,000 decibels. The said elf gave the small red-haired child a resentful sideways sneer that would have put Elvis to shame, before placing the cigarette to her lips one last time, then dropping it on the floor and twisting the ball of her foot on it. Eve was itching to respond to the seven-year-old with the same volume.

'I don't know, sweetheart. I think Santa should kick that elf's backside because she's not exactly doing a great PR job for him.' But the elf looked very big, very butch and that short cropped hairdo said 'New Hall prison' more than 'North Pole'.

'Santa will be back in a minute,' said the elf grumpily when the little boy at the front of the queue asked where he was. Eve half expected the elf to go on to explain that he had gone for a piss.

She wouldn't be surprised at anything after what she had seen so far. It was all so fantastically, brilliantly awful and super-tacky.

'Let's go for a look around and come back later,' said Eve, taking Phoebe's hand. 'And let Father Christmas get on with his jacking up,' she added under her breath.

The 'White Christmas' theme park had made all the national papers recently for being a total and utter rip-off, earning it the nickname 'Shite Christmas'. So, in Eve's opinion, there was no better place to do some market research than here, especially with the aid of Phoebe May Tinker, who was a cross between Simon Cowell and Hedda Hopper in judging children's entertainment attempts. A half-dead pilot light inside Eve coughed into certain life when she read about Shite Christmas on the internet. She knew it was going to be awful but never anticipated it could be quite this bad.

Young Phoebe May Tinker was seven going on forty-five. She was an intense child with the big, wide inquisitive eyes of an old wise owl and nothing got past her. She was a mini-me of her ridiculously intelligent father, Rupert, whom Alison had met at Oxford University when she was studying classics and Rupert was studying something scientificky and genius-sounding like 'advanced nuclear physics and chemical extra science'. Alison was now expecting a boy and Eve had no doubt that he would emerge into the world as flame-haired as his parents and correcting Einstein's theories.

But Phoebe, funny little dot that she was, was also a darling of the highest order, and she was one of the very few people that always managed to make Eve smile. Eve loved the feel of her little hand seeking out her larger one and finding security there. She had always wanted children one day. Phoebe, along with Alison's unborn son, were going to be the closest she ever got to that ambition being fulfilled.

Not many of the parents were smiling much, having paid out forty pounds per head for the 'Lapland Experience'. Well, if this was anything like Lapland, no wonder Santa disappeared for 364 days of the year; he was probably in therapy. Eve was now panicking that she might have scarred Phoebe for life with this day out.

The ticket man at the front door couldn't have smiled less if he'd tried. His 'Welcome to White Christmas' was delivered with as much cheer as a funeral director commiserating with relatives of the deceased. He would have been superb had this been 'Halloween World' with his gaunt, pale, Hammer Horror face.

The 'snow-covered paths' were grey-white painted concrete. A very noisy snow machine was spitting out snowflakes from behind the tallest tree in a copse of plastic fir trees. At least they were supposed to be snowflakes – but in actual fact were a 50/50 split between ice shrapnel and splashes of water. An engineer in a bright orange suit could clearly be seen trying to adjust it, and had been heard issuing profanities until one of the elves – a six-foot youth whose green trouser hems had long divorced from his ankles – disappeared behind the tree and was heard telling old Tango-suit to watch his fucking language.

'Rudolf's pen' housed a reindeer with a red flashing nose who was turning his head mechanically from side to side as if in disbelief. Even he was embarrassed to be there and was going to have serious talks with his agent – and he was plastic.

Eve and Phoebe pootled off for an early lunch. The 'Elf Café' made the refectory from Oliver Twist look like The Ivy. The look aimed for was 'rustic', the look achieved was 'workhouse'. The menu was 'alternative-delicious', Eve thought with a delighted smirk: chicken nuggets, chips, hotdogs, cheap-quality beef burgers with or without cheese . . . Rubbish. There wasn't a bit of thought or imagination which had been put into it – and yet it was heaving at the gills – even after the slating it had received in the nationals. Eve's palms started itching with the anticipation of heavy amounts of profit touching them.

Phoebe bit down on a chicken nugget and chewed it delicately.

'What do you think?' asked Eve, giving her a nudge.

'Do elves really eat chicken nuggets?' asked Phoebe, her forehead creased with thought. 'I'd like to think that they do.'

'I think some of them eat rather a lot of chicken nuggets,' thought Eve, looking at the gigantically fat elf operating the till. He had fingers like thick pork sausages and a selection of chins on display.

'What would you imagine elves eat, Phoebe?' asked Eve, biting down on a chip.

Phoebe considered the question and Eve could almost hear the cogs turning in the big brain inhabiting that little head.

'I think lots of soup and nice bread,' said Phoebe eventually. 'And Polar Bear pie.'

Eve coughed and nearly choked.

'Not sure I'd like to eat a nice fluffy polar bear,' said Eve, hoping to implant some environmental friendliness into the small girl.

'It wouldn't be made of polar bears, silly,' tutted Phoebe. 'It would be called Polar Bear Pie because it was their favourite.'

'Ah,' said Eve. And phew.

'And lots of ice cream,' added Phoebe, after some more thought. 'I think elves would like lots of different flavours of ice cream.'

'Oh yes, they would, wouldn't they?' nodded Eve, thinking, *Bless you Phoebe, you're saying all the right things*. Who needed to pay marketing consultants when you had Phoebe May Tinker in your corner? Seeing a theme park through the eyes of a child was the best way forward.

'And they'd drink snowberry juice,' said Phoebe, reaching for the tomato ketchup in the sauce-covered plastic bottle.

'What's that?' asked Eve.

'It's very cold and white,' whispered Phoebe, as if imparting a great secret.

Snowberry juice. Eve liked the sound of snowberry juice. She envisaged something sweet and slushy and – as Phoebe had said – icy cold.

The only ice creams available in the Elf Café were Magnums and Cornettos. Eve thought of her cousin Violet who owned a beautiful little ice-cream parlour in Maltstone. Violet, whom she hadn't seen half as much as she should have liked and was going to make up for that. 'White Christmas' might have been a disaster, although it pulled in visitors because it had a certain novelty value, but it really wouldn't take much to trump it.

Eve's head was churning with ideas. The theme park didn't have to be all about Christmas – there was so much more to winter than Santa and elves. And thank goodness for that, too, because Eve's brain wouldn't have been whirring that much over a park full of all that sort of twinkly tat.

The husky ride was closed until further notice, much

to Phoebe's disappointment. They did, however, go into the doggy stables to look at the huskies, two of which were snarling German Shepherds and vicious enough to have Santa's leg off as soon as look at him.

'Let's go and try Santa again,' said Eve, hoping to cheer Phoebe up. She had been so looking forward to having a husky ride.

The *Prisoner: Cell Block H* elf was still on sentry duty outside Santa's grotto – or rather his B&Q shed with some cotton wool balanced precariously on top of it. The queue was long, but Eve noticed that it was going down quite quickly. As she neared the front, she saw that the shed was divided into two – *two* Santas. How the heck was she going to explain that one away? Luckily this was Phoebe.

'I don't think either of these are the real Santa,' whispered the little girl, as one of the Santa's heads popped out of the front door to see how long the queue was. Underneath the very bad beard and wig ensemble, his dark-brown hair could clearly be seen, and his youthful unlined face.

Blimey, chuckled Eve to herself. I must be getting old if Santa looks young.

The convict-elf eventually directed Phoebe and Eve into the right-hand side of the shed with a flick of her head. Their Santa had a big red nose and make-up on his hands, which didn't quite cover up the LOVE and HATE tattoos.

'Ho ho ho,' he said, doing the fakest laugh in the world. 'And what's your name, little girl?'

Phoebe's eyes were glued to his nose.

'My name is Phoebe May Tinker,' she said. 'Is your nose real? Do you have high blood pressure?'

Santa spluttered and moved swiftly on. 'And what am I going to bring you on Christmas Eve?'

Still staring at his veined conk, Phoebe replied, 'Well, you won't be bringing me anything, because you're not Santa, are you? The real one will be bringing me a bike with a basket and a Snow White princess costume.'

Santa looked mightily relieved to be rescued by another elf making an entrance through the door at the back of his half of the shed holding a camera. This poor elf was plagued with acne and Eve just hoped that Phoebe didn't draw attention to it.

'Your ear's just fallen off,' said Phoebe, reaching down to pick up a plastic pointed ear.

'Cheers,' said the spotty elf with a heavy sigh. 'Elves' ears are always doing that.'

'Your ear can't fall off if it's real. And this one is quite obviously plastic,' humphed Phoebe, and her unimpressed face showed as she posed for a snap with Santa. The elf disappeared again to process the photo whilst Santa delved into his sack and pulled out a pink package with 'Girl – under 10' written on it. It didn't take an idiot to see it was a book, but that was okay because Phoebe loved books. She had ripped off the paper before Santa had even started to say, 'Put it under your tree at home.' Her lip curled over to see that the book was *Thirty Facts You Always Wanted To Know About Aircraft*.

'Oh dear,' said Santa, baring his teeth. He reached into his sack again and pulled out another book labelled 'Girl – under 10'. This time he made sure he asked her to put it under her tree before she opened it. Santa's cheeks were growing as purple as his nose. There was a vein in his neck throbbing so much that Eve thought they ought to get out before it exploded.

Eve took Phoebe's hand and led her out of the back of the shed where the spotty elf with the dodgy ear was waiting for them, holding a photograph of a very unsmiling Phoebe and the tattooed Santa.

'That will be five pounds please,' he said, holding his palm out.

'Do you eat a lot of chocolate?' Phoebe asked, staring up at his face.

Oh God, thought Eve. 'Er, isn't a photo included in the price?'

'Ooh no,' said the elf.

'It's okay, I don't want it, Auntie Eve. He's not the real Santa,' said dear Phoebe. But Eve paid up. She wanted this photo very badly. She would put it on her desk as a reminder of the start of it all – the moment when she realized that Great Aunt Evelyn wasn't as barmy as she first thought.

Chapter 4

As hoped for, Phoebe was totally and utterly unimpressed by Shite Christmas. In the car on the way home, Phoebe was only too happy to give a list of all the things she hated about it: plastic reindeer rather than real ones, no husky ride, very ugly elves with droppy-off ears. Although she did give the chicken nuggets nine out of ten.

'Phoebe, if I had a theme park like that, would you help me choose what sort of things I would need?' asked Eve.

Phoebe's face lit up as if someone had switched on a 1,000 watt lightbulb behind her eyes. 'Oh, Aunt Eve, can I? Will you have a reindeer like Comet in the *Santa Claus* films that pumps?' And she giggled and made some very impressive farting noises. She was only seven after all.

'Well, er, not sure about the reindeer,' Eve brushed

over that one quickly. She had seen Aunt Evelyn's plans for a reindeer enclosure but that wasn't going to happen. They would smell and need feeding and cleaning out and all that complicated stuff. Far too high maintenance. And possibly a health and safety hazard too with those antlers. She didn't want to get sued because a reindeer had kebabbed a small child.

'You need ice cream,' said Phoebe. 'Lots of ice cream. And chicken nuggets. But you could call them something much more Christmassier, like—' she mused heavily for a moment '—penguins' feet.'

'Great idea,' Eve encouraged, although she wanted to gag slightly. Maybe they wouldn't go with that idea either. Phoebe May had a bit of a way to go in marketing yet, but she was spot on with the ice cream. Eve had made plans to ring her cousin Violet as soon as she got home. Violet was the queen of ice-cream making and it would be a good excuse for a long overdue catch-up. Once upon a time they had been nigh on inseparable, but since Jonathan had blasted into Eve's life, turned it upside down and left her so suddenly, Eve had been embarrassingly lax about seeing her family and her friends. She had been reminded, after visiting Alison, how good it was to talk and have a coffee too – and how little time it took up really. Her business hadn't collapsed for taking a few hours off – she could have seen more of Violet and her mother – Auntie Susan – if she had really tried harder.

'Lots of Christmas trees with sparkly lights and snow,' continued Phoebe, on a roll now. 'And nice shops and cakes and elves and a real Santa's workshop. And mince pies and rides and white horses.'

'If I got this right, I could be sitting on an absolute goldmine,' Eve mused as Phoebe reeled off a list of essentials from polar bears to snowball-fighting arenas. Shite Christmas, with its smoking elves and Father Christmases not old enough to start shaving was a revoltingly brilliant money-spinner despite being absolute rubbish. So how much revenue would a really good, top-notch, winter theme park bring in?

Phoebe fell asleep an hour into the journey, exhausted from thinking up all her ideas. Eve's brain was in overload. Having visited Shite Christmas, she saw first-hand just how much work was involved in running a theme park, but boy was she excited about getting started.

'I put it to you, Eve Douglas, that you could do this,' said that silky, seductive barrister voice in her head. 'If anyone can, you can.'

And Eve knew that was true. She was a master at organization and covered every base. She had built up a reputation of being a shrewd, resourceful businesswoman who left nothing to chance – her clients trusted her to do a polished job and she delivered every time.

Eve hadn't really known what she wanted to do when she left school, so drifted into office jobs and then to a building society where, eight years ago, she took a voluntary secondment into the Events Coordination department and found her niche in life. When the secondment ended, she knew there was nothing else she wanted to do but more of the same and took a leap of faith by starting her own events-organizing company. She'd been lucky, as one of her first clients had been let down at the eleventh hour when the organizers of his wife's fiftieth birthday bash went bankrupt. Eve found a barge, caterers, comedian and a band, set up a bar and had the boat decorated in pink balloons and bunting all within eighteen hours. That client was delighted – and very well connected. Bookings began to fill Eve's diary and recommendation followed recommendation.

If people wanted a James Bond party, Eve Douglas didn't just supply the music and a gold statue, she drafted in lookalikes of Bond villains complete with white cat, arranged for vodka martinis (shaken not stirred) to be served on arrival, Aston Martin taxis, and on one occasion engineered an appearance by Pierce Brosnan. Eve went the extra mile with everything she did and the result was that her accountant was a very happy man. Eve's Events was a profitable and growing business and she had been approached on three separate occasions the past year alone by companies wanting to buy her out. She had kept their details, never thinking she would open the file. But Eve knew that she couldn't run Eve's Events and Winterworld. Well, she could at a push, but Eve's style wasn't diversifying – she liked her energies channelled to one place. She would need to think very carefully about which path she was going to take.

Eve carried a sleeping Phoebe into Alison's lovely barn conversion of a house.

'She's out for the count,' she smiled, putting Phoebe down on the sofa in the lounge.

'Come and have a coffee,' said Alison, waddling into the kitchen. 'I'm not letting you go without giving me some more details on your inheritance.'

Eve took a seat at the island in the centre of the huge kitchen/dining room and watched Alison making coffees. She had never seen her usually tall and waif-like friend so round – or as content. Serenity was coming off Alison in waves.

'You look so beautiful,' said Eve.

'Piss off,' laughed Alison. 'I haven't seen my feet for weeks and I'm ravaged by heartburn and backache. Tell me something to take my mind off things.'

'What do you want to know?'

'I want to know everything. I still can't believe it all. Rupert thought I was drunk when I told him.'

'I know how he feels,' chuckled Eve. 'I can't take it all in myself. Aunt Evelyn of all people, with all those secrets under her belt. It's . . . crazy.'

Alison brought over two mugs and an opened biscuit tin.

'Dunk one of those chocolate ginger biscuits, they're to die for,' she commanded. 'Are you still going to keep Eve's Events running?'

'I don't see how I can. It's more than a full-time job and I can't do two full-time jobs. I've had a couple of offers to sell over the years, so I'm going to put out some feelers.'

'That's a shame,' said Alison. 'You've worked so hard.'

'Well, I took a leap of faith starting it up so I'm just going to have to take another one letting it go,' Eve sighed, reaching for a biscuit. 'Oh and I haven't told you the best bit. Aunt Evelyn only left me half of it. The other half she left to a total stranger – A Mr Jack Glass. I can't wait to find out who the hell he is.'

'Pardon?' Alison stopped mid-biscuit chew.

'You heard right. Aunt Evelyn never mentioned him at all. But yet he's one of the main beneficiaries of her will. And that is as much as I know about him. Until I meet him in a few days.'

'And she never mentioned the name to you?'

'Not once.'

'When was the last time you saw her?'

'Two months before she died,' replied Eve with a small cough. Usually she visited her aunt once a month but her work commitments had been so heavy recently she'd missed a visit and rang Aunt Evelyn instead. She felt rather ashamed of that now – especially as it would only have cost her a couple of hours of her time and she could have spared that really if she'd tried. Her Aunt Evelyn looked forward to seeing her so much.

'Dear God,' said Alison, resuming scoffing of biscuit. 'Your aunt really did have a lot of secrets in her life, didn't she?'

'So many that I don't think I knew her a quarter as well as I thought I did,' sighed Eve.

As soon as Eve got home, she unfolded her aunt's simple plans and those far more detailed drawings by the architect over her large dining table; she saw more possibilities every time she did so. In the middle of the land, her aunt had foreseen 'an enchanted forest' of Christmas trees with a twirly path cutting through the middle. Evelyn had drawn a horse and trap on the path along the route with the word 'snow ponies' written above it, and a miniature railway line was also present. At the left side of the forest was a reindeer enclosure and stables. To the right were a collection of log cabins, one labelled gift shop, one a restaurant and some unnamed. At the far end of the development was a funfair dominated by a sketch of a huge carousel. Santa's grotto was one of five more log cabins next to the funfair. Three of the cabins were bracketed together and called 'honeymoon cabins'. One was marked as 'the wedding chapel'. Eve peered at it while shaking her head. Surely her aunt wasn't that batty as to think that anyone would seriously want to be married in a theme park? This was South Yorkshire, not Las Vegas after all. A vision of Santa in black sunglasses and tassels, singing 'Suspicious Minds' whilst smelling of peanut butter and burgers, suddenly came to mind. It wasn't a pretty image.

Eve put her pen down and closed the book. Organizing a black-tie corporate event with dancing waterfalls was one thing – seeing that this ridiculously ambitious theme park was built, marketed, advertised and managed was another.

Eve looked up at the ceiling and imagined beyond it, right up into the stars, where her aunt would be sitting with Stanley looking down at the havoc she had caused in her great-niece's brain. She would know that Eve wouldn't be able to resist the challenge she had set her.

'You wicked old bird,' said Eve to the sky. 'What the hell have you done to me?'

Ideas were crowding to get into her brain. She

needed that smoking elf to keep them at the door
and let them enter one at a time. But first things first
– she better meet up with this 'Jack Glass' and suss
him out as a business partner. Eve worked alone as a
rule, but for 'quite a few million pounds' she just
might be persuaded to see if she could put up with
the man.

Chapter 5

Over the next few days Eve worked on tying up the future of Eve's Events, as well as overseeing a fortieth birthday party and sourcing a consignment of green-tinged champagne for an Irish wedding. If she were going to sell up, she wanted to make sure that the right people took over and things went as seamlessly as possible for her clients. She met with the three companies who had expressed interest in buying her out. By far the best offer was from the biggest of the three: 'Paul's Parties'. Paul Hoylandswaine was a local entrepreneur with his finger in more pies than a room full of Little Jack Horners. He was a bruff but straight man who didn't do bidding wars or time-wasting: he knew what he wanted and went straight for the jugular. He said that if Eve was serious about letting her enterprise go, she wouldn't find anyone who would look after it and continue to build it up more than he would, and he'd have contracts drawn up in two days for her to sign. Eve hadn't wanted to move quite that fast, but Paul Hoylandswaine said he wasn't going to 'fanny about' whilst she hummed and ha-ed. The deal was on the table with a now or never sticker on it; he didn't stop balls rolling when they were in motion. Eve had a massive moment of panic. If Winterworld folded, she would have nothing. She knew where she was running Eve's Events, but Winterworld was a trip into the dark, scary unknown. But the moment passed and Eve found her hand extending to shake his and the deal was done.

Winterworld would have to be a success, because Eve didn't go backwards — at least not in business. She might have been stuck in the past in her personal life, but in her career, she would only ever allow herself to move forwards. She wasn't a natural gambler but this was an extraordinary business which merited out-of-the-box thinking. As she signed on the dotted line she knew that however much of a knobhead this Jack Glass turned out to be, she would have to get on with him now.

Eve loved working for herself with no boss to answer to and she was disciplined enough to do that. Winning new clients excited her; earning lots of money thrilled her. People liked her and trusted her and found her easy to deal with — that was indicative in the repeat custom she received. She knew she was taking a massive gamble on Jack Glass being the same. What if he was an obnoxious cretin whom no one wanted to do business with?

She remembered taking Jonathan off to a very expensive hotel in Denmark for the weekend after banking a particularly massive cheque. These days she hadn't anything as exciting to spend it on though. All her money went into the bank and sat there twiddling its thumbs.

She had scribbled quite a few alterations on Aunt Evelyn's plan for the park as well. The wedding chapel had been changed to a second gift shop and café, for a start. Food, that's where the money was – not in silly whimsical chapels that would probably bring in one booking a year and be a total waste of a building. The reindeer enclosure had been changed into a coffee shop and picnic area. Livestock only ran up vets' bills although it did, she supposed, make some commercial sense to have the ponies, if they were to be working and earning their hay or straw or whatever they ate pulling hired carriages and were not just stuck in a field pooing. She even wondered if there was any mileage in the idea of selling snow-pony poo to gardeners (it was just a thought). She had also claimed one of the log cabins near the restaurant as an ice-cream parlour. If she could get Violet on board that would be fantastic. Not just because she made the best ice cream in the world, but because she would have an ally firmly in her camp in case Mr Glass turned out to be a right old tosser with no business acumen at all. Any friendly weight on her side would help in levering him out. She would be meeting him tomorrow anyway. And all the many questions she had about him were at last going to be answered. Or so she thought.

Chapter 6

Sitting in Mr Mead's office, Eve rolled *his* name around in her mouth. The spelling, she had learned, was *Jacques Glace,* not Jack Glass. She imagined a number of personalities which that name would suit. A fifty-something French fop with frilly cuffs, a giant quiff and a blue rinse. Carrying a toy poodle. Or a very young, arrogant, nerdy-student type with a big coat and a Masters in philosophy, a long Dr Who scarf wound around his neck. Eve still couldn't work out how Jacques Glace had managed to jointly inherit a very valuable chunk of land from her aunt. She considered the possibility that Aunt Evelyn had acquired a young, slim, six-packed Jacques Glace as a gigolo, and the land was his payment for 'services rendered'. She dismissed that immediately as being totally daft and so out of character for Aunt Evelyn it couldn't be taken seriously for a second. Then again, everything she had learned about her aunt recently was out of her character – did she really know old Evelyn that well? The disclosures of the past couple of weeks had made her wonder. The sweet, quiet Aunt Evelyn who lived surrounded by very old sepia-coloured memories and had a penchant for Mr Kipling cakes was not the woman she recognized from all the recent revelations. It was how Lois Lane must have felt when she discovered who Clark Kent really was.

Eve had thought of nothing else but plans for the park since she had visited White Christmas. But she wanted to run it her way and not have to make joint decisions. Maybe – she hoped – he'd be willing to act as a silent partner and let her get on with it. With two cooks, the winter broth was more than likely to get spoiled. Anyway, Mr Glace would soon realize that he couldn't be as imaginative or good at organizing as she was; and when he saw that he would recede into the shadows and go and buy a boat to live on and ring up every year to check on the profits. She could live with that arrangement, she supposed.

Eve looked out of the window at a very rainy, bitter October day as they waited for the arrival of Jacques Glace. The Christmas lights were already up, strung across the central Barnsley street. If the start of Christmas became any earlier, Britain was going to end up being like Aunt Evelyn's house and not bother taking its decorations down. The shops had been filling up with Christmassy things since early September, forcing everyone to start feeling the pressure. Eve could have quite happily taken a flight to somewhere hot and sunny as soon as she saw the first Christmas card on a shelf and not returned until 2 January. However, Christmas for Eve's Events was a lucrative time – she had to stick around and be tortured by it.

As she sat waiting for Mr Glace to turn up – he was already late by an annoying ten minutes – she mused about Christmases past. She supposed she must have had some happy memories about the season, but they were buried beneath the weight of the unpleasant ones. For every recollection of being at her Auntie Susan's, stuffed full of good food, there were five of her mother either drunk, sleeping off a party or snogging like a teenager on the sofa with a transient boyfriend. Eve remembered having fish fingers for Christmas lunch once because her mother was too stoned to cook anything else. Ruth Douglas flitted from man to man and home to home like a not-alto-gether-there butterfly and Christmas was an excuse to become even more of a sybarite than usual. Eve always felt as if she were outside a huge snow globe looking in at other people's merriment and enjoyment of Christmas whilst being unable to be part of it. The memories of her Christmases past were scented with cannabis, stale beer, and cheese and onion crisps. And the one Christmas which she felt might herald her entrance into that giant snow globe was the unhappiest and most terrible of them all.

Footsteps thundering up the stairs disturbed her reverie and ruled out the possibility that Mr Glace was a light French fop. He sounded more like a carthorse with Dutch clogs on.

Whatever she expected Jacques Glace to be like it wasn't the man who blustered into Mr Mead's office with a knitted hat on, complete with ear flaps and woven woollen plaits. He had an Arctic explorer coat on, the collar pulled up to his nose, and the biggest padded gloves that Eve had ever seen. The weather, however bad it was, didn't warrant that amount of anorak. This was Barnsley town centre, not Antarctica.

'Ah, Mr Glace,' said Mr Mead, standing and holding out his hand. 'Isn't it a cold one today?'

'*Oui*,' said Mr Glace. So he *was* French then. How the hell did Aunt Evelyn end up leaving half a theme park to a French man with hypothermia?

Eve took him in from top to bottom, and then back up again, where she found his eyes waiting for her. And very blue they were too. That was a bit embarrassing, she thought, him watching her watching him.

'Mr Glace, this is Miss Douglas.'

'*Bonjour*,' he said, holding his huge gloved hand out. Eve held hers out and his mitten totally engulfed it. And it was puddle-dropped-in soggy. His hand-shake was energetic to say the least – she was surprised her arm was still in its socket by the time he had released her. Eve pulled her hand back and tried to dry it surreptitiously on her trousers but she wasn't subtle enough and she heard a muffle of three syllables which could have been 'so sorry'.

'Do take a seat,' said Mr Mead, indicating the chair next to Eve.

'Muffle muffle,' Mr Glace replied, but no one could understand what he said. Eve felt herself sighing impatiently as Mr Glace wrestled with the zip on his coat, then decided that he might need to take his gloves off first, but seemed to be having some difficulty doing that. Eve wouldn't have been surprised to find that his gloves were threaded on a string through his sleeves. Mr Mead and Eve waited until the ridiculous Mr Glace tried to gain some purchase on one glove with the other. He tugged hard to no avail, then harder, with the result that the glove flew off and hit Eve square in the face.

'Mom mom mom mom,' was the sound that came out of the big coat.

'It's fine,' said Eve, in a voice that intimated it was anything but fine. She lifted the glove with one finger and handed it back to Mr Glace as if she had just picked up a dead rat. Then she dabbed at her face to dry it whilst Mr Glace took off his other glove and unzipped his tent of a coat.

Eve's brain had not been in appraising mood for a long time. If it were, she might have found her pupils dilating at the face of the newly uncovered Jacques Glace, because he was a handsome man. His eyes were indeed very blue and there was a mischievous light dancing in them. His mouth was generous and rested in an upward curve as if he had laughed so much it had become its normal set. There was just the right amount of deliberate stubble on his strong jaw to say 'very well groomed' and it was greying, like his cropped short hair, and both suited him well. Oh yes, he had 'charmer' written all over him. She had yet to find out if he had charmed or conned her great aunt − or both. As he pulled off his coat to reveal a pair of big shoulders, a waft of aftershave passed over Eve. Something foresty and − yeurch − reminiscent of Christmas.

Jacques sat down on the chair and rubbed some life into his hands. They were the size of shovels, Eve noticed. He wore a ring on the third finger of his right hand. She wondered if that was a wedding ring and maybe the French wore them on that finger?

Mr Mead pressed the button on an intercom on his desk.

'Barbara, would you bring the coffee through now. Mr Glace has arrived.'

'Ooh, lovely,' said Jacques Glace, in a voice as French as a Yorkshire pudding. 'I'm parched.'

It made Eve's head jerk towards him. 'You're not French?' she asked.

'Half,' he said with a sparkle in his eye. 'The bottom half.'

Eve felt her top lip twitch into a sneer. One of those men who thought he was really funny and God's gift to women. Well, he wasn't. She wondered if his real name was Jack Glass after all and he was just being a pretentious prat with the spelling.

Mr Mead's secretary pushed open the door holding a tray of three tall china mugs of coffee with impossibly tiny handles. Eve foresaw a disaster and tried to move her chair ever so slightly further away from the half-Frenchman before he ended up spilling his drink all over her skirt.

He didn't even attempt the handle though, she noticed. His hand circled the top of the cup and he lifted it to his lips. She was most surprised that he didn't slurp, or pour the coffee into the saucer and drink it that way.

'Sorry if I've held you up by not being able to meet earlier in the week,' said Jacques both to Mr Mead and Eve. 'I've been away.'

Eve wondered if he'd been at a slapstick convention.

'So, how do you know my aunt so well that she left you in joint possession of a one-hundred-and-fifty-acre plot of land?' asked Eve, trying – but failing – not to sound cross about that.

Jacques Glace had the audacity to ever so slowly raise his finger to his nose and then tap it twice. How dare he, thought Eve. It wasn't exactly an unreasonable question in the circumstances.

'Mr Glace, you've looked in more detail at the plans for Winterworld, I presume?' said Mr Mead.

'*Oui*,' said Jacques. 'And I've got some great ideas to contribute. I can't wait to start working on it with you, Miss Douglas,' he added, turning towards Eve and giving her a wide smile which showed off nice, even white teeth. The smile of a charming crocodile, thought Eve to herself. Well, any attempt to seduce her with soft words would fall on deaf ears. She knew his type. She came across them in her job often: men who thought a big smile would get them a massive discount. The only thing they actually did get was a 'dream on, buster' smile in return.

'Do you have any experience of theme parks, Mr Glace?' Eve wondered what line of business he was in. She couldn't imagine he was running ICI.

'Only going to them,' came the reply. She wasn't surprised. She could imagine Jacques Glass sitting on a roller coaster like a big kid, with his giant hands raised above his head, shouting 'wheee'.

'So you're not a builder then?' Eve tried to pry subtly.

'*Non.*'

'Or an engineer.'

'*Non.*'

He was being deliberately obstructive. Enjoying it too, judging from the twinkle in his eye as he delivered his monosyllabic answers.

Eve went for the direct question.

'So what exactly is your line of work, Mr Glace?'

Jacques Glace swivelled in his seat. 'I haven't worked in ages,' he said, clearly delighting in the look on her face.

Eve was shocked: her aunt had left half an unfinished theme park to a jobless joker. She wondered if this might contravene the 'being of sound mind' part of writing a will.

Mr Mead pushed two sheets of paper across the table. 'These require your signatures to officially allow you to be in charge of Winterworld Ltd,' he explained. 'All funds will then be available, although as I said, you do need both parties' approval as well as my own on items of major spending.'

Good, thought Eve. Jacques Glace didn't look trustworthy with money. She had visions of him running amok with a chequebook and spending it all on sweets.

Jacques politely indicated that Eve should sign first.

'Your aunt ran Winterworld from the Portakabin on site until the staff quarters were completed,' said Mr Mead, taking the signed papers and sealing them in a brown envelope. 'The grounds are patrolled by Pitbull Securities. They've been expertly secured.'

'Yes, they would be,' said Eve, half in the open, half to herself. Pitbull Securities had been in the game a long time. Keith Pitt the younger was an ex-boxer and local hard man whom anyone would be an idiot to cross. Keith Pitt the elder used to have a scrapyard in the seventies, patrolled by a lion that he'd bought from a circus because he was sick of stuff getting nicked and his Alsatians couldn't keep up. He'd got the idea from someone who kept a bear in his yard, but he couldn't find one of those. No wonder some people thought Barnsley was a bit rough. Her Uncle Jeff once told her that the lion kept getting out and was often to be found leisurely walking down Burton Street. Keith Pitt used to freeze sheeps' heads for the lion to nibble on in the summer like big ice-pops, and it would play football with a box around the yard. On occasion it even went in the car with him, hanging over the back seat watching the scenery pass by. 'Leo' made the *Barnsley Chronicle* on quite a few occasions over the years. Funnily enough, no one ever robbed the Pitt scrap-yards again.

Eve shook her head at the thought of her aunt

having an office, which was even more insane than the idea of guard-lions. The vision of Evelyn going into work with a briefcase was totally unbelievable. She laughed aloud, not meaning to.

'I'm sorry,' she excused herself. 'I still can't take it all in.'

'I understand,' nodded Mr Mead. 'It must have been quite a shock.'

'I mean, Aunt Evelyn doing all this. It's unthinkable really.'

'I can imagine it quite well,' interrupted Jacques. 'She was a sprightly old bird. Sharp as a razor with an incredible head for business. If only she had known she had that potential earlier in her life. She could have been President of the USA.'

Eve gave a half-gasp, half-dry chuckle, and felt a spiral of fury course through her. How dare he intimate he knew Aunt Evelyn better than her own flesh and blood did? The cheek of the man. She sat on her anger and tried to talk sweetly.

'And from where did you gain your insight of my aunt?' she asked with a deadly smile.

'From many, many hours of conversation,' was all Jacques Glace gave away. He spoke teasingly slowly as if delighting in keeping Eve in the dark.

Mr Mead handed over two identical sets of keys.

'These are for the Portakabin,' he said. 'And the front gate. I don't know what the others are for I'm afraid, nor can I tell you how far she was in the project; but as I understand it, her files were expertly kept and, knowing Miss Douglas, all should be very straightforward.'

'You're telling me,' said Eve. In the files she had so far studied, everything was documented down to when the snow machines were arriving, the staff she had set on via an agency, how much they were to be paid, even where she had bought the reindeer from, although Eve had every intention of getting a refund on the animal.

'So, we need to go into the office and pick up where she left off,' Jacques stated. 'I suggest we synchronize our watches and meet at nine a.m. on Monday morning.' He turned to Eve for affirmation.

'Yes, I was going to say the same,' said Eve. 'I'll be there at eight a.m.'

'Oh, make it nine,' Jacques responded with a flap of his hand. 'Don't want to kill ourselves, do we? And it will be *Monday* morning. Yuk.'

Eve doubted that Jacques Glace would be in danger of killing himself with work.

They exited Mr Mead's office together, both holding their set of keys.

'Where are you parked?' asked Jacques.

Eve pointed to the left. Thank goodness he was parked to the right, so she wouldn't have to endure walking beside him.

'I'm looking forward to working with you, Eve,' Jacques sparkled.

'I'm looking forward to picking up the project,' said Eve, unable to make it plainer that working with him was not something she was relishing.

He let loose a low peal of laughter then pulled in a lungful of cold air and noisily let it go. 'Ah, it's going to be fun one day,' he said. 'Full of sparks and fire.'

'What is?' said Eve.

'Being married to you, because nothing surer, it will happen. Please remember that,' he said. 'See you on Monday, Miss Douglas.' And off he went, leaving a stunned Eve in his wake.

Chapter 7

Eve went straight from the solicitor to her cousin's ice-cream parlour for a coffee and a rant. And an ice cream. At least she could draw some comfort from a caramel apple-pie sundae. Violet really did make the most gorgeous ice cream.

'Crikey, it must be "national visit Violet day",' she laughed with delight. 'I've only just waved Bel and Max off.'

'Are they both okay?' asked Eve. She didn't know Bel and Max very well, but what she knew of them she liked enormously. They'd been very kind to Violet when she'd needed good friends.

'Same as always,' Violet grinned. 'Max is planning her wedding and well . . .' She shook her head. 'If it doesn't end up in the *Guinness Book of Records* for being the flashest event in history, I'll eat my hat and yours. She's supposed to be on a diet, as she's trying on dresses later, but she's just wolfed down four scoops of my summer pudding and clotted cream. And Bel wasn't far behind her with three scoops of chocolate velvet.'

'Ooh, they both sound nice,' said Eve. She wondered if Violet had ever considered making a winter pudding ice cream.

'Sit down and I'll fetch us some ice cream.'

Eve didn't wait to be asked twice.

'You know, I think I'm still gobsmacked about the theme park,' said Violet, after bringing over a small scoop of ice cream for herself and a sundae for Eve. Violet's was lavender flavoured. It was a delicate shade of mauve with scented sugar crystals sprinkled on top. She nodded with approval at her experiment. It had turned out better than expected, as Violet Flockton's ice-cream trials usually did. 'When you told me what Evelyn had left you, I did wonder if you'd been licking LSD tabs.'

Eve nodded. 'I can understand that. I don't know what Aunt Evelyn was playing at. She can't have been of sound mind for ages. People with sound minds do not build theme parks in Barnsley and then leave half of them to idiot idle strangers. She should have been locked up for her own safety.'

'You sounded like Granny Ferrell then,' laughed Violet.

'Don't.' Eve formed her fingers into a cross and

held it up against the thought of their joint maternal
grandmother – Pat Ferrell. Violet's paternal nan used
to say that if they shaved Pat's hair off, they'd discover
a trio of sixes.

'Any idea what you're buying her for her birthday?' said Violet. 'It gets harder every year to find
something she likes.'

'Blimey, Violet, it's not her birthday until next
month.'

'I know, I know. I don't really know why I stress
about it so much – whatever we get for her she
hates.'

'Cheer me up talking about her, why don't you?'
said Eve. If anyone could make her mother look like
an angel by comparison, it was Granny Ferrell. Violet
had been lucky to have the experience of a lovely
granny in her Nan Flockton – her father's mother.
Eve, alas, never knew her real father. She doubted
even her mother, Ruth, knew him that well. Carl
Douglas married her in a fug of cannabis smoke
when she was six months pregnant and left her a
week before she gave birth, never to return. As the
baby was born on 24 December, Ruth called her
Eve, a decision which was to come in quite useful
later. Because when Eve was eight years old, Susan
received a surprise letter from a lady calling herself
Evelyn Douglas, who had been trying to trace Ruth
without success. She was the aunt of Carl Douglas

and, though no longer in touch with her wayward nephew or his parents, had only recently learned from a branch of the family that a Douglas baby had been born who was named after her, and she desperately wanted to get in touch.

Ruth, sniffing money in the air, was very keen to make the point that the baby had indeed been named after her – oh happy coincidence, she thought, especially as old Evelyn Douglas was a childless spinster. In truth, she hadn't a clue what any of Carl's relatives were called or how many he had. Her only interest in him had been his ability to get his hands on really good weed and, when they weren't too stoned, his incredible appetite for sex. Ruth took her young daughter on the bus to visit her long-lost great-aunt but soon lost interest in the monthly trips when it was quite obvious Evelyn Douglas had no fortune to leave. But Eve liked the old lady, and so she used to go alone and drink tea out of her fine bone china cups and eat far too many Mr Kipling cakes. Eve wasn't allowed pets because Ruth couldn't be bothered with them, so sitting on Aunt Evelyn's plump sofa stroking her purring cat, Fancy, was a treat in itself. Eve didn't mind that the old lady showed her the same photographs over and over or told the same stories about her brave Stanley; she just loved her, the bungalow, the cakes and the cats.

'What about a bit of jewellery for her forthcoming cruise holiday?' asked Violet.

'Or some polish for her horns?'

Violet chuckled. 'Do you think Auntie Ruth will come over for it?'

'Don't be daft, Violet.' Eve held her hands out with imaginary weights in them. 'A meal with her old bat of a mother or remaining in a sunny commune in Spain. Hmm . . . let me think.' The hand holding the Spanish sunshine dropped heavily. Duty would never be as weighted as pleasure for Ruth Douglas – including anything to do with her daughter. Ruth Douglas was a hedonist of the highest order.

'When did you last hear from your mum?'

'My birthday last year. Except she rang on the twenty-second of December.' Once upon a time, Eve had doubted that anyone could forget their only child's birthday, then she started watching Jeremy Kyle. She half expected her mother to be on that one day, drifting on stage with a kaftan, being lectured by JK not to smoke as much wacky baccy. That thought was replaced by one of Susan, who still sent her a home-made birthday cake.

'I just don't know how your mum turned out the lovely way she did,' Eve said, not for the first time. Violet gave her cousin an affectionate nudge. She didn't know herself, to be honest. Life hadn't been easy for her mum, brought up in a loveless household, expected to play a parental role in the raising of her sibling whilst Pat gallivanted off with her fancy men as a kick-back for Grandad Ferrell running off with a young barmaid. Then, when happiness eventually came to Susan in the form of the lovely Jeff Flockton, he was taken away from her much too soon with a stroke.

'How's your mum doing with Mr Sausage?'

That was their pet name for Patrick, the big, friendly butcher who was courting Susan.

Violet chuckled. 'She's very loved up.'

'Good,' said Eve.

'It's so nice to see you, Eve,' said Violet, her voice suddenly flooded with affection. 'You've been a stranger for too long. Mum would be delighted if you just called in. She was only saying the other day how we should force you to come for Sunday lunch.'

'I know,' nodded Eve, feeling a stab of shame. After all Auntie Susan had done for her over the years, she shouldn't have shut her out. She loved her cousin and her aunt. Spending time with them was a pleasure she had denied herself for too long, and she intended to do something about it.

'Ladies, is everything all right?' asked the tall, dark-haired man in an apron appearing at their table.

'No,' said Violet. 'I need to complain to the manager.'

'I'm so sorry about that. I'd bring her over to hear

your complaint, but she's too busy sitting around and eating,' he replied. He winked and touched Violet's cheek with the back of his finger before going back behind the counter again.

'You look as if you're melting more than your ice cream,' said Eve, looking at the dreamy look on her cousin's face. 'How's Pav doing these days?'

Violet looked across at her handsome partner being charming to a couple of small children who wanted tubs with all the trimmings.

'He's good,' said Violet quietly. 'His chest still aches when he lifts anything heavy though. He'll never go back to working on building sites again, but I'm kind of glad about that, if I'm honest. He loves being in the shop and he's got loads of painting commissions. He still works too hard, though, and tires himself out. I despair sometimes. He doesn't rest as much as he should.' She sighed and shook her head at him. But there was love and pride in her eyes as she did so.

Pav was Polish and came over to England to work as a builder with his brother. Violet met him when she advertised for an artist to paint fairground horses on the walls of her ice-cream parlour, Carousel. She had nearly lost him in a fire the previous year but miraculously, he had survived. She loved him so much it hurt sometimes. His merry ways and warmth constantly made her heart sing. She only wished Eve could find someone who had the same effect on her. She had been in limbo for so long, Violet wondered if she would be permanently trapped in the state. She was too young and lovely to still be so sad. But Eve was resolutely stuck in the past and would not be budged out of it.

Violet tentatively voiced what was in her mind.

'You could do with a Pav yourself,' she said.

Eve smiled. 'He's lovely. You're lucky. But then so is he.'

'Maybe you'll end up falling madly in love with your new business partner.'

Eve ha-ed at that. 'I haven't met the man yet who could fill Jonathan's shoes. And if I have, I can guarantee you that it wouldn't be Jacques Glace and his cheesy line in banter.' And his big soggy flying gloves, she added to herself.

'The newspapers are awash with stories of those who have fallen in love with people they once disliked,' said Violet, sticking her spoon into her ice cream.

'Yeah well, I'm okay being single, thank you.'

'Has no one taken your eye in the past few years, Eve?' asked Violet, knowing she was straying onto dodgy ground. She and Eve might have been related, but Eve's broken heart and subsequent empty love life had always been off-limits.

'I haven't even looked. Anyway – to business,'

said Eve, changing the subject quickly. 'I want you to supply the ice cream for Winterworld. What do you think?'

Violet's big violet eyes rounded with delight. 'You're joking.'

'I'm not,' said Eve, thinking how beautiful her cousin was – more so because she hadn't a clue how lovely she looked.

'Jeez, Eve, that's just fab.' Then a sensible thought tugged at the sleeve of her elation. 'Won't you have to clear it with Mr Glace first?'

'I suppose,' replied Eve, with a snarl playing on her lip. 'But I can't see there being a problem. No one makes ice cream like you.' And like he would dare to override her on this. Or anything else come to that.

'I've got some lovely Christmas flavours,' said Violet. 'And they've got edible glitter in them as well.'

'Winter,' corrected Eve. 'Try and keep Christmas out of it as much as possible.'

'Oh Eve, if it's a winter theme park, people will expect it to be Christmas-heavy.'

'Well, they're going to be disappointed then, aren't they?' said Eve, licking the last of her ice cream from her spoon. 'I'll ring you as soon as I've spoken to him on Monday.' She imbued the word 'him' with all the charm of a disease-ridden clown. 'You'll be able to run a second parlour, won't you?'

'Yes, yes of course,' said Eve. 'Janet wants full-time work rather than part-time so I'll increase her hours, get her some part-time help and then Pav and I will set up the new place.'

'I see it just like this,' said Eve, looking around her at the beautiful horses painted on the walls. It was ice cream heaven as far as she was concerned.

'Only with a Christmas theme, I presume,' Violet put in.

'*Winter*,' amended Eve. 'Yes, just like this.'

'Pav would be delighted to paint more horses on walls,' smiled Violet. 'He loved doing these. I can safely speak for him on that score.'

'Good, that's settled then,' said Eve. 'And now I must be off.'

'So soon?' said Violet. But she knew she was lucky to see Eve at all these days. She was always working, never stopped. Never gave herself time to relax – or think. Or grieve properly as she should have done.

Violet hurried across to Pav to tell him the good news about having a new parlour in Eve's theme park. He was delighted, as she expected, that there would be more horses to paint. White ones, he envisaged. Like Christmas horses made of snow. And Violet knew they would look wonderful.

It didn't look as if there would be any more customers that day, so they decided to finish early. Pav turned the sign around on the door to read 'closed'. Then he crossed over to Violet, put his big arms around her, pulled her close to his chest and kissed her long and softly. Violet still felt butterflies inside her stomach flutter their wings with delight when his fingers threaded into her long silver-blonde hair. To think once she had been about to marry a man whose kisses and touch she avoided at all costs and would have committed herself to a sad, dry life. She sometimes dreamt that she was still in that stifling, choking relationship, and woke up in a cold sweat only to see the sweet form of Pav at her side. She had always thought love like this happened to other people, not to her.

'Marry me,' said Pav. 'I want you to have the same name as me. I want you to be Mrs Nowak, not Miss Flockton. I'm an old-fashioned boy.'

Boy. It was the loudest word in the phrase.

Violet laughed and prepared to fob him off as usual. 'One day. What's the rush?'

'Always you say the same thing,' said Pav, releasing her from his hold and throwing up his arms into the air. For the first time, Violet detected that there was none of his usual humour in the gesture.

She loved him so much. And of course she wanted to be Mrs Pawel Novak, but she was afraid of her own happiness. He might have looked like a man, but he was so much younger than her – nine years. She feared that he would wake up one day and realize how young he was, how much living he should do before settling down. She didn't want to fetter him as her ex-fiancé had fettered her. She never wanted him to feel trapped and unable to breathe the way she had once felt with her ex.

'I do love you, Pav,' she said, feeling suddenly incredibly choked up. 'It's not that I don't.'

'I know,' he said, and nodded slowly. 'But this is the last time I will be rejected, Violet. I won't ask you again.'

He turned then and smiled at her and kissed her forehead. 'Come on, let's go home. It's my turn to cook.' He held out his large hand for her to take and though the gesture was full of love and warmth, she felt suddenly chilled from the inside out.

Chapter 8

The Daily Trumpet *would like to apologize to Mrs Bunty Smith for an entry which appeared on Monday's page three. We did, of course, mean that Mrs Smith was one of Asda's most popular ex-workers, not that she was one of Asda's most popular sex workers. We do apologize to Mrs Smith for any distress caused and to Asda Barnsley for all the resulting nuisance phone calls.*

Chapter 9

The first thing Eve did when she got home was fire up her computer to google the name Jacques Glace again. It was a pretty distinctive name – or so she thought, but so far she hadn't found any trace of him. Apart from a whole host of restaurants picking up the 'glace' word, and a lot of French entries, there was also a huge Canadian company which took up pages. She widened the net slightly and typed in 'UK' with as much success. There was a Jean-Jacques Glace, a decorated war veteran with one leg, and if there was one thing Eve was definite about it was that Jolly Jacques wasn't brave military material. Plus he had two legs, which ruled him out. There were lots of references to Glace Bay in Nova Scotia but nothing about a large oaf with a 'French bottom half'.

Then she struck gold. Or rather glass.

She tried the alternative spelling 'Jack Glass'. She

found a Jack Glass in Barnsley born in 1826. Then an article archived in the *Weekly Bugle* from eight years ago:

PENSIONER ROBBED OF LIFE SAVINGS BY 'MAJOR' CON MAN

A Leeds pensioner was conned out of her £40,000 life savings by a man claiming to be a long-lost relative of her deceased son. The pensioner, who asked not to be named, said the man claimed to be an army major who was stationed with her son before his untimely death.

Mrs X was living alone and recovering from cancer when the man, who called himself Major Jack Glasshoughton, made contact. 'He said he had fallen on hard times after being honourably discharged from the army and that my son and he had planned to go into business together. I wanted to honour my son's promise to this man,' she said.

Mrs X gave 'The Major' eight instalments of £5,000 in cash, which he promised to return with interest. 'I thought I was dealing with a man of honour, like my son,' she said. 'I'm going to lose my house because of this now.'

Det Sgt Piers Clemit from West Yorkshire police said that con men were well practised at choosing potential targets and often worked to befriend victims who were isolated and alone.

'From investigations that I've carried out, it appears that a man of this description has conned at least two other

fragile pensioners. He has gained admittance to their homes pretending to be a policeman and a gas engineer and taken money and jewellery worth over £6,000.

'The ideal victims that they go for will be people who live in a community but are effectively on their own,' said Det Sgt Clemit. 'They are expert at saying what the victims want to hear. They target areas where there are small houses and bungalows that show telltale signs such as hand-rails, uncleared gutters and unkempt gardens, which are all indications that the property is home to an elderly, vulnerable person. Uniforms can easily be procured and are not a guarantee that the person wearing them is in a position of trust.'

Police are warning the elderly to be on guard. 'The Major' is six foot plus, of very smart appearance, short dark hair, with a neutral accent. Police are linking this man with the names Jack Glasshoughton, James Glass, Jackie Glass, John Glasier and James Jackson. If anyone is familiar with these names or has been approached by this man, please call the Crimesmashers number at the bottom of this page.'

Eve sank back in her chair. 'Well, well, well,' she said aloud to herself. Now that was too much of a coincidence. She made a few notes, including the detective sergeant's name. She would email and find out if they'd ever caught 'The Major'. She wouldn't have been surprised to hear that they hadn't, because he sounded a greasy, shifty character. Maybe he had laid low for a few years and was now back in business, preying on old ladies who lived in bungalows with his tried and trusted modus operandi. Were Jacques Glace and Major Jack Glasshoughton one and the same? She'd bet her share of the theme park they were, and she would go all out to prove it. Yes, she knew there was something shifty about Jacques Glace all right. He was too smiley, too cheerful, too easy-going, too secretive.

From the corner of her eye, she saw the candle flame flicker. The candle which Jonathan had bought for her and placed in her window and told her that as long as it burned, she was his and he was hers. He told her this on the last day she ever saw him.

'Oh Jonathan, who is Jacques Glace?' she said. 'Is he really Major Glasshoughton? Did he con Aunt Evelyn into writing him into her will?'

Why couldn't life be simple? Why was life so full of questions, like how did Aunt Evelyn end up with a theme park? Who was Jacques Glace? Why had he made that stupid joke about marrying her? Why couldn't she have married the man she loved? Why was she sitting here talking to a candle – the only thing that signified she was loved in this world? Tears welled up in her eyes and she fought them back because Eve Douglas did not cry. But she couldn't push back that surge of sadness and pain that her man was on the other side of an impenetrable barrier. Her brave, lovely, wonderful, Corporal Jonathan Lighthouse. Killed in action on Christmas Day five years ago – three days before he was due to come home from Helmand Province. As if another man could ever measure up to him. Jacques Glace less than most. Jonathan was brave and brilliant. Jacques Glace was a maverick who didn't work and had about as much dress sense as a blind court jester. It was an insult for him to even think he had a chance at charming her. He wasn't even fit enough to wait in the queue to clean Jonathan's shoes.

Chapter 10

'I can't find a single Jacques Glace on the net, but I did find a Major Jack Glasshoughton who conned an old lady out of her life savings. And when I rang the police, they told me that he's never been found. What do you think about that then?' said Eve, pulling on her car handbrake at the side of the Winterworld gate.

'Sorry, what?' said Violet, lifting her eyes from the newspaper where they had been glued.

'What's the matter? You look cross.'

'It's this damned paper. I don't know who the editor in chief is, but I suspect it's someone in Broadmoor.' She passed over the *Trumpet* and pointed to the top of the page.

The Daily Trumpet *would like to point out that the popular ice-cream parlour, Carousel, will be open*

3pm–5pm Tuesday to Sunday and not 3pm–5pm Tuesday to Sunday as previously published.

'They're useless,' said Eve, shaking her head. 'I can't believe you agreed to advertise with them.'

'I didn't,' replied Violet. 'They took it upon themselves to wreck my business single-handedly. Anyway, what were you saying about Jacques Glace?'

'I said that I wonder if that's his real name. I suppose I'll find that out for definite when "I get married to him". I still can't believe he said that. The cheek of the . . . well, I don't know what to call him. Man doesn't seem to be the right word.'

Eve harrumphed with such indignation that her cousin Violet barked with laughter. That caused Eve to give her a withering look.

'It's so not funny, Violet.'

'I'm sorry,' said Violet, trying hard to straighten her face and failing dismally.

'I thought I'd find some sympathy with you of all people.' Eve sniffed. 'If that was his attempt to seduce, I'm quite safe.'

Violet straightened her face. 'I think it'll be fun working with him and trying to get to the bottom of who he is. He sounds a tonic, and you need an adventure. Get your Miss Marple hat on,' she said. 'You could put your wedding notice in the *Trumpet*: "Steve Berry, aged sixty-five, marries Gus Jackman, aged fifteen".'

'Very droll,' said Eve. 'And tonic isn't a word I'd attribute to him. I don't trust him, Violet. How can anyone trust a man who has managed to wangle half of my aunt's inheritance from her after two minutes' acquaintance? Look at this.' With a certain amount of smugness, she pulled a photocopy of the article about the Major from her handbag and handed it over to her cousin, waiting patiently until she had finished reading it.

'You do know the *Bugle* got closed down for reporting just about every story it reported wrongly. Then it rose like the Phoenix from the ashes with the same editor and a new name: the *Daily Trumpet*,' was Violet's only comment.

'Well, they got this story right because I checked with the police. They never did find Major Glasshoughton. Major *Jack* Glasshoughton.'

'And is Jacques as tall and dark as this Major?'

'Very tall. Not dark though, but he could have easily gone grey in eight years. I'm going to ring the police again and report him.'

Violet looked horrified. 'Eve, you can't go around accusing people without good reason.'

'Well, I'm going to tell Mr Mead anyway and see what he has to say about it all. I knew there was something fishy about the man. Do you know, I could quite happily bring Aunt Evelyn back to life just to kill her,' said Eve, scratching hard at her stomach. 'How could she be so careless and then leave me to sort all this out?'

'Got lice?' Violet nodded towards her.

'They've obviously been buggering about with the formula for shower gel again,' Eve answered. 'I appear to have become allergic to my own knickers.'

'Don't tell Jacques Glace that one,' giggled Violet. 'He'll suggest you take them off.'

Eve shuddered. 'Don't even joke.'

'Come on then,' said Violet, clicking off her seat-belt. 'Let's go and check out your inheritance. I'm so excited. My cousin owns a Christmas theme park.' She clapped her hands together with delight.

'Winter theme park, please,' said Eve, mumbling in a very disgruntled way to herself. She had been non-stop poring over plans for Winterworld and now had a very definite idea of what it was going to be like: oodles of quality, less kiddy and more adult orientated than the rubbishy 'Lapland-type' theme parks which had garnered so much bad press for being gawdy and, well, crap. Winterworld was going to be a much classier act. She had dragged Violet along for half an hour to get a sneak peak of the plot before tomorrow's big day: her first day at work there. Violet was always so full of puppyish joie de vivre that it would be useful to see things through her eyes, Eve thought. Violet was the equivalent of an adult Phoebe May Tinker.

Eve stood peeping through a slit in the high build-er's barricades, trying to imagine the park open and running before December if she had her way. She might have had more success imagining herself as Angelina Jolie.

Violet was squeaking with excitement and the sound made Eve smile. She had felt so terribly guilty that Violet was trapped in an awful situation last year and hadn't been able to talk to her about it, espe-cially as they were virtually inseparable as children.

'Come on, then. Into the unknown,' said Eve, taking out the large key and slipping it into the lock on the large iron side-gate. A security camera fixed to a nearby pole swept around to them.

'Oh God, are we going to be mauled by Rottweilers or lions in a minute?' asked Violet.

'No, I rang Mr Pitt and told him I was coming,' replied Eve. 'So don't worry.' And the two women walked through, one slender as a reed and very blonde, the other dark, taller and curvier. Eve was very much in the mould of her aunt Susan with her big bosom and the nipped-in waist of a fifties film starlet, whereas Violet was like the women on the Flockton side – pale skin, bluebell-coloured eyes and a fragile frame.

Before them lay a concrete path leading up to a wood full of huge Christmas trees. To the right were log cabins. There looked to be a lot of land. Violet summed it up in just one word: 'Blimey.'

'Give or take the F-words, that's what I was think-ing,' gasped Eve. 'Look at all those Christmas trees.'

'What's that building over there?' asked Violet, pointing towards a large log cabin. She unfolded the map which Eve had photocopied. 'Ooh, it must be the café.'

'Yes it is. And that one behind it is going to be your ice-cream parlour,' Eve said, feeling ever so slightly faint. Standing here in the midst of it all was a curious mix of daunting and exciting. On one side, the sheer implausability of tackling a project of this size, on the other, the challenge, the adrenaline rush, the sense of achievement, because Eve knew she could make this work better than anyone else ever could. And then she'd be able to retire in six years' time when she hit forty.

'It's a lovely idea having honeymoon cottages for the people who get married in the chapel,' sighed Violet. 'That would be so romantic, spending your first night as Mr and Mrs in a cabin on the edge of that pretty forest of Christmas trees.'

'Like anyone will want to get married here,' huffed Eve. 'The chapel isn't going to happen, you can bet your life savings on that one. It's a total waste of a building.'

'Can you alter the plans like that? Don't you need permission from your partner?'

'I'll get permission, don't you worry,' said Eve,

knowing that she easily would. When Eve Douglas put her mind to something, it happened.

'I'm looking forward to opening another branch of Carousel. Does that make me a magnate?' asked Violet with a smile on her lips. 'What do you think the *Daily Trumpet* would call me?'

Eve chuckled. 'That newspaper is just unbelievable. You do realize they'll refer to you as a "magnet".'

Violet giggled. 'I have some great flavours that will go down really well – Snowflake, Mince Pie, Brandy Butter. Christmas . . .' Violet paused as Eve raised a finger.

'Figgy Pudding,' she corrected. 'Sounds better than Christmas Pudding anyway.'

Violet shrugged without saying that she thought Figgy pudding sounded very old-fashioned in a wrong way. She wished Eve would let a little of the festive season into her heart. Five years was way too much time to be shut away inside oneself. Violet didn't want her cousin ending up like poor old Evelyn – alone and lonely for many, many years with only the cold comfort of ever-fading memories.

'This place could be a goldmine in a couple of years if I get it right,' said Eve.

Violet winked at her cousin. 'If *you* can't make it happen, Eve, no one can,' she said.

Then behind them came the thunderous sound of someone bellowing 'hello'. They turned to see a grinning, waving giant in a very familiar coat: Eve's fellow will beneficiary.

'*Bonjour*,' he shouted. 'Fancy meeting you here. Aren't we on a wavelength? That bodes well.'

'Who's that?' whispered Violet.

'It's *him*,' Eve replied under her breath. And from the way she said 'him' and that her hair appeared to be standing up on end like a pissed-off cat, Violet knew this must be the mysterious Jacques Glace. Violet was intrigued. She had wondered what he looked like. From Eve's description she had imagined a cross between Nosferatu and Frankenstein's monster, not this smiling, handsome silver-fox with shiny blue eyes and very nice, generous lips curved up into a smile. Jacques strode towards them.

'Don't let him shake your hand, V,' warned Eve quickly. 'I've only just managed to get my arm back in its socket.'

'So here we are on our land,' said Jacques, managing to imply intimacy with the way he said that. 'Huge, isn't it? Look at those trees – wow. How strange you should be here at the same time as me. That's a good sign, don't you think?'

His damned eyes were twinkling mischievously again. Eve didn't ask what that was a good sign of. She wasn't in the mood for another of his stupid jokes about marriage. He was a charmer all right, but she was safe. Forewarned was forearmed.

'Hi there, I'm Jacques Glace. No doubt you've heard all about me from Eve.' He winked at Eve and she felt her lip curling over her teeth. He held his paw out towards Violet, seeing as no introductions from Eve were forthcoming.

Eve flashed a warning at Violet as she was taking his hand, but Jacques shook it very gently. It was the sort of handshake that spoke volumes to Violet. She got a very good vibe from him, however much of an obvious downer Eve had on the man.

'Sisters, I presume?' asked Jacques, flicking his finger from one to the other. Despite their different builds and colourings, that wasn't as ludicrous as it might have sounded, because there was a distinct similarity in the shape of their large black-fringed eyes – even if Violet's were the shade of May blue-bells, and Eve's Christmas-tree green. They also had identical smiles – but Jacques wouldn't have noticed that because he hadn't seen Eve genuinely smile yet.

'Cousins,' said Violet, in a voice that told Eve she was a little charmed by Jacques. Traitor. She wouldn't be that charmed when Eve exposed him for ripping the arse out of old ladies' savings.

'Ah,' said Jacques, and he turned to Eve then and raised his eyebrows in such a way that she felt duty bound to make introductions.

'Mr Glace, meet Violet,' said Eve. 'Violet makes

ice cream. I am hoping I can persuade her to supply Winterworld.'

'Oh, I love ice cream,' beamed Jacques with all the enthusiasm of a five-year-old child faced with a giant Mr Whippy cone studded with twelve flakes in it. 'My grandmother used to make the best ice cream in France. And a gorgeous orange and cinnamon sorbet at Christmas. Do we get free samples?' He rubbed his hands together and somehow reminded Eve of the big, daft red setter puppy which used to live a few doors down from her mother in one of the houses they had lived in. That's what Jacques would be if he were suddenly turned into a canine. She wished. He'd be easier to control that way. Then again, thinking of that hyper dog that never seemed to calm down – maybe not.

'I'm sure I could rustle up a tub or two for you,' said Violet. She had the temerity to smile. Eve couldn't believe it – her cousin was borderline flirting with this man.

'Ace,' beamed Jacques and held up an approving thumb. Then his attention shifted to Eve. 'So, shall we commence a grand tour of our park then?' He held out his crooked arm for her to take. She ignored it and walked forward towards the first log cabin.

Jacques followed behind, unfolding a map from his pocket.

'So that's the café then?' he said, trying to peer in

through the boarded-up windows; then he tried the door. As if it would be open, huffed Eve, consulting the map as she strolled on. She would have had serious words with the builders if it was. She heard Violet laughing behind her at something Jacques was saying and felt a prickle of betrayal.

Eve swept her eyes over the not-quite-finished buildings in front of her and began to visualize how it would all look when it was completed. It was mid-October already. Could they really get enough of it ready to open for this Christmas? Maybe – if the workmen were here 24/7.

As if Jacques – perish the thought – had delved into Eve's head and seen her thoughts, he said, 'It could be ready for this Christmas if we get our act together.'

'Surely not,' said Violet, visualizing the amount of work that would take. She looked to Eve for her reaction and was surprised to see her head slowly nodding an affirmative.

'All the major building work is done and if we draft in more builders to work around the clock to finish everything off, I don't see why not. Obviously it'll take a few years to build up to its full potential, but I reckon there will be enough here to merit an entrance fee this year. It's going to be close – mid-December I'd guess – but, yep, it's possible,' Jacques went on.

'I agree,' said Eve. Not to cash in on the major money-making period around Christmas would be an epic failure – and Eve didn't do failure. In the light of Shite Christmas's questionable success, other winter theme parks would spring up like pesky dandelions on a lawn, and Winterworld needed to be up and running and bloody fantastic, grabbing all the limelight. Yes it could be good, and now was the ideal time to do it, with so many builders out of (and desperate for) work. They could make this happen.

Eve walked on, imagining the completed park – *over there the fast-food restaurant, the souvenir shop and ice-cream parlour.* She tried not to think about the must-have Santa's grotto. Maybe she could leave that with Jacques Glace to sort out. She imagined he'd be very good at playing with toys.

'I was just telling Violet,' said Jacques, coming up behind her and using her cousin's name as casually as if he had known her for years, 'that apparently the only completely finished building on site is the wedding chapel. He grinned and stared at her with a look that was longer than necessary. 'Wonder why Evelyn put that top of the list? It's behind the enchanted forest.'

'God only knows,' Eve exclaimed. Damn.

'I think I might have guessed,' he said. 'I bet your aunt thought we'd get along very well.'

Eve ignored that.

They walked along the path to the first of more log cabins – the one with a tower and a single bell hanging in it. What a ridiculous thing to have built – and built first, thought Eve. It didn't make any good commercial business sense. Her aunt had really slipped up there.

'I need to get inside,' said Eve.

'I like your enthusiasm for getting down the aisle,' Jacques winked. 'That bodes well, too.'

Eve refused to be party to his infantile wedding jokes, and walked around the outside of the chapel getting her sensible Hunter wellies even more caked in mud. Behind her she could hear Jacques talking to Violet about ice cream. At least he was in agreement with her idea to bring in Violet and Pav. As he would soon be in agreement with all her other plans.

The chapel was bolted shut and they didn't have a key for the padlock on the tiny, gothic arched door.

'What a shame,' said Jacques, leaning over and saying for her ears only, 'we could have had a practice run.'

And for his ears only Eve said, 'I don't know what your game is, Mr Glace, but please be assured that your puerile, unfunny jokes are falling on very deaf ears.'

'Who's joking? I always mean what I say; you would be as well to remember that, Miss Douglas,' he said, so close to her ear that she felt his stubble brush her lobe. She moved away and scratched at it as if it had just been touched by an irritating insect – which wasn't too far away from what she thought about her mysterious business partner. Then she moved her scratching attentions down to her side and stuck her nails into her skin because the itch there was still driving her mental. She was going to write to Procter and Gamble when she got home and complain that they shouldn't mess around with their lemon shower gel formulas without informing the public.

The grotto had a protective fence around it so they couldn't even see the outside, never mind the inside of it. Not that Eve was anxious to. Santa held no attraction for her. It was a stupid thing to believe in anyway.

'What do you think we should call the ice-cream parlour?' asked Violet. 'Santa's Ices, Santa's Pantry . . .'

'Why should it be Santa's anything?' Eve replied with a weary snap in her voice. 'It's Winterworld, not Christmasworld. We should concentrate primarily on the season, not the holiday.' Why was everyone so obsessed with it being all about Christmas?

'So you're just going to cut out all references to Christmas?' said Jacques, doing a very French-like shrug. 'Who would you prefer to have running the grotto then? A child catcher?'

'Don't be silly,' said Eve. 'Of course, we'll have to

have a Santa. But we need to emphasize the winter aspect more than the Christmas aspect. It's commercial sense. No one would want to come to a Christmas theme park in July.'

'I would,' said Violet, raising her hand as if she were in class. Then she realized that she probably shouldn't have said that from the withering look Eve gave her.

'I beg to differ also,' said Jacques. 'Some people have Christmas in their heart all year round. Your Aunt Evelyn for instance.'

'Who was quite obviously more unhinged than I'd thought, looking at all this,' said Eve under her breath. Well, she'd get her way in the end. She had years of business experience behind her and only an idiot would try to convince her that she was wrong in wanting to adhere strictly to the 'winter' theme. But she was thinking more and more that she was going to have a battle on her hands with Jacques Glace. He was a Christmasphile and he'd have the park full of festive tat given half the chance. Well, he wouldn't get that chance. When Eve found out what his dubious connection to Aunt Evelyn was, she would use it to drive him out of her business.

The track for the miniature railway had been laid already at the side of the path through the forest.

'This is going to be so pretty,' trilled Violet. 'What

a shame you couldn't get the reindeer to pull a sleigh too, along here.'

'There won't be any reindeer,' Eve returned. She thought she had said that under her breath but Jacques heard it.

'No reindeer?' he boomed, making Brian Blessed sound like a horse whisperer. 'Of course there will be reindeer. You can't have a Christmas park without a reindeer.'

'It's not a Christmas park,' Eve clung desperately onto her calmness.

'Oh yes it is,' Jacques laughed.

'Oh no it isn't,' Eve replied.

'Oh yes it is,' Jacques said again, and Eve was just about to argue when she realized he had deliberately dragged her into a pantomime exchange. The man was incorrigible.

'It is a *winter* theme park, Mr Glace. There is a marked difference. And though there is a crossover, there must have been a reason why my Aunt Evelyn called it "Winterworld" and not "Christmasworld". Trust me, she will have thought of that. You must see my point.'

'I do see your point,' Jacques nodded sagely. 'But Evelyn called it Winterworld because the name Christmasworld had been taken by a company who threatened to sue her if she used it. Trust *me*, I know what she wanted. Santa, reindeers, elves, snowmen and a ton and a half of glitter.'

'How do you know that?' gasped Eve, flicking at some loose strands which had broken free from her tied-back hair.

'Because she told me,' he said.

Eve didn't answer because she felt as if she might blow up if she opened her mouth. How *dare* this man whom she didn't know from Adam tell her what her own aunt wanted. An aunt she had known for twenty-six years as well. Who was he to do that? She needed to know a lot more about Mr Jacques Glace – or should she say Major Jack Glasshoughton?

'Well, I think I've seen enough for now,' said Jacques, grinning as if he was pleased at throwing a spanner into Eve's works. 'See you bright and early in the morning. *Au revoir, mademoiselle,*' he said to Violet. 'And *au revoir, ma cherie,*' to Eve.

Infuriated, she gave him the briefest of dismissive nods and turned her attention back to the plans whilst he walked off whistling 'Winter Wonderland'.

'That was a bit rude, you not saying goodbye to him,' said Violet.

'I don't like him and I don't trust him,' said Eve. 'When I find out who *he* is, I might be more inclined to speak civilly to him.' She was totally convinced that Jacques Glace was a man with more secrets than three Aunt Evelyns.

Chapter 11

The house was freezing when Eve got in. The central-heating clock had reset itself and thought it was the middle of the night and switched itself off. It was a cold house at the best of times, far too big for one person rattling around in it. Then again, when she and Jonathan had bought it, they'd had plans to fill it full of friends and parties – and, in time, children.

Eve altered the clock on the control panel, heard the rumble begin in the pipes and stood by the window, holding her hands over the hurricane glass with the large candle burning brightly inside it. The heat touched her fingers and warmed them like a caress.

She tried to imagine how Jonathan's hand used to feel when it held hers and she couldn't, however much she tried. Life had robbed her of her fiancé and if that wasn't enough, it whittled away at her remaining memories, stripping them of tiny details day by day. They thought they had all the time in the world to record the progress of the house renovation on the camcorder, but they didn't. Just one fifteen-second film bite remained on her iPod of Jonathan, in his uniform, lighting the candle in the window before he left for Helmand Province.

Eve played it for the millionth time and smiled as he appeared on the screen, so slim and handsome in his uniform. He struck a long match and held the flame to the thick white pillar candle.

'As long as this burns, Evie, remember I'm with you,' he said, and blew a kiss at the camera. See you soon, honey. You look after yourself. And look after my candle.' Then the film ended. Five minutes later, he was gone, and she never saw him alive again.

The candle had been replaced many times over the five years, but she had never let that flame go out, never gave up the thought that Jonathan, wherever he was, was hers and she was his. The candle was proof that that hadn't changed. No one could ever come close to loving anyone the way they had loved each other. No one. So there was no point in her ever opening up her heart to let anyone else in, was there?

Chapter 12

Whatever Mr Jacques Glace might have decreed, Eve was on her way to work by half-past seven the next morning. She had presumed she would be the first one on site, but was wrong by a long mile. The large gates were open and diggers were operating, and in the car park was an old Jeep with a personalized reg on it. The first five letters read J4CK G. That must have cost a fortune, she thought, quickly followed by: I hope that money didn't come from Aunt Evelyn.

'Ah, good morning, Mademoiselle Eve, ' Jacques greeted her, as Eve pushed the door to the Portakabin open and found him there, drinking coffee, surrounded by open boxes of papers, his enormous feet up on the desk. 'You went for an early start too. Couldn't sleep. Far too excited.' He grinned, then offered: 'Can I make you a coffee?' He pointed to an old-fashioned percolator, on the top of a nearby table, which was spitting and hissing like something that needed the services of an exorcist.

'Thanks, I'll get my own,' said Eve, stripping off her gloves. It might have been frosty outside, but at least the Portakabin was toasty-warm.

'Milk's in the fridge.' Jacques pointed to a tiny box at the other side of the table. 'Sugar's . . . Ah, don't expect you take sugar.'

'Actually, I do,' said Eve.

'That surprises me,' laughed Jacques.

'Why? Why should it surprise you?' snapped Eve. The man knew nothing about her and was pretending he did.

'Because . . .' He drew the shape of a woman in the air with his hands: a woman with a small waist. Eve didn't like that the drawn-in-the-air woman had quite big boobs and hips though. Dear God, she'd only been in the room for five minutes and he had wound her up already.

'Sugar's in the top filing cabinet with the crockery,' said Jacques, an amused smile playing on his lips. Then Eve was sure he muttered something like, 'Alas we're out of Evening Primrose Oil.' She didn't give him the satisfaction of asking him to repeat it though.

'I've found loads more files,' said Jacques. 'I've left them out on your desk for you to look at.'

Eve bristled again. There were two desks in the Portakabin and already Jacques had decided which was hers and which his. Admittedly, the one he pointed to was by the window in the nicer position but still, he had chosen and that's what rankled.

'Thank you,' she said, managing to sound not in the slightest grateful.

Eve poured herself a coffee, splashed in some milk and added half a teaspoon of sugar. Then she went back to the desk which Jacques had *so kindly* selected for her and lifted up one of the files. It bore the label: 'Reindeer'.

'Well, we're not having those,' said Eve in a low breath, and put the file back down.

'You can't have a Winterworld without reindeer,' said Jacques.

'Of course, you can,' said Eve, picking up the next file: 'Elves'. 'Dear God,' she said. 'We are most certainly not having elves.'

'Too late. Evelyn employed loads of them and they've all got contracts.'

Eve laughed mirthlessly. 'How can you employ elves? They don't exist.'

'People willing to dress up as elves do. You'll be saying next you aren't having any snowmen.'

'Snowmen are allowed,' conceded Eve.

'Goodness. We agree on something,' chuckled Jacques, chalking a point up in the air with a licked finger. 'Gets the blood going, doesn't it? A bit of verbal fencing in the morning.'

Oh, here we go again, thought Eve. Well, she would ignore his silly, childish flirtations. He would get tired of it eventually. They were going to be far too busy for such silliness.

As if able to read her thoughts, Jacques said, 'We've got a meeting at eleven with the site manager. Nothing to worry about, just touching base. I've already had a word with him about drafting extra men.'

'Oh, have you?' He was showing off, she decided. Trying to make out that he was super-efficient. Incompetent people usually tried that tactic but they soon became unstuck.

'Yep.'

'What did you know about Winterworld before the will reading?' Eve asked, chewing the end of her pen. 'Didn't Aunt Evelyn ever say anything to you about it, during your "many, many hours of conversation"?'

'She talked about it non-stop,' said Jacques, 'but not as something she was actually doing, but rather as something she always wished she could have done. In our "many, many hours of conversation" she spoke about it as someone else would talk about wishing they had enough money to buy a huge house by the sea or try their luck in Hollywood. I never for a moment thought that she was actually in the process of building a real theme park. She was always drawing little sketches and coming up with new ideas for it – but I thought it was a harmless fantasy. A diversion.'

'And where did you have these "hours of conversation"?' Eve asked tightly.

'Some in her house, some in mine, some in other places.'

'How long did you know my aunt, Mr Glace?'

'Long enough to know when she passed away what she would have wanted.'

'And what was that?'

Jacques leaped up from the desk, wheeled his chair into the middle of the room, positioned an anglepoise lamp on his desk to shine directly on his face, then quickly sat down.

'Okay, Mrs Gestapo officer. I'll tell you everything. Just promise not to tickle me.'

Very unamused, Eve looked at the man in the chair who was pretending that his arms were tied behind his back. She didn't know how to deal with him. The man was insane. Talking of tickling, her side was still itching like mad. The calamine lotion she had put on the previous night had made it worse if anything. She hadn't slept very well at all. Lack of rest wasn't helping her temper.

'Mr Glace. Old ladies do not leave fortunes to

strangers. Who are you? Where do you come from, and why are you so bloody secretive?'

Jacques stopped pretending to be tortured and for the first time she heard him talking seriously.

'I'm exactly what it says on the tin, Miss Douglas. I'm Jacques Glace and whatever your aunt did was as big a surprise to me as it was a shock to you, but she was a fine judge of character and I consider it an honour that she trusted me to help fulfil a dream that sadly came too late for her to see to fruition. I'm half-French, half-Yorkshire, as I said, and I will do my damnedest to make sure your aunt's dream comes true, and that is all you need to know about me.' He stood up then and took two long strides to the door. 'If you'll excuse me, I have some straw for the paddocks arriving in approximately ten minutes. I'll be back at eleven with the site manager, Effin Williams.'

And with that he walked outside with his big boots on, leaving Eve wondering if she was actually locked in a bad dream after eating far too much cheese late last night.

Effin Williams looked like a weeble. Eve thought that if she were to push the little round man, he would wobble but not fall down. He had shoulders wider than his short legs were long but when he shouted, his workforce jumped to attention. His voice was from the Welsh valley of Carmarthen but sounded as if it was full of coal rather than daffodils. He had a name that suited him down to the ground as most of his workforce called him Effin Williams to his face and effin Effin Williams behind his back.

''Ere is the reindeer park.' He stabbed a stubby finger down on the architect's plan. 'Miss Douglas wanted a stable for them, so a stable is what she has 'ad.'

'Hmm,' said Eve under her breath, sounding like a very unimpressed Lord Sugar. As soon as this meeting was over she was going to ring up and see what the situation was about cancelling the reindeer.

'Is there any other livestock coming?' asked Eve, casting her eye over the map and doing a double-check for anything with the word 'penguin' scribbled on it.

'Only reindeer and white ponies, and I do believe there was some talk about rescue snowy owls,' said Effin. 'Oh, and the polar bear. Not sure if Miss Douglas was *jo-kin'* or not about that. We certainly haven't built an enclosure, so if one arrives, it'll have to bunk up *eyor* with the reindeer, until we can build him a cage.'

Eve saw Effin give Jacques a sly wink, and she bit down on her lip to stem her annoyance. She hadn't liked Effin Williams any more than she had liked Jacques Glace on sight. She had a feeling that

Effin was wondering what she was doing out at work when it was such a good drying day for the washing.

'What stage is the restaurant at?' asked Eve, trying to sound super-efficient and super-in-control and not super-pissed-off.

'Wiring – check, plastered – check, painted – check, floorin'– check,' said Effin, using his short, fat finger to cross off an imaginary checklist in the air. 'Kitchen equipment being delivered' – he looked at his clipboard – 'Thursday this week for fitting.'

'The caterers are on stand-by. They're a very good firm. Friends of mine actually,' put in Jacques. 'I recommended them to your aunt.'

Eve's head whirled suspiciously around. 'Oh, did you really? I thought you didn't know about this place before she died.' Ha. He'd tripped himself up there good and proper.

'I didn't,' said Jacques. 'She asked me one day if I knew of a catering firm who could run "a friend's café" as she told me. I put her in touch with the people I know. I hadn't a clue she meant this place.'

Did Eve believe him? Not really. It was all a bit too convenient for her liking.

'Can you let me know if there's any hold up with anything. We're on a very tight schedule,' Jacques said to the squat little foreman.

'No hold ups at all, Captain,' said Effin.

Eve huffed. Captain? That was rather close to Major.

'I know some very good caterers myself,' said Eve. 'I had in mind to ring them—'

'Evelyn booked them already,' said Jacques. 'I sometimes wonder if she knew she was near the end. She must have worked like a demon to arrange all the things she did.'

Eve tried not to look as drowned with information as she felt. What the hell was her aunt thinking of, taking on a project of this size at her age? Gutsy old bird as she was, even Eve felt totally overwhelmed with the amount of work there was to do and oversee. In truth, she felt uncharacteristically drained. Physically as well as mentally.

'I reckon,' said Effin, slurping noisily on the last of his coffee – a huge pot mug bearing the wording *Welsh men are the best lovers, isn't it?* – 'we'll just about do it for a couple of weeks before Christmas. Everything will be signed off and perfect. I've drafted a load of Poles in. Work like bloody 'ell they do.' He turned purposefully to Eve. 'Then it's just down to you to pick the curtains for the cabins.'

Eve felt herself rearing. Just because she had boobs he was presuming that her major role was to choose the bloody soft furnishings. And the ironic thing was that his boobs were probably bigger than hers. She heard a weird short squeak and realized it was Jacques trying to hold in a laugh. Boy, was she going to show effin Effin Williams and effin Jacques Glace what she was capable of. They'd be eating those cushions along with their own words shortly.

When Effin had left, Jacques watched Eve stomp around the office a few times between boxes.

'So, do you want to pick the curtains for the cabins or shall I?'

He held up his palms in surrender as Eve whizzed around and tried to burn him with her eyes.

'Joke,' he said. 'Evelyn arranged for a team of interior designers as well. As you'll know if you read the files.'

'Yes, I knew that,' said Eve, scratching her side. The itching pain there was driving her mental and making her very snappy.

Outside they heard the Carmarthenshire tones of Effin ring across the yard and drown out even the noise from the digger engine.

'Brysiwch y jiawled diog. Siapwch hi! And for you non-Welsh bastards who didn't understand that, I'm not telling you it's bloody tea-break time. I'm telling you to hurry up you lazy gits and shape up.'

Jacques half winced, half laughed. In a past life, Effin would have been beating galley slaves. He was only glad the little gaffer didn't get PMT weeks.

'Oh, and as far as the stocking of the gift shop

goes, I can manage that by myself, if you don't mind, Mr Glace.'

Jacques turned his eyes to her. Big and blue with a gaze so laser-intense, she found herself blinking and having to drop contact with them before they incinerated her irises.

'Miss Douglas,' he said, in a patient and highly amused tone, 'may I remind you that there is no "I" in team.'

'But there is a "me",' countered Eve.

'And a "meat",' said Jacques.

'What on earth does that mean?' Eve threw back.

Jacques shrugged. 'I don't know, actually.'

Was there any wonder she felt unable to work with him?

'I think it might be best if we head up half the projects each rather than try and do them together. That way, we can play to our strengths.' *And I can see you as little as possible.* 'As I say, I have contacts in the gift-shop trade and the ice-cream shop, as you know,' said Eve sweetly. 'And if you have contacts with Santa, you take over the grotto.'

'Okay,' Jacques replied, those blue eyes twinkling. 'If that's how you would prefer to operate, then we will do that.' He held out his hand to shake on the deal. A bit superfluous, thought Eve, and said so.

'Is that necessary?'

'A gentleman always shakes on an agreement,' he

answered. 'Plus it gives me a chance to hold your hand.' She wished his eyes would stop twinkling. It was as if he was going to play a practical joke on her at any minute. She almost felt as if she should check his palm in case he had one of those electric buzzers lying in wait for her.

Eve took his hand, intending to shake it quickly with as little contact as she could get away with, but he held on firmly and gave it a hearty shake. The man didn't know his own strength. But if it got him away from her and busy on his pet projects she would let him shake her hand on the hour, every hour, for a week. She would let him get on with his side of things for now whilst she carried out her investigations on him. If he thought she trusted him, he would start to act. Very possibly money would start being syphoned off, so she would keep a close eye on the accounts. Whatever he was planning to do, she'd find out and expose him – nothing surer.

Eve sat down at her desk and opened up her address book whilst she tried to shut out the sound of Jacques Glace humming 'Rudolf the Red-Nosed Reindeer'. Not surprisingly, he was word-perfect.

Chapter 13

Eve immediately fixed up a meeting with Nobby from Nobby's Novelties for the next day. He sounded out of puff just from answering the telephone. He could supply all they needed for a theme park gift shop – colourful child-attracting items with a high profit margin.

She went to bed that night worn out but happy with her progress – and woke up the next morning feeling as if she had been kicked in the back by a horse. She must have slept in a very twisted position, she decided.

Winterworld was a hive of activity when she got there. Big trucks were rumbling through the gates. She arrived at the Portakabin, loaded with ibuprofen because her back pain wasn't subsiding, if anything, it was getting worse. And that damned rash was spreading too, but she hadn't any time to go to the doctors because she had the heavy-breathing rep to meet with. What a great start to the day. And if that wasn't enough, Effin Williams was standing there watching her get out of the car, hoping for a flash of thigh, no doubt.

But despite his chauvinistic ways, no one could take away from him that he was a damned good foreman. There was no lounging about on long, infamous builders' tea breaks when he was in the area.

She imagined his Welsh eyes burning into her bum as she climbed the four steps into the Portakabin. The office was full of the smell of fresh coffee; Jacques had beaten her in again, it seemed. She hoped he would bugger off and not be hanging around when Nobby Scuttle arrived. She poured herself a coffee and sat down, because the pain in her back really was dragging her down. It felt as if she had been thumped by a hammer. She wasn't in the mood for Jacques' jolly '*Bonjour*' as he blasted into the office with a giant flying jacket on, and she hoped that was indicative of him making a flying visit. But he settled on his chair, threaded his fingers, and looked as if he didn't really know what to do with himself next. He started whistling – a syncopated, annoying version of 'Away in a Manger', which made Eve lose her thread of concentration.

'It's going to be great, isn't it? I love Christmas,' he enthused. 'If we weren't spending it on my grandparents' farm in France, we were at home with lots of relatives staying over. Big fires, lots of laughter, kids, animals, games.'

'Sounds wonderful,' sneered Eve.

'Oh, it was,' nodded Jacques. 'We used to have a twelve-foot Christmas tree and every visitor had to bring a bauble for it.'

'Wowee.'

Jacques studied Eve.

'You don't like Christmas very much do you, Eve?'

'No,' she replied flatly. 'But I do appreciate its commercial attraction, which we are here to cash in on. Which brings me to the point that I need the office to myself for an hour or so,' she said in a clipped tone. 'I've got a meeting with a novelty man at ten.'

As soon as she said it, she saw Jacques' eyes spark up with mischief. 'A novelty man?'

Before he could give her some smart-aleck comment she clarified, 'A man who sells novelties. For the gift shop. So if you could . . .'

'Yep, no worries,' said Jacques. 'Absolutely no worries at all. I need to oversee some tree-cutting so I'll be pretty busy all morning.'

'Good,' she said, lifting her laptop out of her bag whilst Jacques quietly sipped his coffee. She was just thinking how very quiet he was when he started talking again.

'Bet that is great fun, looking at novelties for the shop.'

Eve carefully underplayed it. She didn't want him to think it was such an exciting job that he would abandon his forest duties for it.

'It's not really,' she said with a shrug of her shoulders. 'I think making an enchanted forest out of a load of trees is a far more pleasant job than picking out shop stocks.'

'Yeah, I'll go and see what's happening there when I've finished my coffee,' he said.

Eve tried to concentrate on her computer screen but was aware that Jacques was watching her. 'What is it?' she snapped. 'Why are you looking at me?'

'Would you rather I totally ignored you?' he laughed.

'Yes,' she said. 'It's off-putting having you stare at me.'

'You're very nice to rest my eyes on,' said Jacques.

Here we go again, Eve thought, tutting loudly. She didn't dignify that with an answer.

'You remind me of your Aunt Evelyn sometimes,' he said. 'You have some of the same mannerisms. You blink a lot when you concentrate.'

'I do not,' refuted Eve, although she knew that her Aunt Evelyn did exactly that.

'Yes, you do.'

'If you say so.' He wanted to draw her into

conversation and she had no time nor patience for him. This gnawing ache at her side was starting to make even breathing a chore. She hoped if she continued to look as if she were concentrating very hard at her screen he would take the hint, and so it was with a huge amount of relief that she watched him drain his cup and stand up.

'Right, I'll go and oversee some forestry. What time is your "novelty man" coming?'

'Ten,' said Eve.

'Ten,' he repeated, and was gone.

'Thank God for that,' Eve said when the door closed on him.

'I heard that,' said a loud voice behind it.

At 9.50 Jacques returned, much to Eve's chagrin.

'Everything is going well in tree land so I thought I'd sit in on your meeting with the novelty man.'

'I don't think you will,' she said crossly.

'Oh, go on,' Jacques punched her arm gently. 'I need some negotiating tips from a master.'

'You patronizing—'

'Patronizing? *Moi*?' Jacques' eyebrows rose to the ceiling. 'Not at all, dear lady. Besides, I want to see what a "novelty man" looks like.'

Eve's face was just going a lovely shade of scarlet when there was a sharp rap on the door. Nobby had arrived and Eve didn't want to argue with Jacques in front of him. Plus she didn't have the energy for a verbal tussle. It would be easier just to let him sit in and play with some of Nobby's free samples. Hopefully a wind-up toy might engage his tiny brain and distract him from making any comment.

Nobby Scuttle was a very wide man with an unhealthily ruddy complexion. He made even Effin Williams look like a twig. The block-black toupee he wore did nothing to reclaim any of his youth; in fact it gave him more than a passing resemblance to an old music hall ventriloquist's doll. And one that had been sitting too close to the fire. His suit had damp patches under the arms, despite the early hour of the morning, and he wafted in with breathy wheezes and a cloud of sweat and very strong cologne. It was a heady mix at the best of times, but in a very warm Portakabin and not feeling her best, Eve hoped this was going to be a very short meeting. She had to decide quickly on some novelties to keep children who visited the park happy. It shouldn't be too complicated a job, then she could send him on his way.

After damp handshakes, Jacques took it upon himself to pour coffees whilst Nobby Scuttle wheezed a bit more as he leaned over to get inside his brief-case. He sounded like a broken pair of bellows.

His fat sausage-fingers handed over a brochure with lots of Post-it notes stuck between the pages, highlighting things which Nobby had recommended. There was nothing out of the ordinary: rubbers, pencil sharpeners, cheap-looking spiral-bound pads.

'Anything you see in the brochure will be emblazoned with your logo.' He swept his hand through the air as if touching some invisible lettering. 'We supply to all the main theme parks and the zoos. You won't find any better on price.'

He let that information – and some more sweat-smells – sink in. Eve felt the annoying presence of Jacques peering over her shoulder.

'Bit ordinary, isn't it?' he sniffed, saying exactly what was in Eve's mind, yet still she felt like huffing. It was up to her to deliver that line if anyone, not him.

'People just want to buy anything with the name on it. You don't need to put a lot of effort into choosing things. They'll sell anyway,' Nobby winked confidentially. 'Kids have bottomless pockets in these sorts of places.'

'I don't think Santa would agree with that,' said Jacques. Eve closed her eyes and blew out her cheeks. Nobby Scuttle gave an amused little laugh, presuming Jacques was joking, even though his expression said he wasn't.

'Beg pardon?' he asked then.

'I think he means that we are actually looking for

some "less ordinary" ideas as well. That other people don't supply,' suggested Eve, before Nobby rang for some men in white coats for Jacques.

'Well, I mean that and—' began Jacques, but Eve cut him off.

'We do need a lot of these cheaper-end items but—'

'We don't want any rubbish,' Jacques interrupted right back. 'And, er, excuse me for saying, but this is proper rubbish. Can you show us something that no one else has?'

Nobby Scuttle's neck started mottling with purple. His stuff had never been awarded the title 'rubbish' before, obviously. He had presumed this was going to be another lazy sale – palm them off with a few rubbers and pencils and cheap crappy watersnakes – and *ker-ching*.

'Puzzles,' said Nobby, reaching in his briefcase for a sample of a sliding tile puzzle.

'Seen 'em dozens of times,' sniffed Jacques dismissively, before Eve could pick it up from the table. What the hell was wrong with her? She seemed to be functioning on ever-reducing power. The ibuprofen tablets weren't working at all. Eve stretched out her back and tried to massage the pain surreptitiously. It was getting so bad that finding any respite from the pain was taking priority over telling Jacques to butt out. She was forced to stay silent whilst Jacques dissed everything that Nobby Scuttle pulled out of his briefcase: the souvenir clotted-cream fudge, the plastic reindeer figures, the water pistols.

'This pen doesn't even write,' said Jacques, scribbling on a pad on his desk with one of Nobby's samples.

By this time, Nobby was the colour of beetroot with a blood pressure problem. The smell of sweat was getting very heavy in the air as Nobby's underarms were pouring it out. Eve forced herself to concentrate on the novelty pooing reindeer before she retched and both insulted Nobby and showed herself up.

Nobby took the pen from Jacques, none too gently, and tried it himself. It didn't write, however much he ground the nib into the paper.

'It was working earlier,' he said in a tone that almost accused Jacques of wrecking it. 'We always check my samples before visiting clients.'

'Have you got another?' Eve asked Nobby. She needed to wrap up this meeting quickly. The pain in her back was wearing her thin.

'Are you all right?' asked Jacques, wondering why Eve was growing as pale as Nobby was turning aubergine. It looked as if he was absorbing all her colour by a process of osmosis.

'Yes, of course,' she said, trying to sound okay and

not as if she was going to collapse into a heap any minute.

Nobby picked out another pen from his magic briefcase, putting it down firmly on the table, resisting the urge to chuck it at the big chap who seemed intent on sabotaging his pitch.

That pen didn't work either. Nobby grabbed it and started shaking it as if the ink had crawled up the shaft deliberately. Jacques sat there watching him, arms folded across his chest, an amused smile playing on his lips.

'I wonder if you'd care to leave the samples with us and let us discuss them,' said Eve. If she didn't get out of this Portakabin and get into a bath to ease this muscle pain she was going to pass out.

'I'll bring you more samples,' said Nobby, also keen to get out and return with higher price-point items if that's what they wanted. He'd kill his assistant when he got back to the office, sending him out with broken goods.

Eve stood to usher Nobby and his briefcase out, but the next few minutes passed in a blur because all she could think about was the gnawing ache in her body. Nobby was taking an eternity to say goodbye to them and then decided to drag an enormous diary out of his case to pin them down to another meeting. Eve couldn't even remember what she arranged with him then as he and his sweat-cloud were gone and she slumped into the chair, pulling in some heavy, calming breaths before reaching for her handbag and checking her car keys were in there.

'You look grey,' said Jacques. 'Are you feeling okay?'

'Perfectly,' said Eve, mustering every bit of strength she had. 'However, I appear to have hurt my back, so I'm going to have to go home to rest it.'

'Do you want me to drive you?'

Eve had a sudden picture of being in a car with Jacques. A clown car with doors that blew off, and a dashboard where flowers sprang out whilst he took corners at G-force and honked a giant horn.

'I'll manage,' she said, putting a brave mask on and walking out to her car. She knew that Jacques was standing in the doorway watching her and so made a monumental effort to walk normally. She wanted to turn around and tell him that it was all right, she wasn't going to collapse, but the effort would have been too much because half of her really did believe that if she didn't get home fast enough, she definitely would collapse in a heap.

Chapter 14

'Shingles,' declared Dr Gilhooley in his soft Irish brogue. He appeared very impressed as he examined Eve's right side. 'And quite a beautiful specimen of it, too.'

'Shingles?' Wasn't that something old people got, thought Eve.

'I'm presuming you had chicken pox as a child,' said the doctor as he wrote out a prescription.

Oh yes. She'd had chicken pox one Christmas. She'd been in bed feeling lousy whilst the sounds of her mother's party from the floor below filtered up to her. People kept coming into her room thinking it was the toilet.

'Well, the virus doesn't leave your body. It stays there waiting for a time to spring back into life again,' went on Dr Gilhooley with all the drama of a Shakespearean actor.

'I've got grown-up chicken pox?' Eve questioned. Never. She felt as if she had been run over by a steamroller.

'I thought it might be shingles when I saw the rash and heard the symptoms. Jeff once had it in the same place,' said Susan. Eve hadn't made it all the way home when she set off from Winterworld. The pain had forced her to curtail her journey and make a pit stop at her aunt's in the hope she could borrow some more supplies of ibuprofen. Susan had taken one look at her niece and pushed her into Violet's old room, then she rang for the doctor. Dr Gilhooley seemed almost smitten by the superior rash on her stomach. He appraised it like a Van Gogh masterpiece.

'Stress sometimes brings it on,' said the doctor, handing over the prescription he had just scribbled to Susan, who was already putting on her coat to go to the pharmacy for it. 'Give her some ibuprofen to start with. There are some strong painkillers on that prescription. She'll need them.'

'I remember my Jeff getting it,' returned Susan. 'He was absolutely felled by it.'

Eve was so tired.

'I'll just have a little nap, Auntie Susan, then I'll be out of your hair,' she said. Susan and Doctor Gilhooley both gave a highly amused bark of laughter.

'You're going nowhere, young lady. For a start, you're highly infectious and secondly, you will need to rest.'

'She doesn't know what rest is. That's why she's got shingles, most likely,' said Susan, turning to the doctor. 'But she sure as hell is going to learn.'

'I can't rest,' said Eve, struggling to keep her eyes from shuttering down. 'I've got too much work to do. I've got novelties to find, reindeer to cancel . . .'

'Never mind all that,' said Dr Gilhooley, presuming she was hallucinating. He closed up his old-fashioned Gladstone bag. 'You can lie back in bed for the next couple of weeks and dream about them instead.'

'Couple of weeks?' Eve tried to swing her legs out of bed but the pain in her back was just too much.

'Oh, at least,' said the crusty-voiced doctor. 'You'll have to let someone else do the running for a while now.'

'You can make one phone call,' said Susan, reaching for Eve's handbag, 'then I'm confiscating your mobile.'

'I'm allowed one phone call? Have I suddenly been transported to prison?'

'Yes,' said her aunt sternly. 'Until you're better, you are in my prison.'

Eve weakly hunted in her bag for her mobile but Susan had to help her in the end. As her aunt followed the doctor out, Eve rang Jacques' number with a feeling of dread as heavy in her stomach as the ache in her back was.

'Ah, Lady Douglas. How are you? Feeling more comfortable I hope,' came his annoyingly joyous voice.

'Never felt better,' said Eve, yawning. 'Apparently I have shingles and am going to have to take a couple of days off.'

'Ooh, nasty,' he drew a long intake of breath. 'Well, don't worry, Winterworld is in safe hands with me.'

About as safe as an orphanage would be in Herod's.

'I took some papers home to look at and sign last night. I need to get them back to you to counter-sign,' said Eve.

'Don't worry about that. I'll get hold of them somehow.'

'I'll give Violet a key to my house. I'll ask her to get them for you,' she said, in case he decided to break in.

'Go rest,' he said. 'And don't worry about a thing. I'm in charge.'

Words which would have instantly made Eve panic, had she the strength to start shaking. She so wanted to sleep, to claim some oblivion from this ache in her back.

'Jacques, please remember the word "winter".

Don't even attempt to think you can convince me to turn this into a purely Christmas extravaganza.'

'As if,' said Jacques, sounding about as convincing as a dieter holding a pork pie in each hand.

Eve clicked off the phone. She would prove Dr Gilhooley wrong. All she needed was a good sleep, then her shoulder would be back at that *winter* grindstone before her so-called partner ran amok. Work was all the medicine she ever required. She had Nobby to meet with again and then she had to sort out the food kiosks. The last thought on her mind before she lost consciousness was 'Would it be feasible to sell reindeer burgers?'

Chapter 15

Three days later, Eve awoke with as much of a jump as her exhausted body would allow. *The candle*. It would be nearly out, if it wasn't already. She tried to sit up, but it wasn't happening. So she tried rolling over, which was more successful except that she couldn't stop and ended up on the carpet, where she found herself stuck. She heard Auntie Susan's footsteps thundering up the staircase.

'Goodness gracious, Eve, what do you think you're doing?' said Susan brusquely, but her hands were kind and caring as she hoisted up her niece and deposited her back in bed.

'I've got to go home,' said Eve.

'Whatever it is you think you have to go home for, it can wait,' said Susan, lifting up one of the bottles of pills on the bedside table and unscrewing the lid. 'I don't know, I hardly see you for years and you're in a hurry to get away from me. Anyone would think this was a remake of *Misery*. I might have to hobble you if you decide to escape again.'

Eve might have laughed at that had she not felt sick and as if someone had stolen all her bones and replaced them with jelly.

'Anyway, you timed that fall out of bed beautifully, your next meds are due. I hate having to wake you up to give them to you. I remember Jeff saying that sleep was as good as it gets when you have shingles.'

'The candle flame will go out,' said Eve. She felt so weak and wobbly and useless as the tears began to flow out of her eyes.

'Ah,' said Susan, understanding now. 'Well, I'll ring Violet, shall I?' She lifted a tablet to Eve's lips and then a glass of water. 'Don't you worry about your flame, we'll sort that out. You need to rest. Take a drink, love, then settle back down. I'll try and get hold of her now.'

'The house keys are in my bag.'

'I'll find your keys, don't you worry. Now, don't you dare get out of that bed again. You sleep, young lady.'

Eve heard her aunt on the phone talking to Violet. 'It's urgent,' she was saying. 'It's the candle.' She was once again asleep before she heard any more.

Chapter 16

Violet clicked off her mobile and looked across at Pav who had his big strong back towards her as he painted the fifth snow pony onto the wall. It reminded her of when he was painting the walls of Carousel. Except he was working considerably faster in her cousin's café than he was in her own. A point which she felt duty bound to mention.

'Ah, but I wanted to hang around in your café as long as possible,' he said, turning around and grinning at her. 'Here is it not so important to be slow because when the work is done, I know I will still see you.'

'Crafty,' Violet smiled as he winked at her. As always, being in his presence made her feel so warm and loved. Alas she did not add 'safe' to the list. One day, when she was forty, Pav would have his head turned by someone twenty years younger than her, she was sure. He was hers to enjoy for a little while, then he would go and leave her heart in pieces.

'I'm going out for a bit,' she said. 'I need to collect some things from Eve's house.'

'Okay,' said Pav. 'How is she?'

'Wobbly,' said Violet. 'And fretting about the flame. Poor thing.'

As she opened the door to go out, Jacques had his hand on the other side of the handle to come in. She had only been introduced to him days ago and yet she felt as if she had known him for years. Both she and Pav found him affable, cheery and charming, and anything but the annoying twerp that Eve had painted him as. Around the park people referred to him as 'Captain' because they found him to be an able leader, a confident and capable boss. He was well liked, he rolled his sleeves up and wasn't above being hands-on. She didn't buy into Eve's theory that Jacques and Major Jack were one and the same. Con men like that wouldn't risk exposure by working front line with lots of people.

When he entered the café his grin seemed to make the temperature rise by ten degrees.

'Hi,' he said.

'Hi and bye,' laughed Violet.

'Something I said?' chuckled Jacques.

'I've got to go and pick some things up from Eve's house, and I need to do it rather quickly,' Violet said.

'How is she?' asked Jacques.

'Poorly,' sighed Violet. 'I can't imagine she's very pleased about being incapacitated.' Actually, that was an understatement. She imagined that if Eve was in any state of being compos mentis, she would be furious to be confined to bed. Not least because of what her partner would be doing in her absence – and with good reason. The man was a walking dynamo. Eve was going to be livid when she found out what he had been up to in the past few days, left to his own devices. Huge wooden candy canes had appeared everywhere, and he had been experimenting with adding glitter to the snow machines so the snowflakes were extra sparkly.

'Did Eve mention anything about some papers she took home to sign? She said you'd get them for me, Violet. It's quite important I have them,' said Jacques.

'I'll have a look, of course,' replied Violet, thinking that she wouldn't have a clue where to start looking for those. She headed out to her car, only to find that it was blocked in by two of the workmen's vans. The people working on the park seemed to be doubling by the day. She would have to ring for a taxi – it would be quicker than trying to find out which workmen the vans belonged to.

She doubled-back to the ice-cream parlour to ring for a taxi because her mobile was low on battery. She found Pav and Jacques engaged in merry conversation. Jacques was fascinated by the white horses that Pav was painting on the walls. Violet was dreading telling Eve that 'the Captain' had decided the ice-cream parlour was to be called 'Santa's Snow-Cones', although she loved the idea. Jacques seemed a genuinely great bloke and she wondered how Eve could possibly have taken such a dislike to him – she was usually a very good judge of character.

'No need to ring for a taxi, I'll drive you,' Jacques volunteered. 'My car is parked at the front. They wouldn't dare block me in.' He laughed his big booming Brian Blessed laugh and Violet followed him out.

His car is just like him, thought Violet as they headed off down the main road. Warm, clean, big and safe. It smelt lovely too – the air in the car was scented with his pine-forest aftershave. She liked a man who carried a nice scent – Pav always did.

'So Eve is going to be off work a little longer than she anticipated, then?' he asked, interrupting her musings.

'Yes, and I'm not really surprised,' Violet nodded sadly. 'They say you can get shingles if you're run down and that's what I think is wrong with her. She never lets herself have any rest.'

'Workaholic, eh?'

'Too right,' Violet agreed. She knew that Eve

kept herself busy so she wouldn't have time to think too much. Eve wasn't very kind to herself and a little part of Violet was actually glad – in a strange way – that she was being forced to recharge her batteries. She hadn't grieved over Jonathan's death. Grieving was a way of letting go, and Eve refused to grieve because she hadn't let him go.

Eve's house was only a twenty-minute drive away from Winterworld.

Jacques looked at the house he had just pulled up in front of. 'Darklands', read a sign above the door-bell. It was a large Victorian villa with a huge front picture window. It wasn't at all what he expected of Eve's house. He imagined something swish and stark and pristine, not a tired-looking building with a scraggy front garden.

As if Violet knew what was going through his mind, she said, 'I wish Eve would sell it and buy something easier to manage. The back garden is enormous. She keeps saying she's going to get a gardener, but it never happens.' She always thought the name of the house summed it up perfectly. It was a dreary place and a bit spooky, if she was honest.

'It has a beautiful façade,' said Jacques kindly, accentuating the positives.

'Yes, I suppose so,' nodded Violet, looking at the ornate stonework above and around the door and the bay window. It was grand, there were no two ways about it, but it wasn't 'Eve'. At least not this present lonely Eve, who should have been in a cosy cottage – like Violet's own beloved Postbox Cottage. The vivacious, laughing Eve, with the wonderfully clever soldier-fiancé, who was going to restore the house to its former glory fitted here – but that Eve with the big smile was as dead as the dashing soldier was.

'Would you like to come in with me and see if you can find your papers?' asked Violet. She hated the feel of the cold house and the comforting presence of Jacques would be a blessing. Her mum had told her to bring some clothes for Eve too whilst she was there.

Jacques seemed only too happy to accompany Violet inside. He was intrigued to see more of the house. He'd always believed a house was a reflection of the people living in it.

Violet unlocked the heavy front door and pushed hard at it as there was a bank of letters behind it. She picked them up and put them in her handbag to take to her cousin. Jacques strode in behind her, looking at the chunky oak staircase and the photos of Eve and Jonathan that hung on the walls. Ah, that's what she looks like when she smiles, he thought to himself. Smiling, happy Eve looked years younger than suspicious, over-worked Eve. Whilst he was looking at the photographs, Violet went into the office to sort out the candle. Not only was it still lit, but there were days of wax left. The candle took a month to burn and it wasn't even halfway down yet. She looked on Eve's desk but didn't see any of the papers which Jacques might be looking for.

'I can't find any documents in her office, so try looking in the kitchen. I think Eve works on the big table on her laptop in there,' said Violet, pointing to the kitchen door. 'I'm just going upstairs to get some clothes.'

There was nothing on the kitchen table, so Jacques took it upon himself to look in Eve's office for himself. It was a large square room with a high ceiling, dominated by a big wooden desk already gathering a sprinkling of dust. He found what he was looking for weighed down by a heart-shaped frame on a shelf. The photo inside was the handsome soldier and a grinning Eve. Jacques picked it up and studied it. Her hair was loose and the wind was blowing it. Her eyes were cat-green and sparkling with life. She hadn't a clue what was around the corner in that photograph.

Just after Violet had filled up a small hold-all, the realization hit her that she had permitted a total stranger to walk around her cousin's house – a stranger that Eve didn't trust. Eve would have been furious to think that Jacques Glace of all people was looking at her things, her photographs. I really shouldn't let him roam around the house unaccompanied, she then thought to herself, and hurried down the stairs to find Jacques in the kitchen looking at a sepia photo of old Evelyn on the wall, and not burgling the place. He was holding some documents under his arm.

'You found them, then?'

'Yes, thanks. I'll countersign these so they can be actioned. I have some papers in the car that Eve needs to sign pretty quickly too,' said Jacques. 'They can't wait for her to get fully better I'm afraid.'

'Give them to me and I'll get her signature for you.'

'She was a lovely old lady, wasn't she?' he said fondly, glancing up again at the photo on the wall.

'I never met her,' said Violet. 'But I know how incredibly fond of her Eve was. How long did you know her?'

'About a year and a half.'

'How did you meet her?' asked Violet, in her gentle conversational way that bore no hint of prying.

'Hospital visiting,' said Jacques. 'Bringing a bit of company to the infirm. She made me smile a lot, did old Evelyn.'

'Ah,' Violet said. So there was no more mystery to it than that. She smiled, recalling Eve's wild theories that Jacques had hypnotized Aunt Evelyn or tricked her, Harold Shipman style, into leaving him half her fortune, when the reality was that he had simply done a stint at being a hospital visitor and ended up chatting to a lonely old lady. That would tie in with the time when Evelyn went into hospital with the mini stroke that seemed to give her a new lease of life.

'I know it was her fantasy to build a theme park; she had a great deal of fun planning it in hospital. She had books full of drawings and ideas. I must admit, though, I never thought her dream would leave the paper,' said Jacques, a smile curving his lips. 'It was as big a surprise to me as it was to everyone else, and I certainly never expected to inherit half of it.' He seemed to be making the point quite clearly.

'It was Evelyn's money to do with as she wished,' said Violet in response. 'She was a woman very much of her own mind.'

'Like her great-niece then,' said Jacques. 'Only softer.'

He said it factually, not unkindly, but still Violet felt duty bound to jump to Eve's defence.

'Eve's not hard, Jacques, however she may come across at the moment. She's just . . .' Violet realized she might be saying too much. Jacques was too easy to talk to, to trust. If he was a con-man, he'd be really good at it, Violet thought. She shut up and walked over to the fridge to check for out-of-date food that might need throwing away.

'You were saying,' Jacques prompted her. 'About Eve?'

'She's hurting,' said Violet. She had no intention of spilling her cousin's business and being disloyal, but at the same time she didn't want Eve to be judged harshly. 'Eve hasn't been Eve since her fiancé Jonathan died. He was a soldier, killed in Helmand on Christmas Day, five years ago.' She tipped some rather rank milk down the sink and ran the tap to sluice it away.

'Ah,' said Jacques. 'And she can't move on.'

'No,' said Violet. 'She can't.'

She hated the thought that Eve was existing until the day she died to be reunited with Jonathan. She had often thought about blowing out the candle, hoping that Eve would see that as a sign from Jonathan that they must part and she should start to live, but she couldn't bring herself to do it and betray her cousin. She didn't know if that was the right thing to do or not.

'She was always so smiley,' said Violet, not liking that the Eve of today wasn't the real Eve. 'Okay, she always hated Christmas and probably with good reason . . .' Violet pulled the rein hard on herself. Eve's rotten upbringing with a purely selfish mother wasn't her story to tell. 'But she was – is – a great person, with a big heart, a kind, sweet soul. She's just stuck in a rut. And she won't get out of it whilst that flame is still burning.' *And it will burn forever and Eve will end up like Evelyn – mourning until she is an old lady.*

'Flame?' inquired Jacques.

'The candle in her office,' said Violet. 'As long as it burns, she reads that as a sign that Jonathan is still hers and she is still his.'

'Oh no. I've just blown it out,' said Jacques with a gulp. 'I thought it was a fire hazard.'

'Oh God. We have to relight it.' She turned to the drawers behind her and started hunting around for a match. Jacques took the cupboards above.

'Got some,' said Violet. 'Whatever you do, don't tell Eve what you did. In fact, don't tell Eve you were here at all. She'll kill us both.'

They both walked back into the office to see the strangest thing – the light was back and dancing on top of the candle.

Chapter 17

When Violet arrived at her mum's house, Susan was sitting at the kitchen table, laughing at today's apology in the *Trumpet*.

'Listen to this,' she said. "*In Saturday's edition, it was reported that Mrs Christine Buckley was always renowned for being an elephant lady. We did, of course, mean that Mrs Buckley was always renowned for being an elegant lady. We apologize to Mrs Buckley for any distress sustained.*" I'm sure none of them read the newspaper before it goes to print.'

Violet chuckled.

'They must print an apology at least three times a week. Sometimes they have to apologize for the apology because the apology ends up being worse than the original mistake.'

'I should cut them out and collect them,' said Susan, pulling a mug out of the cupboard for her daughter. It was the one with butterflies on it – Nan's old cup. 'I wish I hadn't thrown that one away now that advertised the special weekend offer for an eleven-inch, crusty penis with five toppings of your choice. The owner of Luigi's must have gone barmy at that.'

Violet laughed heartily then clamped her hand over her mouth because her old room was directly above. 'How's the invalid?'

'Asleep. I've just been up to check on her. Don't go up, Violet, in case you wake her. As you know, I'm a great advocate of sleep for the poorly.'

'I promised Jacques I'd get her to sign some documents,' said Violet. 'I'll be as quick as I can.'

A few minutes later, Violet had returned, hating herself for having had to wake up her cousin, stick a pen in her hand and watch Eve sign her name before flopping back on the pillow again. Eve hadn't even checked what she was signing her name to, which was most unlike her.

'Poor thing,' said Violet, lifting up her cup. 'She's zonked out.'

'Nothing better than sleep for the poorly,' nodded Susan, and Violet thought back to the days when she was young and not so well, and Mum tucking her up in bed with a fat, cosy, hot-water bottle. *You get to sleep and let the fairy nurses make you better in your dreams,* Susan used to say.

'I've made sure the candle is fine, and I'll be off in a moment to take these forms to Jacques. He wants them quite urgently.'

'Oh, her favourite person,' said Susan. 'What's he like, this Jacques Glace? She's got a real bee in her bonnet about him, hasn't she? She woke up yesterday shouting out his name, and not in a very complimentary way.'

'I think he's lovely,' said Violet. 'Big, cheerful, friendly, handsome too. He's got short grey hair and nice shiny eyes and big solid shoulders like Pav. He winds her up terribly,' said Violet. 'He is an imp. He keeps making flirty jokes and saying that he's going to marry her. It doesn't go down very well, as you can imagine.'

'Ah,' said Susan. Then she fell so quiet that Violet knew there was something Susan wasn't telling her.

'Mum, what is it?'

Susan didn't answer. She just stared at her cup for a few minutes and seemed to be building herself up for a massive revelation.

'Mum?' prompted Violet.

Susan lifted her head. 'Patrick. Patrick. Patrick,' she stammered.

'What's this – butcher's Tourette's?'

'Patrick's asked me to marry him,' Susan blurted out. Then she waited for her daughter's reaction with a fearful expression on her face.

'That's brilliant!' said Violet, breaking into a big smile and throwing her arms around her mum. 'He's a lovely fella. I'm thrilled for you.'

'Are you okay with it, really?' said Susan, collapsing into a sigh of relief.

'Of course, I am,' said Violet, taking a celebratory swig of coffee. 'You've been on your own for far too long. You deserve to be happy with a nice man.'

'We should make it a double,' said Susan. 'I can't understand why you don't marry that lovely man of yours.'

Violet nursed her cup. 'We're okay as we are,' she said, unable to convey the voice to back up the words. She didn't want the tears to come to her eyes, but they did all the same.

'Love, what's up?' said Susan. 'Don't you love him any more? Don't you keep any more big secrets from me, my girl. I've had enough of that sort of thing for five lifetimes.'

'Love him?' Violet gave a dry chuckle. 'I love him so much it hurts me. But he's nine years younger than me, Mum. Six years ago he was a teenager. He's too young to commit for ever.'

'Oh, Violet, how do you know that?' said Susan, stroking the white-blonde hair back from her daughter's face. 'Your dad and I were only bairns when we married. And we knew what we were doing.'

'Dad wasn't nine years younger than you. Pav

might think he wants to settle down, but one day he'll realize that he's drop-dead gorgeous, married to a forty-something, and twenty-year-old women with pert boobs and no wrinkles will be flinging themselves at him.' Violet pushed the tears back with the tips of her fingers.

'Violet. Listen to me,' said Susan, taking her daughter's hand. 'Love – and I'm talking proper, deep love – doesn't come along as often as you might think. And when it does, you have to grab it with both hands and hang on to the gift that life gives you. You've only got to think of her upstairs if you need any proof of that one. I never thought I'd meet anyone else after your father died. But I have, and I'm lucky for that. I don't know that in ten years' time Patrick won't have an affair or get run over by a bus, but I can't turn down my chance of happiness because of what might never happen. We only have the here and now as a definite.'

Violet nodded. She knew what her mother was saying was right but she was still frightened to commit herself wholly to Pav. She needed to keep something back in reserve to protect herself because otherwise, when the day came when he would leave, there would be nothing left of her.

Chapter 18

The Daily Trumpet *would like to amend the entry made in last Friday's journal. We did, of course, mean that Mr Donald Hill was a famous factory mogul, not a famous fat Tory mongrel as printed.*

We recognize this has caused some distress to Mr Hill and his wife, Brian, and wish to extend our sincere apologies.

Chapter 19

The Daily Trumpet *would like to apologize for the entry made in last Tuesday's edition when we referred to Mr Donald Hill's wife as Brian. This should have read Pamela. We regret any distress caused.*

NOVEMBER

Chapter 20

It took over three damp, miserable, cold weeks before Eve could stand for more than two minutes without the pain in her back dragging her into a curled foetal position. Behind Susan's back one day she got dressed, which took forever, and then opened the back door to see if she could walk to her car. She couldn't. Who would have thought a variation on a childhood illness could have laid her so low. She conceded defeat and got back into bed before her auntie discovered her and slapped her legs.

At least the blisters on her front had dried up, but they itched like crazy and a large tub of aqueous calamine cream was her new best friend. She had smeared so much on that it had seeped slightly through her skirt, but it would have to do; her jacket would cover it up. Auntie Susan had tried to insist that Eve took another week off, but Eve now had just enough strength to stand her ground. Just. Plus she needed to find out what was going on with Winterworld because no one would tell her. Violet was infuriatingly vague. All she would say was that everything was going to plan, according to Jacques, and she wasn't to worry.

'My plan or his plan?' Eve asked.

'It's all looking fantastic,' Violet replied. Which didn't exactly answer Eve's question directly, and made her suspicious.

On the morning of her first day back at work, Eve had to borrow a large safety pin from her aunt as her skirt was too big. She had lost over a stone and a half since coming down with shingles. As Eve stepped through the door for the first time, the fresh air went straight to her brain like a triple shot of vodka and she toppled slightly.

'That's it, you're going back to bed,' said Susan, attempting to shepherd her frail niece back indoors. 'Violet, help me get her inside.'

'Auntie Susan, as much as I've enjoyed your hospitality, if I have to spend one more day in bed, I will scream,' said Eve. 'And I need to get back to Winterworld because you, Violet Flockton, are being very short on detail.'

'With good reason,' Violet returned. 'You needed to rest body and head.' She didn't add that she was terrified to tell her cousin what had been going on.

Eve's adrenaline levels would be up to Usain Bolt's, three seconds before his torso broke the finishing line. Maybe it wasn't a bad thing that Eve was going back to work on this early, sunless, mid-November day so she could see all the changes for herself. Violet couldn't keep up being evasive for any longer.

As Violet drove them closer to Winterworld, the triangular tops of the Christmas trees came into view – all white with sparkling snow. Eve felt the first stirrings of panic. She had – up to this point – imagined that the operation had more or less ground to a halt in her absence. But the closer they got to Winterworld and saw the number of vehicles crowded outside the gates, the more wrong she realized she had been. It was as if she had fast-forwarded a year rather than just less than a month.

As they pulled into the car park and then walked through the gates, she was seeing a very different place to the one she had left, clutching her back. This world was full of trees strung with Christmas lights. Engineers were testing out a snow machine and a flurry of large dry flakes fell on her head for a few seconds. Workmen were hammering inside the log cabins and two of them were fixing a tall, chunky signpost in the ground. Various arrows at the top pointed to Santa's grotto, The Snow Ponies, Santa's Snow-Cones Ice-Cream Parlour – *What?* The Elf Theatre. *The Elf Theatre?* thought Eve. Where the bollocks did that feature on the original plans? There were red-and-white-striped candy canes everywhere she looked as well. Then she spotted one of the arrows pointing to The Reindeer. Damn, she never had stopped its arrival. The sodding thing had probably arrived by now. Then a troupe of midgets in green elf suits passed by carrying brown hessian sacks, causing Eve to shake her head in the hope that the vision would dissipate – it didn't. They were, if the signpost was to be believed, heading for their designated theatre. Effin Williams was barking at a trio of workmen sweeping up some broken glass.

'*Ti mor iwsless a cachu carw!*'

'He says we're as useless as reindeer shit,' said Arfon, one of the Welsh joiners, wearily translating for his Polish co-worker.

Why was everything so bloody glittery? How much tinsel was wrapped around those trees? Who sanctioned a 'bauble market'?

'Well, hello!' came a big booming voice to her left. Eve turned slowly to see her nemesis, or partner, as she supposed she had better call him.

'What have you done?' she said, her voice no louder than a breath.

'I've been busy,' said Jacques with hearty smugness.

'I can see that,' said Eve.

'I'm glad you approve, I'm rather proud . . .'

'I didn't say I approve,' said Eve, her voice finding

some volume. 'In fact, I don't approve at all – not one bit. Which part of "do not turn this into a Christmas extravaganza" didn't you understand? This. Is. Supposed. To. Be. Winterworld.'

'Same thing,' sniffed Jacques.

'No, it is NOT,' said Eve, feeling the rise of temper inside her. Some other workmen were chuntering to each other in Polish as they pulled a huge sleigh loaded with wrapped presents in the direction of the gift shop. Eve watched it pass in front of her with a mouth open in disbelief, whilst Effin was screaming at the men, stabbing his finger in the opposite direction.

'The grotto. I said take it to the bloody grotto. *Dw i erioed 'di gweithio 'da'r fath grŵp o dwats di-glem!*'

'What he say?' asked Mik, one of the Polish sledge-pullers.

Once again Arfon translated it.

'He said that he's never worked with such a group of incompetent twats. We're in the wrong job us, Mik. We should be employed as official interpreters in this place.'

Mik then translated what Effin had said into Polish and Eve watched the Polish workers bow their heads to hide their sniggering.

'Who authorized that sleigh thing? I thought all monies spent had to be jointly signed for,' said Eve.

'Ah, well.' Jacques stroked his stubble. 'The thing

is, we needed to act quickly, and so thank goodness you gave me permission.'

'I most certainly did not,' said Eve. Then her brain caught up. Violet had asked her to sign some forms when she wasn't quite compos mentis. He'd got her own cousin to do his dirty work – the conniving bastard. Oh boy, he was starting to show his colours now.

'This isn't happening,' said Eve, watching a trio of snowmen bumble past her, carrying wreaths of holly leaves and boxes labelled 'baubles'. She was still in the grip of shingles and having a nightmare. Any minute she was going to wake up and see the Winterworld she had imagined, devoid of stupid things like elves, candy canes and bloody reindeer.

'We have even got our first booking for the wedding chapel,' said Jacques with a little wink. Then he sighed. 'Shame it wasn't us, but then again we can wait.'

'More fool them,' she whispered under her breath as she turned away. She had only been in his presence for five minutes and already her heart was thumping with fury.

'Come and let me show you the animal enclosure,' he said, chuckling at her bristling. 'You'll notice something very different about it since the last time you saw it.'

'I hope I will,' said Eve, 'considering the last time I saw it, it was a square of mud.'

'The ponies have arrived and totally settled in,' said Jacques.

'Great,' replied Eve, in a voice that reflected the news was anything but great.

'And she arrived on Saturday,' he said, keeping to her pace.

'She?' asked Eve. 'Who is "she"?'

'Holly.'

'Holly who?'

'Hollywood . . . hurrah for Hollywood!' Jacques started to sing with a very bad Ethel Merman vibrato.

Eve looked blankly at him.

'It sounded like we were doing a knock-knock joke,' he explained.

'Hmm,' hummed Eve, totally unimpressed by his attempt at humour.

'What do you think of the enchanted forest, then?' asked Jacques, pride beaming in his eyes as they entered the small forest of snow-capped firs twinkling with lights.

'It's nice,' Eve nodded with reserved approval, even though she was far more impressed than she let on. The forest looked as if it had been there for ever. There was a magical prickling in the air, like a low dose of electricity, which hung like the lanterns between the trees. For a few seconds it was as if she had wandered into her childhood favourite book, *The Enchanted Wood*, where the trees were a darker shade of green than usual and whispered their secrets to each other with a wisha-wisha-wisha sound overhead. And the smell was like fresh, pine-scented aftershave, though she realized a split second later that it was drifting from Jacques. She didn't like the way his 'enchanted forest' was making her feel. It was dredging up a memory of her Auntie Susan taking her and Violet to see the Father Christmas who visited Higher Hoppleton Hall every year. She had a clear memory of walking into the oak-panelled library and seeing the huge man with the long white beard and small half-moon glasses, and *knowing* he was the real one. That was especially sweet because she had been losing her faith. At school, the class rough-arse Charlene Prince had been mocking her for still believing in Santa, but after meeting him at Higher Hoppleton all her doubts disappeared. Then four days later, she woke up on Christmas morning to find no presents because Ruth had been too plastered the night before and forgot to put them out. Charlene Prince was right after all – he didn't exist, and something in Eve began to die that Christmas. And kept on dying more with every passing Christmas until it died outright five years ago.

A curling path had been laid through the wood for the pony and trap rides. At least Jacques hadn't over-ridden her plans on that score whilst she was ill.

As if reading her thoughts, he said, 'Path okay for you? Does it meet with your approval?'

'Yes,' said Eve, unable to resist adding, 'remarkably.'

'Good,' said Jacques. 'Think how romantic it will be to ride a pony and trap to the wedding chapel through here. Or the betrothed couple could take the mini-train if they so wish. The forest will be covered in twinkling lights.'

'It is already.'

'Oh, this is nothing compared to what it will be like,' said Jacques. 'Romantic with a capital R.'

Eve nodded. He was right, it would probably be the most romantic part of the whole ceremony.

'And there will be snowmen and elves waving at the bride and groom from behind the trees,' Jacques went on.

Eve groaned. 'Dear God. You're not serious?'

The man was a walking joke from a Christmas cracker.

The small, pretty forest began to thin and within a few steps it was behind them and Eve was standing at the side of the reindeer enclosure. She had just opened her mouth to drop a sarcastic comment about how stunning the fence was when Jacques raised his finger to his lips.

'Shhh,' he said. 'Prepare to meet Holly.' Then he started to make a soft clicking noise with his tongue and his teeth.

Just when Eve was about to tell him not to hand in his day job and become an animal trainer, she saw an inquisitive nose protrude from the side of the reindeer shed.

'Come on, girl. Come on,' encouraged Jacques in a voice so soft and quiet that Eve wouldn't have thought it possible to have come from him.

With a two steps forward, one step backwards pattern, the small, barrel-tummied, white reindeer edged outwards and towards them slowly.

'Isn't she lovely?' whispered Jacques. 'She's pregnant. Naughty Olly in her last home cleared a five-foot fence to be with her. But who could blame him?'

The reindeer sniffed the air as if trying to pick up the scent of whether she was faced with a friend or a foe. Her soft, dark eyes told Eve that she wanted to trust them, but was afraid, and Eve's heart lurched in her chest in sympathy.

Jacques held out his hand and Holly backed up. 'It's okay, girl, come on.'

Holly seemed to inch towards his hand, then sniffed and jerked backwards, but Jacques' patience paid off and finally the reindeer pushed her head against his cupped fingers.

'She's been hand-reared,' said Jacques. 'She likes affection. But then, don't we all?' And he took Eve's hand firmly and placed it on the reindeer's cheek.

Eve thought it would be wiry, but Holly's fur was thick and soft.

'She likes you,' said Jacques, taking away his hand and letting Holly rub her head against Eve's fingers.

'Oh, she's lovely,' said Eve, mesmerized by this experience, which wasn't on her list of top ten things to do. Holly's fur was so thick she couldn't get her fingers through it. And she'd presumed the reindeer would be much bigger and clumsier-looking than this, with big, dangerous antlers. Eve suddenly became very aware of being watched and turned to see Jacques staring at her, wearing a grin so cheesy it should have come free with a packet of Jacob's crackers.

'You've taken to her big-time, haven't you?' he said. 'You'll be heading up a chorus of 'Rudolf the Red-Nosed Reindeer' any minute now.'

'Don't bet on it,' said Eve, letting her hand drop. 'When's she due to give birth?'

'Could be any time. She's very big,' said Jacques.

'Does the local vet help reindeer give birth?' Admittedly it was a change from diagnosing wet-tail in hamsters. 'I presume you've asked?'

'Believe it or not, I have that covered,' said Jacques. 'You'll have to get up much earlier than that to catch me out. Mr Fleece did a stint at a wildlife park. He can handle a delivery of a reindeer baby when it comes.'

'Mr Fleece?' Well, that was a great name for a vet, thought Eve. On more than one level.

'Yep. He's a jolly good fellow,' replied Jacques, deadpan.

Eve was just about to ask what on earth he was on about when she got it: *Fleece a jolly good fellow*. She shook her head, tried not to groan, and turned her back on both Holly and him. Poring over the accounts book was preferable to his stand-up comedy routine. Pulling her own teeth out would have been preferable to his stand-up comedy routine, if she was honest.

In the distance, Effin's Carmarthenshire tones were splitting the air as he showered abuse on his workmen – Welsh and Polish alike.

'I think in a past life he was Attila the Hun,' said Jacques. And Eve smiled, though she didn't want to. She quickly recovered.

'Right, if you can take me through all that you've done since I was last here, I'd be very grateful,' said Eve, trying not to sound as in need of a sit down and a rejuvenating coffee as she was.

'Certainly,' said Jacques. 'Come and look at the ponies. Shame the traps haven't arrived yet, we could have tested out that romantic drive through the forest.'

'Thank heaven for small mercies,' said Eve, moving towards the horses.

She didn't want to like them, really – they were just animals who were going to make her money, but she couldn't help herself. The 'snow ponies' were delightful creatures, five old white ponies, and sharing their paddock was a twenty-five-year-old, huge white Shire Horse called Christopher – all of them had been destined for the knackers yard before Aunt Evelyn stepped in to rescue them. She had arranged stabling for them all until the park was ready to take them. The stables they were now being housed in at Winterworld were the equine version of a Hilton.

'Your Aunt Evelyn loved horses, didn't she?' said Jacques.

'Erm, yes,' replied Eve, but in truth she didn't know if her aunt had or not. She had only ever heard her talk about cats.

'The people at the stables were very sad to hear she'd died. She went to visit the ponies every week, apparently.'

Another side to Aunt Evelyn that Eve hadn't a clue had existed.

'They're so friendly,' said Jacques as Christopher lumbered to the fence and Jacques reached out and stroked his muzzle.

'He's very big, isn't he?' said Eve, hoping the thing wasn't going to suddenly jump over and trample them to death.

'He's a softy. Stroke him.'

Eve showed willing and put her hand on the horse's head. He seemed to like it, because when she stopped he nudged her hand, wanting more.

'Not sure he's had a lot of love in his life,' said Jacques. 'But we'll make up for it here, won't we, fella.'

'Touching,' said Eve drily. 'Okay, show me the rest.'

They headed back into the lovely man-made forest, and once again she was visited by that sweet ache of a rare Christmas memory which she could think of without wanting to run from it.

Jacques must have had the ability to stop time, was Eve's only thought, as he showed her all that had changed in the past month. It wasn't possible. Well it was, with the amount of workmen they had, but still . . . The log cabins were complete and ready to be furnished, the restaurant was equipped, the gift shop fully stocked with really nice stuff, which he obviously hadn't got from Nobby Scuttle. Eve couldn't remember seeing a conical cabin selling soup and hot chocolate on the original plans, but one had sprung up at the side of the ice-cream parlour. Elf-people were practising their shows and routines in a specially built theatre, snow machines were discreetly placed everywhere and puffing out practice sprays of snow. To say that Eve was over-whelmed by the changes was putting it finely. She didn't like the idea that her absence had shown her to be almost expendable, because she hadn't thought anyone could have powered a project like her, but Jacques Glace – the idiot buffoon Jacques Glace – had surpassed anything she could have done in less than a month. He left her in the Portakabin needing a sit down and a coffee, and exited with a smiling sense of pride that he had gobsmacked her with his military-precision organizational skills. He knew it would have rankled that she had met her match as far as making things happen went. That much he had learned first-hand from old Evelyn Douglas.

Eve tried not to be impressed, but it wasn't happening. The man wasn't human. She expected to find the paperwork a mess, but it was exactly the opposite. Everything was accounted for, filed precisely, the figures stacked up to the penny. It's all too perfect, her brain told her. It's so good that there has to be something wrong. Now she was on the mend, she could carry on her private investigations about the serial con-artist who had gone to ground for a few years, and if there was any link whatsoever to Mr Glace, she would have him in a police cell as soon as look at him. Then Aunt Evelyn's will would be altered and Winterworld would be all hers.

She lifted up an invoice for 200 Schneekugel which had been shipped in from Germany. It didn't help that the invoice was in German. But whatever he had bought cost thousands of euros. Maybe, this was it – the first evidence she had of a scam, she thought with some glee. She grabbed the invoice and marched off to find Mr Glace.

After a five-minute fruitless search, Eve went into the ice-cream parlour, which was really taking shape now. Pav was putting the finishing touches to his mural – white glitter paint on the white Carousel horses that adorned the walls. Violet was in the kitchen humming 'White Christmas' as she stirred some edible silver flakes into a white ice-cream mix.

'Haven't seen Jacques, have you?' Eve asked.

'No, I haven't, sorry,' said Violet.

'Any idea what a Schneekugel is, Pav?' asked Eve.

'Yes, it's a ball,' said Pav, struggling to find the words. 'A snow ball.'

'I hope not,' said Eve. 'If I found out Mr Glace has spent three zillion quid on snowballs I might be cutting off his own snowballs.'

'Ah, I remember,' said Pav. 'He is in plot two with the carousel.'

'I might have known he'd be playing on swings,' Eve grumbled. 'See you later.'

Violet watched her cousin stride off in the direction of the fun park area.

'I think Eve protests too much,' said Pav, who had turned to watch Violet watching Eve.

'What do you mean?'

'I think if she let her guard down, she and Jacques would be very good for each other. He's a good man.'

'She never lets her guard down,' said Violet.

'You women always have your guards raised,' said Pav, lifting his forearms in front of his face. 'Like a portcullis. You think only enemies are waiting outside, not friends.'

There was a sadness in his eyes as he turned his attentions back to his painting. And Violet didn't say anything, because she knew he was right.

Chapter 21

Plot two in Winterworld would formally be known as Winterpark when the sign was raised over the great iron arch that marked the entrance. Three of Effin's men were just fixing the 'PARK' part of the name – luckily for Eve's blood pressure, she didn't see the 'SANTA' part that would go up to prefix it – another of Jacques' changes. In the near distance, the first horse was being bolted onto the biggest carousel Eve had ever seen in her life – a horse as white and sparkling as the horses on the ice-cream parlour wall. Eve's heart was stabbed again with a memory of being at a Christmas fair in the park as a youngster, spending all her pocket money on the carousel rides rather than use some of it to hook-a-duck. She remembered waving to her mother, then seeing a man approaching Ruth and taking her attention away. Whenever there was a man on the scene,

Eve was pushed right to the back of the queue for her mother's time and affection.

Jacques' loud singing of 'Let it Snow' with all the wrong words rang out from a nearby log cabin.

'Oh, the weather is really bummy, but the fire is super scrummy . . .'

That was another log cabin that wasn't on the original plan. If she didn't know better, she would have thought Jacques Glace had magicked her into having shingles so he could have his own way on everything.

'*Bonjour, ma cherie*,' he boomed as she walked into a shelf-lined cabin to find him knee-deep in boxes, opening them all with a Stanley knife. His cheery face made her cross, and she shook the invoice at him, which seemed to amuse him and inflamed her even further.

'What are Schneekugel?' she snapped. 'And why have you bought two hundred of them over from Germany at the price of Roman Abramovich's yacht?'

He crossed his arms and looked at her with mischief playing in his eyes. 'What do you think they are?'

He knows he is irritating the crap out of me, thought Eve to herself. She tried not to rise to the bait, but failed.

'I don't know what they are,' she growled. 'Pav

said they're snowballs. Please tell me that's lost something in translation.'

'Didn't you look them up on Google Translate?'

'Wha . . . why . . . Just tell me what they are please, Mr Glace. And why you've bought so many.' Her hand flicked back some stray pieces of her dark-brown hair. 'Aunt Evelyn might as well have burned all her money. And that carousel is enormous.'

'Yes, I know,' said Jacques. 'But what a magnificent specimen it is. I know a man who buys them and restores them.'

'Ah, you "know a man", do you?' humphed Eve. 'Pity you didn't "know a man" who could have let you have two hundred Schneekugel cheap instead of paying this amount of euros,' and once again she shook the invoice.

'Actually I did,' replied Jacques. 'A German man – Herr Kutz.'

Another pathetic joke. Did the man ever turn off?

'Oh, for goodness sake. Just for once, can't I get a sensib—'

'Look at the signature at the bottom,' said Jacques. 'I kid you not.'

There at the bottom of the invoice, in best copper-plate, was the name 'Helmut Kutz'.

'Helmut gave us this consignment at a cut price. One hundred to exhibit, one hundred to sell. And they will sell.' And he pulled from a box something covered in bubble wrap which he peeled off and handed over to Eve: a polished glass globe. 'Schneekugel – snow globes. And you're standing in our new Schneekugelmuseum. I'm guessing you can now work out the translation to that.'

Eve stared at the beautiful scene inside the glass. A formation of Nutcracker soldiers playing instruments, their teeth bared in a fixed grin. She shook it gently and the snow floated around their heads.

'Look at this one,' Jacques said, handing over a smaller globe with a pale-furred reindeer in it, just visible between dark-green fir trees. 'Holly's got her own Schneekugel.'

Eve felt as if someone had ripped her breath away. They were stunning.

'And this.' Jacques handed her a globe which he had shaken so the scene wasn't instantly recognizable. As the snow settled, Eve saw a bride in fur cape, her groom in a sleigh behind her. The bride was smiling, and that smile was full of hope and promise and it was suddenly too much for her. She needed to get out of there before she made a fool of herself.

Eve handed the globe back to him.

'Okay, you win this round, they're lovely,' she said and left quickly, before he saw the tears dripping from her long black lashes.

Chapter 22

Eve returned home that night for the first time in a month. The first thing she did, as always when entering, was to make sure the candle was still lit. Violet had been looking after it for her and all was well.

There was a few days' worth of post to sort through – nothing exciting at first glance, most of it junk, but then she came to a pretty pink envelope with some childish writing on the outside. It was a get-well card from Phoebe May Tinker and a note from Alison in which she apologized yet again for not coming to visit her whilst she was poorly at her aunt's. Eve took her mobile out of her handbag and pressed the speed-dial number for Alison.

'Eve, how are you?' came Alison's concerned reply after two rings. 'I'm so sorry—'

Eve cut her off there and then.

'If you apologize once more, Alison Tinker, you and I will fall out. You couldn't possibly have come to see a woman with shingles when you're pregnant and have a small child, so please shush and let that be an end to it.'

'I half wish Phoebe would get chicken pox and get it over and done with,' sighed Alison. 'Then again, I don't want her to get it. I felt so awful about—'

'Naughty Alison,' Eve admonished her. Then a thought visited her brain like a bee making a surprise detour to a flower. 'Actually, you *can* make it up to me. You can let me borrow Phoebe to come and visit the new theme park soon. I want to see what she thinks.'

'She'd absolutely love that,' said Alison. 'Can I tell her when she gets in from Brownies?'

'Of course,' smiled Eve. 'I am presuming you won't want to trudge around in your advanced state of pregnancy?'

'I am dying to see it,' said Alison, 'but I'll wait until I'm a bit less fat and heavy, if you don't mind. I'm walking like a duck at the moment: any more than twelve steps and I'm ready for a sit down. I'll let Phoebe show me all the pictures she'll probably take with the camera you bought for her birthday.'

'Lovely, it's a date,' said Eve.

'Hope you're okay tomorrow, kiddo,' said Alison,

before saying goodbye. 'I know it'll be a tough one for you.'

'Thank you,' said Eve, feeling tearful that Alison remembered. Tomorrow Jonathan would have been thirty-five years old. Tomorrow they should have been celebrating as Mr and Mrs Lighthouse, doing something romantic. Instead, Eve would be making sure the reindeer and horse dung had been cleared up and spending another day with a buffoon who charmed everyone who met him – even the flaming animals. Everyone but herself, of course.

Chapter 23

Eve didn't usually dream, or at least if she did, she didn't remember them. But that night was an exception – and not the most pleasant one. In her dream, she caught sight of Jonathan in the theme park and ran towards him only for him to disappear. Then she saw him again and the same thing happened. When she saw him for the third time, he didn't walk off and she sped in his direction, noticing that the closer she got to him the more he seemed to change. By the time she reached him, she found Jonathan had become Jacques, but was wearing a soldier's uniform covered in bravery medals, and she was screaming at him to take the uniform off because he wasn't worthy of it, but Jacques wasn't listening.

The dream stayed with her far beyond the boundaries of sleep and she didn't like it one bit that Jacques had had the cheek to morph into Jonathan. Whilst she was having her breakfast, she took a notepad and started to write what little facts she had about Mr Jacques Glace. It barely filled up a page. He had been a hospital visitor to her aunt eighteen months ago and was half-French, half-Yorkshire. Oh, and that he lived in Outer Hoodley. She thought about ringing the hospital to see if they had a formal list of visitors but quickly dismissed the idea. They'd more than likely quote the phrase 'data protection' at her and wouldn't give her any information. With the internet one would have thought it would make it easier to find out information; then 'data protection' came along and counteracted that.

The sum of all she knew about him didn't make for scintillating reading. She decided that she needed to get into his house and snoop.

Violet popped her head around the door of the Portakabin just after two o'clock in the afternoon.

'You okay?' she asked.

'Yep,' said Eve.

'I don't want to fuss you, but you know where I am if you want me.' She handed Eve a small tub and a spoon. 'Try this,' she said.

Eve loaded the spoon with the pale-yellow ice cream and raised it to her lips. It tasted of toffee, burned sugar like the crackling top of a crème brûlée. It reminded Eve of a Christmas fireplace, one with a cosy fire and stockings hung at either side of it. As laughingly far removed an image from all those Christmases she spent with tinny little electric fires as the only heat source in their house as it was possible to be.

'I'm going to call it "Winter Flame".'

'Ah, that's lovely,' smiled Eve. 'That's just what it reminds me of.' If she and Jonathan had had children, she would have made sure they had a grand fireplace which they could have festooned with holly and stockings. 'Have you got time for a coffee?'

'Yes, of course,' said Violet, stepping inside and closing the door behind her. 'I have if you have. I know you're really bus—'

'I've got time.'

'Where's Jacques?' asked Violet.

'Up at the Carousel,' replied Eve. 'I haven't seen him all day.' *Thank God.* 'He left a note on my desk to say that's where he was if I wanted him for anything. Which I don't.'

'It's very quiet in here without him,' chuckled Violet. 'I've never met anyone who was as loud in my life. Even when he's quiet, he's noisy.'

'Tell me about it,' said Eve, pouring out two coffees and handing one to Violet.

'I think a bit of his distraction would have been better for you today, rather than this silence.' Violet took a drink of coffee and let out a long, contented sigh.

'Distraction, maybe,' Eve agreed, 'but not in Jacques Glace form. I can't understand why there is absolutely no information about the man to be had anywhere. It isn't possible in this day and age. If I didn't know any better, I would have thought he was an alien who had been dropped onto earth eighteen months ago, with the express purpose of ripping off my aunt.'

'Isn't that unfair?' said Violet, wishing Eve would let it go.

'Probably,' Eve admitted. 'But why is he so guarded about me knowing anything about him? Surely if he hadn't got anything to hide, he would give something up.'

'Maybe he's just a private person,' said Violet. 'Pav doesn't talk much about himself unless I press.'

'If I could just see inside his house.' Eve plopped that into the conversation like a pebble in water to see how Violet would take it. Violet, as she suspected, looked horrified.

'You can't break into his house.'

'I have no intention of breaking in,' sniffed Eve. 'All I am saying is that if the opportunity arose where I could gain access to his house . . .'

'Break in, you mean,' parried Violet.

'Okay then, break in,' replied Eve. 'I wouldn't take anything. I just want to get a measure of the man and make sure he isn't a crook. You must admit,

V, that it's more than slightly odd that Evelyn left him so much money – and Fancy's and Kringle's ashes – after such a short time. You must. And don't forget the article about that con man . . .'

'Eve, Jacques Glace is not that con man,' said Violet firmly. 'Con men like that are sneak thieves. They don't take up high-profile business positions like running theme parks.' Jacques Glace didn't set off one alarm bell inside her. After all that had happened to Violet in the past couple of years, she thought that if Jacques Glace had been someone to be wary off, she would have felt something.

Violet had a point, Eve conceded. Although, as a counter-argument, con men were often narcissists, arrogant enough to feel they were above suspicion. Double-bluffers.

Eve huffed impatiently. 'Why does everyone have to have so many bloody secrets? What harm would it do to just tell people things?' And Violet knew she wasn't talking about Jacques any more.

'I take it you've had no news from Jonathan's parents?' she asked tentatively.

'No,' said Eve, flatly. 'They've changed their number. I rang a few weeks ago and it was just a dead line.'

Violet sighed. 'They were never going to tell you, Eve. You have to let it go.'

'What harm would it have done to tell me? What

did they think I would do if I knew what they'd done with him?' Eve snapped, then immediately apologized for it. 'I'm sorry, Violet.'

Violet came over and put her arm around Eve. 'It's beyond cruel,' she said softly, giving her cousin a big hug. 'But you don't need to know where Jonathan's ashes are, because wherever they are, he's not there with them. You still have your candle flame.'

'And he is there, isn't he?' asked Eve, wanting Violet to affirm that he was. 'It would have gone out by now, wouldn't it, if he wasn't?'

Violet thought about Jacques inadvertently blowing the candle flame out and it mysteriously relighting itself.

'Yes,' she said. 'He's watching over you.'

The Portakabin was too quiet that afternoon. Eve's eyes were reaching the bottom of a document and not taking in a word. Her brain was teeming with thoughts of Jonathan and what they should have been doing now – together. Then realizations, like tidal waves, kept crashing into those thoughts, that however many fantasies she had, they would never happen because Jonathan Lighthouse was dead and would never return. Yet that flame kept burning at home and that meant he was still out there somewhere, letting her know that he loved her. There was a membrane between their two worlds, an impenetrable barrier that he was behind. But if she found it, they could be together, couldn't they? Her brain ached from the philosophical arguments as she reached into the trunk of corporate gift samples, which sat at the side of her desk. Looking through that little treasure box for a few minutes and giving her head a break might get her back on track. She pulled out the world's ugliest lump of paperweight, which never failed to amuse, and a giant paperclip, then her hand fell on the half-bottle of whisky with the personalized label. She didn't like whisky at all, couldn't even get her nose past the smell of it to have a taste usually, which is why this bottle was still unopened after a year. But today, Eve unscrewed the top and tilted it into her mug of half-drunk coffee, then she lifted it to her lips and tipped it down her throat. It burned. But not quite enough to offset the pain that was unbearably messing up her heart. Maybe if she drank a little more . . .

Chapter 24

Ten minutes after meeting Corporal Jonathan Lighthouse in a bar in March, six years ago, Eve felt a seismic rumble within her. The man who had tapped her on the shoulder was slim, sexy, fit, with soft grey eyes and a melting smile that made her underwear want to drop to the floor. She was hooked from the off.

'Can I buy you a drink?' was all he said for her heart to start thumping more than it had done for anyone else – ever. She couldn't even speak, she had to resort to nodding. He carried her wine and his beer over to a suddenly available niche away from the volume of music and they sat and talked for hours.

Then, at the end of the night, as Eve knew she was seconds away from receiving a kiss that would send explosions tripping along every nerve in her body, Jonathan confessed that he had a girlfriend.

It could have quite easily been a line that he then delivered: 'Look, I really wasn't expecting to come out tonight and meet anyone like you. You've turned my world upside down.'

But as much as Eve wanted to believe him, she also didn't want to move in on someone else's man, and so she kissed him lightly on the cheek and said, 'Goodbye, soldier.'

And that, she presumed, was the end of it.

She didn't expect that the following week a huge bouquet of flowers would arrive at the small office room she rented then when Eve's Events was just turning a corner. And with it an accompanying card saying: 'Ring me, new girlfriend' and a mobile number.

She was trembling when she pressed in the numbers and shaking even more – with delight – when she heard his voice.

'Meet me for dinner,' he said. 'I'll explain all.'

And so she did. And over a meal in a very nice restaurant he told Eve that after meeting her he knew that he wanted to be with her. He couldn't shake her out of his head. And the following night when he saw Marie – his girlfriend of three years, fiancée of four months – he knew he couldn't be with her any more, and ended it just like that.

Of course, Marie was devastated, but what else could he do? He wasn't normally a creature of impulse like this, and he knew it was crazy, but he was a man of straight lines and it wouldn't have been fair to carry on in a relationship with Marie when his head was so full of Eve.

Within six months Jonathan and Eve were engaged and were about to complete the sale on a house together, but Mr and Mrs Lighthouse still refused to meet the woman who had stolen their son's heart. They had considered Marie as a daughter and would not allow her position to be usurped, especially as Marie was so totally heartbroken about the split.

'They'll come round,' promised Jonathan. 'You watch, we'll all be sitting around the table at Christmas laughing and pulling crackers.' But they didn't. Because three months later, when Christmas Day arrived, Jonathan was dead.

Chapter 25

By four o'clock, after quite a few nips of whisky, which she had rather hoped would have dulled the pain of her memories about the cold Lighthouse seniors, Eve found herself more than a little tipsy. Which is why she found herself heading for some air, through the enchanted forest and ending up outside the reindeer enclosure.

There was no one around. Not even Holly seemed to be there. Eve called to her.

'Holly, Holly – are you in there?' and she attempted to make the clicking sounds that Jacques had made to lure her forward. It worked. Holly emerged from her shed, tentatively looking around to see who was calling her. She disappeared back inside, making Eve wonder if that was another rejection to add to today's list, then Holly stepped out and walked slowly over to her, making her snuffly, strange piggy-like noise.

'Hello, girl,' said Eve, stretching out her hand and wishing she had a treat for her. What did reindeer eat? Polos, like horses? Carrots? Elves? The thought of a small pair of green-clad legs hanging out of Holly's jaws made Eve suddenly giggle. She wondered where her aunt had recruited all the dwarves and midgets – were they from an agency? Evelyn had contacted a firm specializing in accounts to deal with all the staff. There was very little the woman hadn't thought of.

'So how's your day been?' said Eve, enjoying the white deer pushing and nudging at her hand. 'Mine's been a bit shit, if I'm honest.'

Holly swung her head around and worried at her side before returning her attention to Eve. Her eyes were big and brown and shiny, and so very sad, Eve thought. She recognized that look. It was the look her own eyes had when her mother whisked her out of primary school and into another one in Sheffield, after they'd moved in with one of her boyfriends, though Eve couldn't for the life of her remember his name. No one would talk to her in the playground and that first fifteen-minute break period seemed to last an eternity. And a week later, one of the girls made a point of giving everyone in the class a Christmas card except her. She felt like a total duck out of water for weeks – until Ruth fell out with her boyfriend and moved them back to Barnsley again in the New Year.

'Do you miss naughty Olly, Holly?' asked Eve. In the background she heard the tinkly, slightly off key sound of carousel music. It made her feel tearful for a reason she couldn't quite pinpoint, as if it signalled a time before her heart became so sad.

'Life should be much better as a single woman without all that romance stuff, shouldn't it, Hols? But I miss it. I used to like waking up with someone.'

Jonathan used to mumble in his sleep. He would make her laugh with some of the nonsense things he came out with. Once he sat bolt upright in bed and announced: 'The sweetshop will be closed until further notice and all NCOs caught in possession of soap will be arrested.'

That memory plunged the ever-present knife into her heart a little deeper.

'He would have been thirty-five today, Holly,' Eve sniffed. 'I only had him for one birthday before he went over there. I made him a cake. It had Cadbury's Buttons all over it.'

Holly nudged her sides again, as if something were hurting her there.

'We made plans to go to Mexico after that Christmas. We were going to buy our wedding rings there. But he died. Roadside bomb. He never thought it would happen to him. He thought he was invincible. '

She had imagined the noise of that bomb in her head so many times, seen Jonathan fly into the air, his arms and legs flailing, before he landed on the ground a beautiful whole corpse. She never let herself think that his end wouldn't have been like that. The army sealed his coffin before they sent it home. Jonathan had made no will, so his next of kin were his parents. The army told Eve of his death but she thought it right and proper that his mother and father took charge of the funeral. Still, they didn't even tell her when it was. She might never have known had one of his friends not rung to tell her.

Eve remembered the many messages she had left on Mr and Mrs Lighthouse's phone. They never picked up, they never rang back. The first time she met them was at Jonathan's funeral.

There was no mistaking the couple immaculately dressed in black, huddled around a weeping, skinny blonde woman whom Eve recognized from Jonathan's old photos as Marie. Eve remembered the narrow-eyed scowl Mrs Lighthouse gave her when someone whispered to her that Eve had arrived. Even the memory of that look burned her. She had the same grey eyes as Jonathan. It was hard to see those eyes viewing her with so much hatred.

They weren't so disingenuous to tell Eve she was not welcome at Jonathan's funeral, but they didn't have to – they made that perfectly clear by ignoring her, concentrating on comforting the distraught Marie and accepting condolences from Jonathan's friends.

'I was terrified to go up to them,' said Eve, stroking Holly's furry head. 'But I had to, I wanted to. I waited until after the ceremony.'

'*I know who you are,*' said Ann Lighthouse when Eve attempted to introduce herself.

'I had all this stuff rehearsed, but all I could manage to say was that I loved him so much,' said Eve, tears rolling down her cheeks. She remembered Mrs Lighthouse bending over and speaking in her ear.

'*Then you should have left him alone. He was happy with Marie, but within months of meeting you, he is dead.*'

'It was like she was telling me I'd killed him,' said Eve. 'She said that they didn't want to know I existed. They wanted to "consign me to the obscurity in which they wished I'd stayed". She said I was a temporary madness from which their son would have recovered. "We do not acknowledge you".' Every frozen word had ripped into Eve like razor wire.

'He was my life,' Eve had sobbed quietly, not wanting to draw attention to herself. She didn't know how many more people hated her. For a moment she imagined they all did.

'*He was our life for a lot longer than he ever was or would be yours,*' snarled Ann Lighthouse, the weight of hatred evident in her voice. '*Ours and Marie's.*'

Tears tickled Eve's cheeks but she didn't wipe them away.

'She laughed when I asked if I could have some of his ashes. A teaspoon of them would have done. "He will come home with us where he belongs," she said to me. "ALL of him."'

Eve remembered then how Ann Lighthouse turned away from her and Eve reached out to touch her arm.

'Will you let me know what you'll do with him then, please,' she had said. 'So I can think of his resting place.'

But Ann Lighthouse had stared at the dark-haired woman reduced to rubble in front of her, wiped her sleeve very pointedly where Eve had touched it, as if it were now disease-ridden, and said a very cold, '*No.*'

The reindeer was looking in Eve's eyes now as if she was really listening. She had never told anyone before what happened at the funeral and yet she was pouring it all out to a pregnant animal.

'I tried ringing them after the funeral but they never answered. So one day I drove to their house to ask them again, and Gregory Lighthouse called the police.'

Indignity was poured on top of the pain. The police were kind but firm and told her to go home.

Jonathan and Eve had joint insurance on the house,

which paid out but brought no comfort to Eve. She gave a huge anonymous donation to Help for Heroes out of the monies, but what she wanted most of all was to know where Jonathan was resting. She didn't take the pension that she could have claimed, signing it over to Jonathan's parents because she didn't feel it belonged to her, but not even that softened the Lighthouses to her.

'I'll never know, Holly. I'll never know where my Jonathan is resting.' She was overcome by a fresh wave of tears and wished she could stop them because tears came from a place where all her pain was stored and she couldn't close the lid on it. It was as if the tears swelled the sealing door as surely as if it were made of wood and she didn't want to cry, didn't want to let all that hurt out because there was too much of it to bear. 'It just gets worse, not better, Holly,' Eve said. 'Time is supposed to be a great healer, but it isn't working, and I don't know what to do any more. Any ideas?'

Holly looked at Eve with sad brown-eyed bewilderment and made a loud honking sound, like an upset goose.

'I know they blame me, Ann and Gregory. They think I changed the course of his fate. People find it easier to blame someone, then they have a target to direct all their hurt. I know it's human nature.' Ann's words had stuck to her like a sugar bomb, then burrowed deep inside and done their most damage in her brain, because more than a little part of Eve wondered if Mrs Lighthouse was right: that if Jonathan had never met her, he would be living still, content with Marie.

I feel alive with you, Eve. More alive than I've ever been with anyone else. You make me believe I could live for ever. He had told her more than once. Did he feel so invincible that he took his eye off the ball? That would make it her fault, wouldn't it?

'Oh Holly, I miss him so much. I miss him more with every passing year.' Eve wiped her eyes and then laughed at her ridiculous self. 'How bloody stupid am I, talking to a reindeer?' But somehow it didn't feel as barmy as it should. The kind-eyed beast offered no comment or judgement, just allowed her to dump a huge lump of sorrow off her chest.

'I don't know how to stop thinking about him, Holly,' she said. 'I don't want to stop thinking about him, even though people think I should. I don't want to go for counselling. I want him to know that he is mine still and always will be, that my love wasn't cut off by his death. Is that so bad?'

Holly offered no comment. Not even when Eve's tears reached the ground. There was no one around to embarrass herself in front of, so Eve let them. Eve didn't cry usually. She had learned from an early age to stuff her emotions away. Only when Jonathan came into her life did the cupboard door on them unlock, and she felt truly able to let her vulnerable self peep out.

Holly flumped heavily to the ground.

'God, don't say I'm boring you,' said Eve. 'Although you must be tired, carrying that weight around.'

Holly curled her great head around towards her bottom, biting at her sides and braying loudly. And Eve knew.

'Oh, you're not are you?' said Eve, looking around her to see if anyone had miraculously appeared to help. She was no reindeer expert but this was looking a bit obvious.

Holly was shuffling around on the ground and looking in discomfort.

'Wait, hang on,' said Eve. 'I'll get the vet.' She reached in her pocket for her mobile phone, then realized she didn't know which vet Jacques had contacted. She thumped in his number.

'Hello,' came his voice after two rings, sounding more Leslie Philips than she liked.

'I think Holly's started giving birth,' she said, feeling as sober as if someone had just chucked a gallon of water over her head.

'I'll be right there,' he replied.

He must have run like Linford Christie from the carousel because he was there in warp-speed seconds.

'Have you rung the vet?' asked Eve in early panic-mode.

'Not yet,' said Jacques. 'I've just been busy doing a four-minute mile.' He took his phone out of his pocket. Eve raised her eyes heavenward, noticing the SpongeBob SquarePants case it was stored in.

The half of the conversation she heard wasn't very encouraging.

'Well, when will he be back then? There must be someone you can send . . .'

'Don't tell me they aren't sending a vet out,' growled Eve.

'Well, they're saying Mr Fleece is on another job, and they've got a rush on.'

He held his finger up as Eve was about to interrupt him again. 'However, they are also saying that it's unlikely we are going to need him anyway. Nature knows what it's doing.'

Jacques put his phone back in his pocket.

A gooey-covered head was pushing out of Holly's rear end.

'Oh look, it's coming,' said Eve, deciding she must have bored the baby reindeer out of its mother. They watched as the next quarter of its body slithered effortlessly out, then Holly struggled to her front feet and the calf plopped softly to the floor.

'It's out! Oh, well done Holly! Congratulations, girl.'

Congratulations? Did you say that to a birthing reindeer?

Eve felt joyously cheerful. It shouldn't have been a lovely moment with all that goo but the tiny reindeer looked like Bambi, albeit Bambi in a big rubber balloon.

'Now watch, she'll take all that jelly off,' said Jacques. But Holly didn't. She crumpled back to the ground, her neck strained towards her back, and then Eve noticed something protruding from her back end.

'What's that?'

'There's another calf in there,' said Jacques.

Holly swung her head around to her side and butted herself.

'Oh God, Jacques. She can't get it out. You need that vet.'

The usually silent Holly gave another distressed bray right on cue.

'Jacques, do you have the keys to the enclosure? We have to get in with her.' Even as she was saying it, Eve didn't believe what had just come out of her mouth. But whether or not it was the whisky talking, she felt the compelling need to offer the poor animal anything she could of comfort.

With one hand Jacques scooped out a jailer's hoop of keys from his pocket, and with the other his phone. 'It's the big one with the green top,' he said, whilst dialling the vet yet again.

Eve fumbled with the lock and then the bolts and went inside the enclosure where she dropped to her knees beside the newly born calf, pulling the greasy vernix from his face so he could breathe, before turning her attention to Holly.

'It's not a head that's stuck, I'm sure it's a leg. No, wait, it's the calf's back end, I think.'

Jacques relayed the information down the line.

'Well, if you can't send a vet here, let us know what to do. Please get get someone to talk us through it,' he said, his voice raised enough to be taken note of.

There was a lull in the conversation as the woman on the end of the line went to find a vet and seemed to be taking ages about it. He tapped the back of the phone impatiently.

Luckily the calf was breathing and trying to get up. So young and already getting to its feet, thought Eve. Nature really was something else.

'Ah, thank you,' said Jacques, obviously re-engaged in conversation. 'Yes, it is a bottom . . . So what you're saying is that we need to use one hand, reach in and push the butt end of the calf forward then reach in with the other arm, following the leg until you reach the foot.'

Eve's head whirled around. 'You have to be joking,' she said. The look on Jacques' face told her that he was doing anything but.

'I'm not joking, Eve.'

'I can't do that . . .' said Eve.

'Eve, look at the size of my hands. I most certainly can't.' Jacques held his spade-like mitt up. If he put those in, Holly would be singing soprano just before she split in half.

'I can't. I just can't,' said Eve. She hadn't had enough whisky to consider that to be a possibility. 'There must be another way.'

'Yes, we let her die.'

Then Holly brayed a really pitiful noise of pain and Eve shook her head.

'Okay, tell me again.' She couldn't believe she was about to stick her hand up a reindeer's backside. 'I need to wash my hands.'

'There's no time. Put your hand in and push the calf's bottom.'

Eve puffed out her cheeks and raised her hand. It wavered near Holly, then pulled back. She told herself she couldn't do it, then that she could. She took another deep breath and pushed her hand in. It was easier than she thought to push the calf forward, although the sensation of seeing her hand disappear into a glob of gel wasn't on her list of things to do again in a hurry.

'Now, put your other hand in and find the leg.'

Eve grimaced and pushed her other hand in gently, searching around, and thankfully found it straightaway.

'Now, trace the leg to the hoof and cup your hand around it to prevent it tearing her.'

Eve was enjoying this marginally less than the ever-so-patient Holly.

'Got it.' She was astounded and squealed with something like delight. 'Jacques, I think I've got them both.'

'Great. Now push gently on the bottom and pull gently on the hooves.'

Eve exerted a slow but definite force, then Holly made an awful noise and Eve's nerve wavered.

'Oh God.'

'Take it slowly, you're doing fabulous.'

'Where's the bloody vet?'

'He's on his way, apparently,' said Jacques.

'Where's Holly's keeper, then?'

'I sent Tim home. His wife is in labour.'

'You're having me on.'

'Nope,' said Jacques with an amused little laugh. 'How are you doing, Eve?'

'I'm pulling.'

'Good girl.' Jacques listened to the instructions coming down his mobile and then relayed them. 'Now ease the bottom in a bit further.'

'If I push the bum in any more it'll come out of her mouth.'

'Just a little bit more, until you can get the hooves past it.'

'Go missus,' said a strange voice. She glanced over her shoulder to see she had an audience. Some of Effin's men were gathered at the fence and more people were coming.

'Oh my God, I think I'm doing it. They're out, Jacques. I've got the hooves out.'

Jacques finished off the conversation with the vet, stuck the phone in his pocket, and bent at the side of Eve. 'Now I can help you pull,' he said. 'Ready.'

'As I'll ever be,' said Eve.

'You can do it, Eve.' Was that Violet's voice she just heard?

'On the count of three; not "three-go" but "one-two", then we go.'

'Okay.'

'One, two . . . three.'

They pulled slowly and firmly. Poor Holly gave a cry.

'It's not budging,' said Eve.

'Oh yes, it is,' said Jacques, in serious panto mode this time. 'Again, one, two . . . three.' The calf slid out, delivered on a slide of two tons of slime and two massive weary cries from Eve and Jacques, and a 'thank the bloody Christ' bray from Holly. Immediately Holly started to lick her newborn calf and then the first one, which staggered towards its mother wanting some overdue attention. There were cheers and claps from the fence. Half the workers were there by now, it seemed.

'Twins,' said Eve, thinking that her outfit was ruined. However much she washed it, it would always remind her of having her arms up a deer's bum.

'That's rare for reindeer,' said Jacques. 'Well done. You were absolutely brilliant, Eve. You should be proud of yourself. She might have died had it not been for you.'

Eve was shaking. She didn't feel proud of herself or brave, she just felt 'what if'. *What if Holly had died alone in her paddock because no one was there? What if she hadn't got pissed and needed some air?* But she kept that inside and said, 'I'm sure she would have been fine.'

'You know that's not true,' said Jacques, and put his hand on Eve's shoulder. 'Eve, you're shaking. Are you all right?'

'Yes, I'm fine,' she said. He must have been able to smell the whisky on her breath. She'd nearly anaesthetized Holly with it. She suddenly felt very embarrassed and attempted to turn away and claim some space between them, but his hand gripped tighter.

'Come here,' he said, turning her around and pressing her into his chest. She got a noseful of his jumper and his Christmas-tree smell and felt his hands warm on her back as they squashed her into him. 'I think you might need a hug after that.' She was amazed that she stayed in the cage of his arms and let him hug her, and she tried not to acknowledge that yes, she did need a hug at that moment.

Eve's legs were shaking more than her upper body was and Jacques' warm, considerate hold on her was the only thing keeping her from falling down into a dark chasm. She had edged near the portal of death again that afternoon, seen it open and be ready to claim Holly and her calf, only to close again unfed, and it had rocked her. But she'd had the power to alter the natural course of Holly's life. It was something that should have made Eve feel better, but all it did was reinforce the feeling that maybe her influence had worked the other way with Jonathan. Just as Ann Lighthouse had said.

Chapter 26

In last week's Margaret Dodworth's monthly recipes, we did of course mean to boil the tin of condensed milk in water and microwave the butter until soft, not to microwave the tin of condensed milk until soft and boil the butter in water. The Daily Trumpet apologizes for any misdirection in this matter.

Chapter 27

It was nearly ten o'clock that night before Violet and Pav got home and far too late to cook, so Violet went for fish and chips whilst Pav laid the table. She was smiling as she walked home, thinking about seeing Eve engulfed in a Jacques hug after the second baby deer was born – a new member of the park family. That sight had made her giddily happy. All the park family, as she called them, had seen a different side to Eve today, which she was thrilled about. They had been wary of her, but after today she had gone up leaps and bounds in their estimations. Violet hoped they'd grow to think of her with as much affection as they regarded Jacques. He laughed and joked with everyone, got his hands dirty with the builders and wasn't above mustering up some coffees and sandwiches for the lads putting up the mighty carousel. Violet was growing very fond of the park family – because that's what it was starting to feel like she belonged to. She would be quite sad when Effin's men had finished and moved on. The Welsh lads were very funny, totally resigned to Effin's screeching at them. Violet wasn't sure she could live without Effin's fantastic Welsh insults very kindly translated for them by Arfon and Thomas, who was in charge of the train. Still, all good things came to an end, and she herself would need to go back to her ice-cream parlour in Maltstone and employ a manager to run the ice-cream parlour in Winterworld when it was up and running smoothly. She thought Janet might be the perfect person for the job. In the holidays they employed her son Robbie too, a big, strapping, handsome boy who might be up for a bit of temporary work when he had finished his exams in the summer.

Oh, it was a jolly ship. There was always laughter to be heard. Violet had never used the word 'guffawed' in her life, but that was the perfect description for the sound Jacques would make when Effin was at full pelt.

One of that day's Effin-isms was an absolute corker.

'He said that the big horse's arse had done more work today than the rest of us have done collectively since we've been here.' The laconic Arfon had kindly translated that one for them as he lifted up his drill. He said it as nonchalantly as if it was something he heard every day – which he did, albeit in different forms.

A couple of the 'elves', not in costume, had come into the ice-cream parlour to have a sneaky look at Pav's horses and hopefully test some ice cream. The elder of the two – Marvin – was a roofer by trade, but at his age the going was getting tough. Landing a job in Winterworld, even if he did have to wear a daft green costume, was like a Christmas gift in itself. It was a delicious feeling knowing that this winter his feet would be firmly on the ground and he'd be warm inside a grotto. As 'grotto guide' his wages wouldn't be as much as they were on building sites, but he didn't care a jot. The hours and comfort of the job far more than made up for that – and the fact that his wife wouldn't be nattering that he'd 'come home dead', as she put it. Apparently Evelyn had sent a recruitment scout looking for 'elves' months ago. She really did have every base covered.

Violet felt a sudden rush of happiness. Today had been a sweet day with Eve trying not to be gooey and maternal over the new reindeer babies, but pride was oozing out of her every pore. It was as if they had defrosted her poor cousin a little – given her something to smile about on a day when she wouldn't have thought it possible. If only Jacques would move into her heart. Because Violet felt sure that if Eve let him, he would. He was just lovely.

When she pushed open the outside door, Violet could hear Pav's voice talking to someone in the lounge, but when she walked into the room it was to see him quickly slam down the phone.

'Wrong number,' he said, smiling at her, and she knew he was lying. She didn't accuse him outright. But when he nipped to the loo after the meal, she rang the redial button and heard a merry female voicemail announcement.

'Hi, this is Serena. I'm obviously not in at the mo, so please leave your name and number after the three beeps. Thank you.' A trilling, ditzy voice that Violet could imagine belonging to a Marilyn Monroe clone. Then Violet tried 1471 and the same automated voice answered.

Violet didn't leave a message.

Chapter 28

The vet was very pleased with the reindeer babies, two little boys. They were tiny and gauche, with long angular legs, but able to stand on them in order to shadow their mother and drink her milk. Eve made them her first port of call the next morning. She had slept solidly for the first time in a long while – no dreams about Jonathan, no nightmares about his parents. That was both unexpected and welcome.

Tim, the keeper's wife, had given birth to a little boy, too. A temporary keeper had been found for now until he came back to work, totally gutted that he had not been there for Holly.

'Great, aren't they?' said Jacques, coming up behind Eve as she hung over the fence and watched the calves unsteadily walking behind their mum. 'Our boys.' He made it sound as if Eve had just given birth and he was cooing over their twins.

'I think you'll find they are *her* boys,' said Eve, moving her hand towards Holly.

'Of course, but they're ours too. I've come over all paternal,' laughed Jacques. 'What shall we call them? I don't think Holly's forte is going to be picking their names out of a hat.'

'I don't know,' said Eve. 'I really don't want the responsibility.'

Jacques' blue eyes began to twinkle. 'Why's that then? In case you pick a wrong one and they grow up with a complex?'

'No, I didn't mean that at all.' Eve flicked a loose strand of hair behind her shoulder.

'You do that a lot,' said Jacques.

'What?' Eve half snapped, suspecting he was going to start his daft flirting.

'Flick your hair back.'

'How can I? It's tied up,' and Eve pointed behind her back at her long French plait.

'I know. But strands work loose and you flick at them. They say if you play with your hair, you're flirting.'

Eve hadn't a clue if she did do that with her hair or not, but she wouldn't be drawn deeper into the conversation and give him the satisfaction of having banter with him.

'Maybe it's just annoying me and in my way,' she said, turning away from him and making a full-stop statement.

'Me or your hair?' Jacques said.

'Both,' replied Eve, and Jacques laughed his big infectious laugh, and Eve had to bite her lip to stop herself smiling because she really, really didn't want to.

Then there was an almighty whoosh sound and they were both suddenly covered in snow.

'Sorry,' called a voice in one of the trees. 'Adjusted the bloody thing too high.' One of Effin's men was fixing a snow machine to the trunk.

In the paddock, Holly and her two little boys raised their heads to the snow drifting down. The way they were closing their eyes made it look as if they were smiling.

'Think you just found a name for one of the twins,' smiled Jacques.

'Silly bloody snow machine?' asked Eve, brushing the wet snow from her skirt.

'Blizzard,' said Jacques, and winked at her.

Chapter 29

'I have to go out,' said Pav, wiping his hands on a towel after tea that night. 'I may be some time.'

He sounded so much like Captain Oates that under normal circumstances Violet would have joked about it.

'Okay,' she said, a lump rising to her throat. Who was he going to see? *Serena with the nice voice? Wrong-number Serena?* She had a sudden moment of panic. She wanted to throw herself onto him and hold him tightly, but she fought against her desperation. She had been in a relationship once with a man she did not love, whom she stayed with because she knew she would break his heart if she left. She did not ever want to have Pav stay unless he wanted to be with her. But just for a moment, she felt the panic that her ex must have felt on a daily basis, knowing that she was slipping away from him.

'Is there anything you want whilst I am out?' he asked. 'Milk, bread?'

'Not that I can think of,' said Violet, pinning on a smile. Come on Violet, get a grip, said a voice inside her. You're growing a big tree from a little seed. It may have been a wrong number after all and Pav rang it back to see who it was. But the other half of her brain was shrugging its shoulders. *If that was a wrong number, I'm Gwyneth Paltrow.* She took a deep breath and tried to deliver the question casually. 'Where are you off to then?'

'I just have somewhere to go,' said Pav. 'Something to do.'

And he kissed her on the head and was gone. The sort of kiss that David Beckham gave Victoria in that first photoshoot after his affair allegations.

Chapter 30

The next morning the Portakabin was freezing because the fire needed a new gas cylinder. One of Effin's men had gone out for a new one and Eve stood huddled in her old black woollen coat by the window, watching Jacques talking to a couple of the 'elf-people' as they liked to call themselves.

Her coat afforded her plenty of warmth but it really needed to go in the bin. The sleeves were going at the elbow and there was a pull at the back. And she couldn't remember how many times now she had had to stitch a button back on. She had bought it new to go out with Jonathan on their first dinner date. That March was freezing and she had been delighted to find a coat that looked smart and was in the sale because she didn't have a lot of spare money to spend on herself in those days. Then again, she was a damned sight happier and warmer back then than she ever was now.

Jonathan had held both sides of the collar when he kissed her for the first time as girlfriend and boyfriend, before his hands had slipped around her back. Her memories were tied up in the threads. The thought had crossed her mind more than once, when she opened up a bin bag to throw in the coat, that she would be throwing a part of Jonathan away if she got rid of it.

But as she tried to recall that first kiss, she found that as soon as Jonathan's hands touched her, they changed into those of Jacques Glace yesterday, holding her as she shook with aftershock from delivering a baby reindeer. Why had she let him cuddle her? Why hadn't she extricated herself from him? Why had she needed to feel someone's arms around her so much – and not just anyone's arms – but *his*. Jonathan was a man of honour; God knows what Jacques Glace was and she had let him hold her like a lover.

She stood at the Portakabin window and watched him holding court with the elf-people. He was amusing them with a tale, claiming their attention as he gesticulated wildly with his long arms. Then his audience fell about laughing together, real laughter, not fake laughter to get on the right side of the boss. Had Eve looked at herself then, she would have seen she was smiling too. She wasn't aware that she was touched by the ripple effect of Jacques' charm. Then one of the elf-people saluted Jacques and he returned that salute, and Eve's jaw tightened. *What right did he have to do that?* Any softening she had done towards Jacques Glace hardened right on up again. He was using a military gesture in a light-hearted, mocking way. She knew she was over-reacting but she couldn't help it. The military was a hair-trigger as far as she was concerned.

Eve knew she needed to get inside his house sooner rather than later, and find out who Jacques Glace was and where he came from. The man was a one-man charm offensive and she didn't want anyone else getting close to him until she had worked out what his game plan was. Charlatans often played a long and sneaky game – she'd watched all the series of *Hustle*, so she knew how polished they could be. But con men in real life weren't nice people turning the tables on the greedy. They knew that people were pre-disposed – wanted – to trust and they used that trust to trample all over people's lives.

So whilst Jacques was still regaling a crowd with his raconteuring skills, Eve quickly rang Barbara, Mr Mead's secretary, to ask for Jacques Glace's address.

'He's asked me to order a chair for his house, and do you know, I can't put my hands on my address book and he's not answering his phone,' she lied with a tinkly, innocent laugh. She felt a soupçon of guilt that Barbara believed her rubbish lie and trustingly recited the address, but still she wrote it on her hand, grabbed her car keys and sneaked out to the innocuous enough address: 1, May Green, Outer Hoodley.

The village was situated off the Barnsley–Wentworth road, although the word 'village' was pushing it a bit. Really, it was more of a hamlet, consisting of a shop, a pub at the side of the river – Dick Turpin's Arms (as if it could be anything else, thought Eve when she saw it) and some very old cottages. Eve pulled up in the village car park and looked round for the presence of a wicker man. These places were curtain-twitching heaven.

She grabbed an old envelope from the car so she could look as if she were posting a letter if anyone asked her 'what she was doing in these parts'. Blimey, it was only a few miles from Barnsley town centre and yet she could have been forgiven for believing that it was *The Hills Have Eyes* territory. It was too quiet, too pretty, too still. Like *Midsummer Murders* land.

May Green was easy enough to find. She guessed that he lived in one of the five houses around a central square of grass with an ornamental maypole in the centre. Each one very different, too: number 5 was a tall, three-storey construction; number 4 had large picture windows and a roof terrace; number 3 was a bungalow, hidden by tall trees; number 2 was a medium-sized house painted white, decorated with lots of hanging baskets; and then there was number 1. Eve hadn't spent a lot of time thinking about what sort of house a man like Jacques Glace might live in, but it wouldn't have been this. It was a double-fronted, but tiny, cottage with a bright-red front door. She noticed that the door knocker was a brass soldier, which made her bristle.

Cream linen curtains hung at all the windows, the paintwork looked fresh, and when she went around the rear, she found a small but impeccably neat garden. She peered in through the back window and saw a tidy kitchen with a wooden work surface. Through the second window she saw a beamed lounge with a battered, but chic, leather Chesterfield sofa opposite a stone inglenook fireplace. There didn't seem to be much furniture in it at all.

'Can I help you?'

A voice cut into Eve's reverie and scared her to death. She jumped and yelped at the same time, and patted her chest to still her heart. For a moment, Eve turned into a human beat-box.

'I'm looking for Mr Glace's house,' said Eve,

growing menopausally hot under the little old lady's hawk-like gaze.

'This is Mr Glace's house, yes,' came the scratchy, suspicious reply.

'I was hoping to catch him in rather than just post this, so I came around the back because I couldn't hear anything when I knocked at the front,' said Eve, all too aware that she was over-explaining. She must have looked as guilty as a Great Train Robber with a bag full of loot and a Ronnie Biggs name-badge.

'He's not in,' said the pint-sized village guard dog.

'No, well, I'll . . . er . . . call back,' said Eve, backing away. 'Thank you.'

'Who shall I say called?' said the old lady, padding towards Eve at an alarming pace.

'No, it's fine,' said Eve. 'He doesn't know me. Thank you, bye.'

She walked off as fast as she could without making it look as if she was running. She was slightly worried the villagers would appear with burning torches if she didn't get out of Outer Hoodley quickly. She slid her key in the ignition and twisted it, thinking that this was the point in horror films when the engine made a tired cough and died. But instead, her car vroomed into life and Eve crunched over the gravel and out of the car park, and in her rear-view window was the little old lady watching to make sure she went.

It wasn't going to be easy to get inside that house if the chance arose. Not if May Green had its own Leo the lion patrolling it. It needed a little planning. And a disguise.

Chapter 31

The Daily Trumpet *would like to apologize to the family of Harold Lamb for the error in last week's obituary. The entry which read, 'To Our Dead Dad', should of course have read, 'To Our Dear Dead'.*

We truly regret any distress caused.

Chapter 32

The chance to suss out Jacques Glace fell so beautifully into Eve's lap, she was almost suspicious that he had planned it himself.

Four days after the little old lady had badgered Eve, Jacques burst into the Portakabin office as he always did. The man was incapable of opening the door and walking in, he had to throw himself in as if he was finding sanctuary from a minus forty-eight blizzard.

'Eve, are you leaving the park today?' he asked.

'Only at home-time,' replied Eve.

'I've got to go out for a few hours, but I'm hitching a lift with Effin. My car needs a new battery and a mechanic in Maltstone is dropping one off and fixing it in for me. If I leave you my keys, would you hand them over to him for me, please?' And he fished in his coat pocket and put his ridiculously loaded key ring down on her desk.

'Could you give me a clue as to which one it is?' asked Eve.

'Yes, sorry, of course. It's the one with the red top. I keep all my keys on the one ring for convenience sake – even if they do take up half my pocket.'

All of his keys? Including his house keys, that must surely mean.

You're joking, thought Eve to herself. He was handing over the bullets which she was going to use to shoot him.

'No worries,' she said, with an inner Dick Dastardly laugh. 'They're in safe hands.'

'I won't be back before lunchtime. I'm going to have to hang around with Effin at a builder's merchants.' Jacques sighed, but his eyes were sparkling with mirth. 'I hope he keeps his temper. He threatened to eat Arfon's liver earlier on. I was tempted to send out for some fava beans and a nice Chianti.'

'Enjoy,' said Eve. 'By the way, when do we have the pleasure of meeting Santa Claus?' She wanted Phoebe to vet him. There would be no more stringent test for Santa than meeting Phoebe May Tinker.

'Nick is coming over on Saturday,' said Jacques.

'Nick?' Eve rolled her eyes. 'Is he really called Nicholas? Have you picked him just because that was his name?'

'I didn't choose him, your aunt Evelyn did,'

replied Jacques. 'And yes, he really is called Nick. Nick St Wenceslas.'

'No.'

'Yep,' smiled Jacques, with that lop-sided easy grin he always had. 'Okay, not really. He's called Nicholas White. Santa Claus extraordinaire. He said he's looking forward to meeting you too. Again.'

'What do you mean, "aga—",' but Jacques had gone with his customary door slam. What a stupid, immature man, thought Eve. 'Again', as if it was the real S. C. and he was going to remember what she used to want for Christmas, like they did on those schmaltzy films. The thing she used to want most at Christmas, which she would never have admitted to anyone, for obvious reasons, was for her mum to fall a bit ill so they could move to Auntie Susan's for the whole week.

Santa was quickly forgotten as Eve picked up the keys and examined them. She heard Effin's voice call out to Jacques and wondered which one of them would come out the winner in a noisy competition. She watched Jacques climb into Effin's truck and it drove off. Then she zoomed out of the Portakabin in the direction of the ice-cream parlour.

Violet looked a little glum when Eve opened the door. She was staring into space and looking as if the cares of the world, wearing weighted boots, had settled on her shoulders.

'V, you okay?'

Violet forced on a smile. 'Yes, I'm fine. Just deep in thought,' she fibbed.

'Where's Pav?'

'Don't know,' replied Violet, shrugging her shoulders. He was disappearing more and more these days without saying where he was going. She wanted to ask him who Serena was, but she was frightened. So she bottled up her fears and they fermented and fizzed horribly inside her.

Eve, however, was too focussed on the opportunity which she had been offered that morning to notice the extent of Violet's angst.

'Violet, I need your help. It's an emergency.'

'Okay,' said Violet, pushing her own problems away. 'What do you want me to do?'

'Just sit in the Portakabin and wait for a garage mechanic, whilst I slip out for an hour. Ring me immediately if Jacques comes back but don't tell him where I am, for God's sake.'

'Eve, what are you up to?' said Violet, narrowing her eyes.

'Can't tell you,' said Eve.

'Can't or won't?'

'Won't.'

'You're going to Jacques' house, aren't you? Eve . . .'

'Violet,' Eve grabbed her small cousin by the arms.

'This is really, really important. I have to know more about Jacques Glace. If I can't find anything, I promise you I'll let it drop.'

And because Violet was a soft touch and because she needed something to fill her mind other than the awful thoughts that insisted on forcing themselves into her head, she sighed in a very resigned way and said, 'Okay then, what do you need me to do?'

Eve stripped the car key from the ring and handed it to her. Then, after leaving Violet in position in the Portakabin, she set off for Outer Hoodley with a clipboard, a set of curtains, a white overall, a pair of Harry Potter wire-framed glasses and a long black wig, left over from a Halloween do. All this had been collected over the weekend and put in Eve's car, ready and waiting for the perfect moment.

Eve pulled in just outside Outer Hoodley so she could dress up. The old lady who lived next to Jacques was like Cerberus, but with only one head, and she didn't want to be recognized. Eve checked her appearance in the wing mirror and found she looked as much like an interior designer as Mr Bean looked like a lifeguard.

Then she drove on into the village car park, picked up her clipboard and the curtains and locked up the car. She tried to walk confidently and innocently towards 1, May Green, with the chutzpah of a person going through customs with twelve bottles of brandy stuffed down their pants.

Eve stole a glance through her wire rims at number 2, but no curtain was twitching. She strutted around to the back of number 1 and tried a key in the lock, taking a deep breath and then another. She didn't know if an alarm was going to go off but would have to risk it. If it did, she would calmly walk back to the car and get the hell out of there.

She twisted the key and the door opened silently.

Eve entered quickly and closed the door behind her, locking it in case the neighbourhood witch came a-knocking. So far so good.

The inside of the house smelled of polish and some sort of spiced-apple air freshener. It was so tidy. There wasn't much furniture, yet it felt cosy and comfortable. The beamed ceiling looked very low; Eve wondered how many times Jacques had cracked his head on it. There were some sealed boxes in the corner. Evidently he hadn't been living in the cottage very long and was still in the process of unpacking.

'Right, no time to lose,' said Eve, slapping her hands together and then opening the single drawer in a long trestle table. There was nothing of interest really: two pens, a plain, unused notepad, a book of stamps, and an electricity bill in the name of Mr J Glace.

There was a file of Winterworld business on a

shelf underneath the coffee table and a well-worn copy of the Robert Harris book *Fatherland*. But on a small wooden tray on the deep window sill, Eve found a hospital appointment card. Apparently, Jacques had been to see a Dr C Khan in August at Norgreen, which was a private hospital in Sheffield. Or was it O Khan? She would google that name and hospital when she got home.

There was nothing at all in the kitchen cupboards and drawers other than what one would expect to find in there, so Eve tried upstairs. The small bath-room was glaringly clean with a residue scent in the air of an expensive manly deodorant. The mirrored wall cabinet housed toothpaste, one toothbrush, soap, razor, shampoo, aftershave and some ibupro-fen. Towels, folded to Benetton-standard, resided in a long cupboard alongside a huge, blue fluffy robe. There was a family of yellow rubber ducks sitting in a line on the side of the bath – *typical*.

There were richer pickings in the bedroom. Again, there were things in boxes not yet unpacked, but still, there was a veritable treasure trove of informa-tion available from what was.

'Oh, this is more like it,' laughed Eve, opening up a huge chunky wardrobe and seeing his clothes. Because on one side were shelves of jeans and jump-ers, and on the other side were military uniforms encased in plastic. 'My God, would you look at this?'

She lifted a red uniform out of the wardrobe. It weighed a ton. The word *Major* came hurtling back to her mind with all the force of a landing airplane. What on earth was he doing with this in his wardrobe? She recognized it as an officer's ceremonial uniform. A very large uniform which must have fitted him.

Eve shuddered as the vision of Jacques Glace strutting up and down in front of the mirror dressed as an officer rose in her head. And oh boy, what was this? She replaced the uniform and lifted out another encased in plastic also: a green, female officer's uniform. It looked very sizeable too. There were other uniforms in there as well, all military ones, but Eve had seen all she needed to of those. She moved over to the chest of drawers at the side of his bed.

The top drawer was full of underwear – very male underwear – no sign of very large stockings or suspenders, thank goodness. The second drawer housed socks, a small box with a watch in it, and some cufflinks. The drawer below though was much more interesting because it was full of military memorabilia. Caps, hats, flat boxes, which Eve opened to find an array of old medals – and in a beautiful red box on a bed of velvet was a new shiny one: a cross suspended from a ribbon of white and purple. She wondered what the story was behind that one. And most worrying of all, underneath the cross, she found an instantly recognizable battered brown box.

Eve's fingers started to tremble as she opened it up, but she knew what was in there already: Stanley's medal. Why would Jacques Glace have this?

Why weren't there any photographs anywhere? she mused, too. She wondered if they were in the sealed boxes, but they would have been impossible to open secretly. Then again, she had seen quite enough for one day. She *had* been right, surely. The presence of Stanley's medal alone proved that. Talk about catching someone red-handed.

She checked that all was as she found it, wiped as many touched surfaces as she could with her sleeve, just in case Mr Glace wore a detective's uniform at weekends and did a spot of fingerprinting, and exited quickly with her head bowed and the curtain over one arm and the clipboard in the other hand.

Back at Winterworld, Violet was disappointingly dismissive about the 'evidence'.

'It's Stanley's medal, Violet,' Eve emphasized. 'Why would Jacques Glace have it?'

'Well, Evelyn obviously gave it to him,' said Violet.

'She wouldn't have given it to him,' growled Eve. 'She would either have given it to me or to the military museum at Higher Hoppleton. He has to have stolen it – I bet you anything.'

'Oh, now, wait,' said Violet. 'You don't know that for definite. And just because he collects all this memorabilia, doesn't make him a charlatan – or a cross-dresser.'

'Oh, come on, V, even you have to admit that there are some things that just don't add up.'

'Have you considered that he might have been in the army and those uniforms are his?'

'Even the female one?'

'Apart from the female one,' huffed Violet.

'Violet, we're talking about a man who keeps his phone in a SpongeBob SquarePants sock. '

'It still doesn't prove anything.'

'I'll tell you what I think, shall I?' Her theory had come to her on the drive back to Winterworld. 'I think he managed to worm his way into Aunt Evelyn's affections using some military knowledge. Look.' She opened the locket around her neck and showed Violet the faded photograph of Stanley. Don't you think there's more than a passing resemblance between him and Jacques?'

Violet looked at the picture and yes, she could see that. Both Stanley and Jacques had very short hair, big shoulders and large bright eyes.

'Someone as lonely as Aunt Evelyn would have been putty in his hands,' said Eve, nodding to herself in a self-congratulatory manner. Move over, Hercule Poirot.

Eve then went over to her computer and googled Dr Khan at Norgreen hospital to find there were actually three Dr Khans working up there – a Dr C Khan in the prosthetic limb department, a Dr C Khan in gynaecology – so that ruled both of those out – but the third, a Dr G Khan was a psychiatrist. Why would Jacques be going to see a psychiatrist? Was he a nutter or a con man? Or perhaps both.

'The plot thickens, Violet,' Eve beckoned her cousin over to look at the screen. 'And I'm telling you, if this plot gets any thicker we'll have to hack it with a chainsaw.'

Chapter 33

After work that night, Eve called in at Alison's house to drop off her birthday card. It was bitterly cold and there was some light, slushy snow on the road. Alison answered the door looking like a sumo wrestler. She seemed to have doubled in size in the six weeks since Eve had seen her last.

'My God,' gasped Eve, pointing at the huge mound pushing out the material of Alison's maternity dress. 'Where did that come from?'

'I honestly don't know,' laughed Alison, leaning over to receive the kiss from her friend. 'Rupert reckons the baby's going to come out riding a horse. Rather worryingly, he's finding me very attractive at the moment, if you know what I mean.'

'Well, of course he does.' Eve followed Alison into her beautiful home. 'You're absolutely blooming.'

'Blooming knackered,' said Alison. 'He's told me

I should aim to keep a few of these pounds on when little Lone Ranger comes out. I think he'll be devastated if my boobs shrink back to nothing.'

'If only all women could find a man who tells them stuff like that,' smiled Eve. 'I presume he's still slaving away in his laboratory earning a crust?'

'Well, he's due back within the next hour or so. He's trying not to work late whilst I'm in my advanced state,' said Alison, opening the door to her amazing window-heavy, south-facing kitchen. The room was bigger than the whole of the downstairs of Eve's house. 'Tea, coffee, glass of wine?'

Eve was going to plump for a tea, but she found herself asking for a glass of red. Alison poured her one whilst having a glass of Sprite herself, and a Gaviscon chaser.

'I tell you, the worst thing about pregnancy is the bloody heartburn. It's a killer,' said Alison. 'I can put up with having to be rolled down to the bathroom fourteen times a night for a wee, and the niggles in my back, but the heartburn is something else.'

'Well, you don't look as if you're anything less than in sublime good health,' said Eve, lifting up a strand of Alison's long golden hair. Would I have been so serene and beautiful carrying Jonathan's baby? Eve thought then. Would Jonathan have put his arms around me and squeezed me, his hands resting on my giant tum, loving us both? She blinked quickly as the vision crumbled as quickly as it had formed.

'You okay?' asked Alison, seeing a dark shadow pass her friend's face.

'Yep,' replied Eve, over-brightly.

Alison nodded 'good', but she wasn't fooled. Oh, how she wished she could reach into Eve and pull out that black sadness that had taken root in her friend's heart. When they were at school together, Eve was the last person that Alison would ever have thought would lose the joy in her soul. Crazy, giggling, funny Eve – the essence of her choked by unspent grief. Jonathan wouldn't have wanted to find her like this – it would have hurt him so much to see Eve's once shiny green eyes as dull as algae on a forgotten pond.

'Bit of light reading?' Eve picked up a huge tome on the work surface: *The Secrets of the Six Wives of Henry VIII*. It wasn't so much a book as a lethal weapon.

'It's very good,' nodded Alison. 'And actually it is a *very* light read considering the length of it. I'm half-way through Jane Seymour.'

'Ah, the love of his life.'

'Well, you say that, but the book makes the point that they weren't really long enough together for the rot to set in. The author's theory is that if she hadn't died after childbirth, her head might have ended up on the reject pile as well. I still maintain that Anne Boleyn was the love of his life. Janey just happened to push out a male sprog and then pop off before all the euphoria had worn thin.' Alison took another long slug of Gaviscon and sighed with relief.

'We'll never know how right or wrong that theory is,' said Eve, convinced the book was talking tosh. 'Where's Phoebe? In her bedroom?'

'She's gone out to her friend Elsie's house for tea,' replied Alison. 'She's due back any time, actually. I wish she'd hurry up, I think it's going to snow.'

'Elsie? Is that an old lady or one of those old names doing a comeback?' Eve laughed.

'It's one of those old names *trying* to do a comeback,' chuckled Alison. 'Except it doesn't quite work, does it? Like Edna or Ernest. Some names are meant to have a renaissance, but a lot most definitely aren't. Anyway, please don't get me on the subject of names. I'm up to here with names.' And she tapped her forehead with the side of her index finger. 'Elisabeth, my mother-in-law, thinks we should name the new baby something singular and Greek. She's been reading this stupid book that intimates if you name your child after an ancient god, that child will inherit the qualities of that deity. Rupert has been less than helpful, actually fooling her into believing that Poseidon is on our list of possibles. He can be so naughty.'

Eve laughed. Rupert sounded as if he had dropped

out of a posh tree with a mouth full of plums, but in reality he had no airs and graces about him at all. His mother, however, was a different kettle of fish. Alison had regaled Eve with enough stories about Elisabeth Derby-Tinker (Rupert had dropped the double-barrel) for her to write a book. Eve had only met the woman once at Alison's wedding – and that was enough to last a lifetime. She was the perfect woman to give redheads a bad name. But awful old bag as she was, she still wasn't in the running to compete with Pat Ferrell.

'I'm terrified Phoebe will turn out just like Elisabeth one day,' said Alison with a shudder. 'I have nightmares about it.'

'Don't be daft,' said Eve. 'Phoebe has you and Rupert to make sure that never happens. It's such a shame she wasn't here. We have a baby reindeer that hasn't got a name and I was hoping she would help me with that.'

'Oh, she'd love to do that,' said Alison.

'None of us can agree on anything,' said Eve. 'We named the other one more or less on the spot – Blizzard – but his brother remains without one.'

'Call him Poseidon,' tutted Alison, breaking open a packet of butter biscuits and tipping them onto a plate. 'Try these, they're gorgeous. I've had such a craving for them through my pregnancy. Spread with Nutella.'

'Do you remember when we first discovered the joy of Nutella?' smiled Eve. 'When we went to that horrible camp in the third year. It had no hot water in the showers, but at least they had Nutella to spread on the toast for breakfast.'

'Oh yes, I'd forgotten all about that God-awful place.' Alison chuckled at the newly awakened memory.

'Forgotten? Blocked out more like. You had the bunk above me and I was crying because I wanted to go home.' And it must have been bad if I wanted to go home, Eve added to herself. 'We got told off for talking in the night.'

'Wasn't it then that we planned to go and live in America when we left school?'

'Yes. New York.'

'We never did manage to get there even on holiday, did we?' Alison sighed. 'I don't know, all those plans you make which you think are set in cement, and really they dissolve when the wind changes.' Then she burst into tears.

'What in God's name . . .' Eve sprang from her seat to put her arms around her friend.

'Sorry. Hormones,' laughed Alison. 'I sometimes worry that I was a crap friend, meeting Rupert so young and not doing all those things we said we were going to do together.'

'That is so ridiculous I could slap you,' said Eve,

ripping off some kitchen roll and passing it to Alison to dab her eyes with.

'I feel like I let you down.'

'Alison Tinker. If you are telling me that you feel guilty that you're happy, you're in big trouble.'

'That's what I do feel.' A fresh wave of tears spurted out of Alison's eyes.

'Oy, have you noticed that I'm not doing so bad. You're talking to the owner of a multi-million-pound theme park.'

'Oh, Eve,' said Alison, not saying what was obvious to them both – that money didn't keep you warm at night. And she so wanted Eve to be as warm at night as she was.

'Moving on from your very silly crying episode,' Eve nudged her friend, 'have you thought of any names at all for the baby?'

'I like Jack,' said Alison, sniffing her tears away. 'Pure and simple – Jack. One of those names which never goes out of fashion. Why did you wrinkle up your nose then?'

'Sorry,' Eve apologized. 'You're right, Jack is timeless. It's just a bit too like Jacques for my liking. My nose tends to automatically go into spasm whenever I hear anything like that word.' And my head starts to throb and my lip starts to curl, she added to herself.

Alison laughed. 'I'd love to meet this Jacques of

yours.' She carried on, despite the fact that Eve lifted up her finger to intimate that this 'Jacques' was most definitely not 'hers'. 'He really has got your goat, hasn't he?'

'He's a charlatan,' said Eve. 'I'm convinced of that more than ever since . . .' Then she stopped.

'Since what?'

Eve didn't answer.

'Since what?' Alison repeated with redhead force. 'Go on.' She studied Eve's guilty expression. She had known her too long not to sense that there had been mischief afoot. 'What have you done, Eve? Tell me now.'

'I know it was wrong,' began Eve. 'But I had to.'

'Had to what?' Alison's hand stilled on the biscuits.

'He left his keys in the office and I drove off and went into his house,' Eve confessed in one breath.

'When?'

'Today.'

'Bloody hell, Eve,' said Alison horrified. 'What on earth made you do that?'

'Gut instinct,' said Eve. 'Something isn't right about that man and I'm glad I did it now, after what I found.'

'Which was what?' Alison leaned forward waiting for Eve's big revelation.

'He's got Stanley's military medal. '

'And?'

'A dress.'

Even as she was saying it, Eve realized it all sounded a bit weak.

'A dress?' Alison said, very unimpressed as she reached for another biscuit.

'A dress for a female soldier was hanging up in his wardrobe. Don't you think that's weird? A very big dress as well.'

'Are you insinuating he's also a transvestite?' said Alison, shaking her head with disbelief.

'I don't know. But it's a possibility, if he's into dressing up. He might enjoy getting in touch with his feminine side and wearing female clothes, like that big cage-fighter on *Big Brother* did. Then again, I didn't see any women's knickers in his drawers . . .'

Alison held up her hand to stem her friend's flow. 'Whoa, whoa, Eve. What do you think you were doing? How would you feel if he'd gone snooping through your knicker drawer?'

Eve tried not to think about that, because she'd have had him arrested. But this was no time for double standards.

'I had to, Ali. I didn't do all this for no reason. He's obsessed with the military. He had uniforms in his wardrobe and drawers of medals and caps and stuff. And eight years ago there was a con man in the area who went by the name Major Jack Glasshoughton. He specialized in targeting pensioners. I found the story on the internet on an old *Weekly Bugle* site. It all adds up, don't you think?'

Alison laughed. 'What I think is that your Aunt Evelyn must have known that Jacques was into military memorabilia and that's why she gave him Stanley's medal. Have you thought of that very simple but plausible possibility? As for the newspaper story . . . how old did you say it was? And when did the *Weekly Bugle* get their facts right? That's why they were closed down.'

Oh, don't you start, thought Eve. Alison was as bad as Violet, refusing to see that there was more to the man than met the eye.

'Explain the dress, then.'

'Well,' began Alison, 'I presume it's part of his collection of memorabilia. Was it the only uniform he had?'

'No, he had some men's ones as well.'

'There you go, then.'

'Explain this, then.' Eve prepared to give her *coup de foudre*. 'He's under a doctor at the hospital. A psychiatrist.' And she gave a smug grin that she was immediately a little ashamed of. Especially as Alison gave her a look of disapproval that wounded her.

'How do you know that?'

'I found an appointment card.'

Alison shook her head. 'Oh, Eve. That's taking snooping a bit too far.'

'Not if he's a nutter it isn't,' Eve defended herself.

'And what if he's just depressed or something like that?'

Boom. Eve remembered – too late – that Alison had a tremendous bout of postnatal depression after giving birth to Phoebe and had seen a psychiatrist as part of her recovery. She wanted Alison's vintage oak flooring to split and swallow her up. It was time to change the subject – and fast.

'Anyway,' Eve waved away that conversation and prepared to start another, 'can I borrow Phoebe at the weekend to come and check the place out and meet Santa?'

'Oh, can I, Mummy?'

A small voice came from behind the door.

'Phoebe?' called Alison. 'How long have you been standing there?'

'I've just hanged up my coat,' said Phoebe. 'Can I go to the winter park? Please please please?'

'She's going through a nosey phase, just in case you're wondering why I'm asking,' Alison whispered to Eve, leaning right over so Phoebe wouldn't hear that. 'You should have taken her with you to Jacques' house.'

'I will next time,' replied Eve, quickly adding, 'Joke,' as she noticed Alison's finger start to wag.

'Please, please, please, Mummy.'

'Well, if you are very good from now until the

weekend, I am sure Auntie Eve will take you to Winterworld.'

Phoebe burst into the room and threw herself on Eve. 'I'll think of loads of reindeer names before then,' she said. And Eve tried to recall how far back in the conversation reindeer had occurred, which would determine how much Phoebe May Tinker had overheard.

Chapter 34

The Daily Trumpet *would like to apologize to a bride and groom who appeared on our 'Newly Weeds' page last Saturday. The bride, Mrs Chelsea Shirt is manageress of Joshua Green's pawn shop and is not, nor ever has been, a porn star. And the groom is called James Shirt and not John Shit as the wording under their photograph read. Mr Shit is a chartered accountant and is not the chairman of 'I Guess That's Why They Call It The Booze' chain of off licenses. As chairman of the Yorkshire Teetotal Society, we understand that this was especially distressful for Mr Shit to read.*

We apologize to Mr and Mrs Shit for any inconvenience and distress and wish them a very happy marriage.

Chapter 35

In the wee small hours, Violet lay awake staring at the ceiling, hoping her sniffing back the tears did not awaken Pav. He had pulled her to bed that evening with more urgency than she could ever remember. They had fallen onto the sheets, undressing each other and kissing madly, and Violet had savoured the feeling of his hardness pressing against her. His lips travelled all over her body and her orgasm was one born out of relief as much as excitement, but when Pav tried to make love to her he couldn't.

'It's fine,' she said, holding him, knowing that it wasn't good at all. He was twenty-five, she thought. Why would a twenty-five-year-old man fail to keep his erection?

There was something on his mind, she knew. Or someone. Had he whisked her upstairs hoping to convince himself that he still wanted her, but his body wouldn't be fooled? And in those cold, dark hours before dawn, Violet listened to the sound of him sleeping and wondered who was there with him in his dreams.

Chapter 36

Anyone watching Eve as she stood at the fence and watched Holly grazing, being followed by little Blizzard and his tiny nameless sibling, would have said, 'She looks a contented woman. One at peace with herself. No one could smile like that, if they weren't pre-disposed to happiness.'

And for a few moments, watching the ridiculously gauche creamy-white calves balancing awkwardly on their long pin legs, Eve forgot the world outside their little bubble. Flakes of snow began to drift down on her head, so perfect that Eve wondered if they were really coming from the skies. As she looked up, she heard a trio of triumphant 'Yeah's.

'At pissing last,' said a Welsh voice from high up a Christmas tree.

'Language, Dai,' said another voice from the ground. 'The boss is over there.'

'Captain or missus?'

'Missus.'

'Shit. *Sori*, missus.'

Were they all calling him Captain now? Had he instigated and encouraged that? It fitted in nicely with his military obsession. Well, if he thought she was going to start saluting him and jumping to attention, he had another think coming. She was only surprised he hadn't started the rumour off that he was a Field Marshal.

She stomped through the forest, joining the white path just as the little train passed her at 125 miles an hour.

'Don't worry, it's being adjusted, missus,' called Thomas, his voice fading to an echo as he sped off through the trees like Casey Jones on whizz. And is that what they are calling me – 'missus'? Eve wondered again. *Missus*. It made her sound at best sixty, at worst like a battleaxe. That didn't help her ratty mood.

Back at the cosy-warm Portakabin, Eve got out her address book to chase the firm who were printing the menus for the restaurant. Kicking some ass would do her good, she thought. And it did. There was nothing like venting your fury on a bit of incompetence to get the blood flowing to all the right areas and blasting fake Captains out of her head. She rewarded herself with a cup of coffee from the snarling machine in the corner, and was just about to sit down and kick some more ass with a sweet supplier when there was a soft tap at the door and a dear, familiar voice said, 'It's only me.'

'Come in, Violet. You don't need to knock,' said Eve. 'Coffee?'

'Thanks,' said Violet. 'And of course I need to knock. You might be in the middle of a meeting.'

'Blimey, Violet, are you okay?' said Eve, handing over a coffee and seeing her cousin's face full-on. She looked as if she hadn't slept for a fortnight. Violet's huge and usually sparkly mauve eyes were as dull as dirty dishwater and she was shivering. 'Sit down,' Eve commanded, and pushed her into a chair.

'I'm fine,' said Violet, sounding anything but. 'I just haven't slept very well.'

'Why?' asked Eve. 'Aren't you feeling well?'

Violet so wanted to open up the floodgates holding everything back. That had been her intention coming to the Portakabin. She couldn't work in the ice-cream parlour, looking at Pav's beautiful back as he put the finishing touches to the last horses. All she could think of was their flop of a love-making session last night, and who Pav might be thinking of whilst he was bringing her to orgasm, something that had always excited him to do before because her pleasure was more important to him than his own, he had always told her. She had lain awake in the wee small hours of the morning torturing herself with pictures of him rolling around in bed with *Serena*, enjoying her much younger, curvier body, as Violet imagined her. But instead, all she said was, 'I'm a bit under the weather, I think.'

'Oh, don't be down,' Eve said, hoping to gee her up. 'You've got too many lovely things in your life to be depressed.'

Violet took in a deep breath. 'I think Pav—'

Then the phone rang and interrupted her flow. Instinctively, Eve picked it up and wished she hadn't. It was the printers reneging on all the promises they had just made to her. She made a 'sorry' face at Violet.

Violet made an 'I'll go' gesture, to which Eve replied with an 'I'll come and find you in a bit' mime. Violet waved an 'It's fine, don't worry' at her, put down the untouched coffee cup and left.

Eve continued with the call and didn't go and find Violet as she had promised. Her head was too full of trying to piece together all the things she knew about Jacques and make them into a picture she could recognize. Later, when she remembered that she hadn't gone to catch up with Violet, she waved it off as unimportant. Violet knew she was busy and would understand. It wasn't as if her cousin, with her gorgeous young artist, thriving business and beautiful cosy cottage, could have that much on her mind now, was it?

Chapter 37

'You think he's what?'

'I think Pav has got someone else,' said Violet, a second before bursting into tears and feeling two arms close around her shoulders.

'No way. Pav isn't a bumhole like that,' said Violet's friend Bel. 'I'd put my life savings on that.'

'What the hell makes you think that?' asked Max, from the other side. The formidable Max McBride. The three women had only known each other little over a year, when they had been shopping for wedding dresses in a strange little shop in Maltstone. A friendship had been struck so deeply between them, it was as if they had known each other in previous lives. So much had happened to them in that year and it had acted as cement on their bond with each other. All three of them were living such different lives when they had first met. But neither

Max nor Bel liked to see that old sadness return to Violet's eyes.

'He couldn't . . .' Violet raised her eyebrows, 'you know . . . last night.' She stuck her finger up in the air.

The tension in both Max's and Bel's shoulders dissipated. 'Is that it?' they both laughed in unison and relief.

'Men aren't machines,' said Max. 'It does happen occasionally.'

Bel nodded. 'You think because he couldn't get it up for one night that he's shagging about? You silly cow. You're both running around like blue-arsed flies trying to get one ice-cream parlour up and running and overseeing the other. He must be under pressure as well as you.'

'It's not just that,' said Violet, as a huge tear plopped down onto her jeans. 'He's been disappearing for hours at a time. He comes in late. And I caught him on the phone last week talking to someone. He put the phone down when I walked in and said it was a wrong number. And when I pressed redial *and* rang 1471 they both connected to the answerphone of a woman called Serena.'

She looked up to see two very blank faces that didn't know what to say. Then Bel leaped up from her seat, 'I'll frigging kill him for you if he's messing you about.'

'Whoa,' said Max. 'Think logically. This is Pav we're talking about. He's adored you from day one. You need to do some more detective work before you set your judgement in stone.'

It was then Max's turn to have two gobsmacked faces staring at her. Max was usually the impulsive, headstrong one.

'Blimey, you've changed. What's *he* done to you? Been putting bromide in your tea?'

Max laughed at Bel. 'The love of a good man makes me see things through much clearer eyes. And your Pav is a good man.' She smiled beatifically. 'Obviously, if he turns out not to be a good man, then I'll hold him down whilst you rip his bollocks off. Have you asked him what he's up to, V?'

'No,' said Violet, drying her eyes on the paper tissue which Bel pulled out of the box on the big, chunky coffee table. 'I daren't. Oh, I'm sorry, Bel. I'm totally ruining your lovely news.'

'Oy, don't be daft. We will have less of that talk or you can forget being joint godmother,' said Bel, who – along with her husband – had just passed the first stage of the adoption process. She couldn't have children of her own and she and her lovely man knew they had a gruelling time of interviews and waiting ahead of them, but also that it would all be worth it in the end. 'I can't see that Pav—'

'Please don't tell me it's my imagination,' cut in Violet. 'I *know* he's up to something.'

'Violet, you need to talk to Pav,' said Max, putting her large hand on Violet's and giving it a squeeze.

'I daren't.' She dropped her head into her hands and Max and Bel grimaced awkwardly at each other.

'Can't you ask your cousin to do a bit of interfering?' said Bel softly.

'I tried to talk to her yesterday, but she's got enough on her plate,' replied Violet.

And though she would never have said it aloud, because she knew how it would have sounded, she felt that Eve was the lucky one out of the two of them – being loved to the end, rather than feeling her relationship slip away and her heart begin to crack a little more each day.

'Ask him,' ordered Bel. 'You can't sit back and suffer like this. It might be nothing.' She was sounding less convinced by the second that this was nothing, and hoped her voice didn't show that.

'I'll think about it,' replied Violet, knowing that she wouldn't. Knowing that she was afraid of the answer he might give. Knowing that by forcing him to admit what was going on, she would push the remaining time she had with him towards the finish line.

Chapter 38

When Phoebe May Tinker walked through the front entrance of Winterworld, Eve could quite easily have believed that her eyes were going to pop out of her little head. Her mouth was still stuck in a perfect O of wonder as she felt snow dropping on her head. Those German snow machines were something else; what they produced was the stuff of Christmas cards – thick, soft flakes that fell onto the trees and made everything look as if it had been sprinkled with sugar.

'So Phoebe, what would you like to see first?' asked Eve, not used to Phoebe being so very quiet. 'Shall we take the train to see the reindeer?'

Phoebe nodded slowly. Eve hoped the train had been adjusted. The previous day it was faster than ever and Thomas was just a blur as he passed her waving. She didn't know what it was running on, but she wished she could have some of it in the morning. Her side and back still niggled and she was still more fatigued than she cared to admit. The shingles virus really had slowed her down these past weeks and she hated not running at full power. The doctor had said it might take years for the nerves to recover.

Thomas and another engineer were deep in Welsh conversation when Eve and Phoebe approached the track.

'Any chance of a ride to the reindeer?' asked Eve.

'Yes, of course,' said Thomas, seeing the little girl and putting on his official cap, which lay on a bench next to a clipboard. 'Climb aboard then, young miss. And missus.'

Eve tried not to bare her teeth. Flaming 'missus'. What a ridiculous title to have. It wasn't in the same league as 'Captain', she thought with an inner snarl. Talking of which, she hoped he wasn't around today. For the last couple of days he had been up at Winterpark helping Effin's men in the children's activity centre, leaving Eve in the office doing what she enjoyed best – sorting out nitty-gritty. Evelyn had set a small army of contractors on to take care of wages and staffing, stuff which would be dealt with in-house in the future, but it certainly made things easier at the beginning because running a theme park didn't come with a manual. That said, Eve was enjoying learning on the job. And though she would hate to admit it, between herself and Jacques, all the 'I's were dotted and the 'T's crossed.

The train kangarooed forward and Phoebe squealed with delight, whilst Eve grabbed onto the safety bar in front of her.

'Is this really safe?' she asked.

'Oh yes,' said Thomas. 'We've managed to adjust the speed now.' Then he set off at G force. The train went so fast that they arrived before they had set off.

'Sorry,' said Thomas. 'It seems to have reverted back to 'ow it was before.' He took his cap off and scratched his head in a totally clichéd way, then plucked the walkie-talkie out of his top pocket and started gabbling in Welsh into it. And back out of it came Effin's Celtic screech.

'*Llai Tomos y Tanc, a mwy Tomos y Wanc!*'

'Oh dear,' said Thomas. 'He says I'm less Thomas the Tank and more Thomas the w—'

'Yes, I think I got that,' Eve quickly spoke over him.

'That was fun,' said Phoebe, her red curls blown behind her. 'Can we go back on the train as well?'

'We'll see,' replied Eve as diplomatically as possible. It wasn't exactly the leisurely trip looking at the trees and all the coloured twinkling lights she had imagined as Phoebe's introduction to the park. 'Anyway, do you want to see the snow ponies first or the reindeer?'

'Oh, the reindeer, the reindeer!' shrieked Phoebe.

'You'll have to be very quiet, Phoebe, as they don't know you yet and might be a little frightened.' Eve took a large carrot and an apple out of her handbag. 'Hold this. Holly loves these. Right now, steady, no sudden movements.'

Eve unlocked the gate and took Phoebe's hand, making the familiar clicking noises which Holly responded to as they walked into the paddock.

'Is she in her stable, Auntie Eve?' asked Phoebe.

Eve nodded and halted halfway across the pen. 'Holly.'

Eve saw the point of an antler poke out of the stable. That was strange – did Holly have antlers?

'We have a carrot and an apple for you,' she trilled.

'Oh good. That's two of my five a day taken care of then,' said a man's voice from inside the stable. Then Jacques' head, complete with an antler headdress, popped out.

Eve jumped a foot. 'What in Pete's name are you doing?'

'I'm cleaning the stable,' said Jacques. 'Daft things prefer to be in here with me as I'm doing it. I've chased them out three times.' He took off the headgear. 'One of the lads left this in here for a joke. Sorry, couldn't resist.' His eyes dropped to Phoebe. 'Hello, young lady, I'm Jacques. You must be Princess Anne.'

Phoebe giggled and Eve thought, *Not someone else charmed by him.* She watched as Jacques strolled over, took off a giant glove and presented his equally giant hand to the little girl, which she shook heartily.

'Jacques,' she said, rolling the word around in her mouth like a toffee. Had Eve not been so focussed on what Jacques was wearing – the world's biggest coat – she would have heard the cogs turning in little Phoebe May Tinker's brain.

'I'm Phoebe May Tinker.'

'My goddaughter,' added Eve, wondering why Phoebe was staring at Jacques' legs so intently.

'So you want to see Holly and her babies. And I do believe Father Christmas is here today in his grotto. Are you going to see him as well?'

'Oh, yes please,' Phoebe yelped, jumping up and down.

'He's here, is he?' said Eve. She couldn't wait to see him for herself.

'Yes, he's here and looking forward to meeting you.'

'Again?' added Eve with a sarcastic grin.

'Of course.' Jacques' returning grin was wide and made his eyes crinkle up. 'Maybe you'd like to ask him for a ring for Christmas.'

Oh, here we go, Eve sighed wearily.

'He's checking his new grotto out for comfort,'

Jacques whispered to Phoebe. Then he turned back to the stable and addressed the animals within.

'Come on, you lot,' he called. 'You've got visitors.'

He made his own clicking noises which seemed to work much faster than Eve's, much to her chagrin. Holly emerged to a gasp of delight from Phoebe, especially as she was tailed by her two almost white babies. Phoebe held her carrot out with a little shaky hand. Jacques closed his hand around her arm and pulled her forward a few steps.

'She knows my smell,' explained Jacques. 'So she's more likely to come over if I'm here.' Infuriatingly, he turned to look at Eve over his shoulder and winked at her.

Holly edged close and Phoebe clamped her hand over her mouth to stop the squeak that almost burst out of her as the gentle reindeer dropped her head and took the carrot from Phoebe's hand. The little girl stared with pure fascination as the reindeer chewed and her two babies sought protection from the stranger by staying very close to mum's side.

'Which one is Blizzard?' she asked Jacques. *Why didn't she ask me?* thought Eve to herself with a humph.

'This one,' said Jacques. 'He's slightly bigger than his brother. We haven't got a name for him yet. Don't suppose you have any ideas?'

'I've already asked Phoebe that one,' grunted Eve. 'Thank you.'

'Hey, do you know there are only twenty-five letters in the alphabet at Christmas?' said Jacques.

Eve waited for the world's oldest punchline.

'That's my favourite Christmas joke,' said Phoebe, grinning. 'No L.' And she pulled a piece of paper out of her Hello Kitty handbag which she proffered to Jacques. 'And it's my number-one favourite name for the baby reindeer.'

'Noel,' Jacques read down the list. 'These are all such lovely names – Snowflake, David, Jingle. But I think you're right, Noel is the one.' He gave a thumbs-up. 'Don't you think so, Auntie Eve?'

Eve narrowed her eyes at him. God, he really was a charmer. Standing there all blue-eyed and Dr Doolittle-like, stroking a reindeer. And weren't animals supposed to be able to suss out what people were really like? Had he managed to pull the wool over their eyes as well? She bet he had a trail of broken hearts behind him. Some daft women would have been mightily flattered by all those marrying references.

However, Eve did have to agree with him that Noel was perfect for the baby reindeer.

'Well done you, Phoebe, we have a name for our baby.' And right on cue, the newly named Noel made a snuffly noise and fell over onto his side as if he'd had a jug of carrot wine. Phoebe shrieked with delight.

'I'm just about finished here,' said Jacques. 'Why don't you go and see the snow ponies next door and I'll catch you up. Then we can all go and see Santa together.'

Eve opened her mouth to give an alternative plan, but she couldn't beat that one because Phoebe was jumping up and down. She gave Jacques a discreet sneer and in return he gave her a smile of triumph. *Bloody man.*

Phoebe fell equally in love with the snow ponies who were greedy for polos, which they could detect in someone's pocket from five miles away. Eve showed Phoebe how to keep her hand flat when she presented a sweet to the ponies so she wouldn't get her fingers nibbled. Big old Christopher didn't use his size to push to the front of the cheeky ponies, but stood patiently with hope in his big brown eyes. Eve wasn't that keen on having drool all over her hand, but somehow the sensation of giving a treat to the old horse offset any yuk factor. She could sense he was content here, which was just as well because he was a huge horse and if he did decide to go off on one, they would be in trouble. Tim the keeper had brushed him till he almost shone. He had to do it quite a lot, apparently, because

Christopher liked nothing better than to roll around on the ground.

'Hi there,' boomed Jacques as Eve was fishing in her handbag for tissues. Phoebe had horse drool all over her coat sleeves as far as the elbow.

'Hello again,' said Phoebe. Eve noticed how intently she studied him as he walked towards them. Her little eyes were travelling up and down over him as if he was a walking *Where's Wally?* book.

'I've been thinking, Eve,' said Jacques.

'Dangerous,' said Eve under her breath.

'How about, when we open the park on the first day, we give all the families of servicemen free entry? I think your aunt would have approved of that, seeing as we're allied to a military charity.'

Eve's head swivelled slowly round to him. She wanted to laugh but thought better of it because it was a generous idea, if not entirely a shock. Was there no end to the man's obsession with the military? From a PR point of view, it was a beauty, of course.

'I think that's a very good suggestion,' she said, unable to quite keep the twist of a smile from the corner of her lips.

'Good, I'll get onto the press, then, and line it up, shall I?' said Jacques.

'You can leave that with me. I'm used to dealing with the press,' said Eve with calm firmness.

'Okay, if you're happy to do that, then it's fine with me.'

Eve felt a tug on her coat sleeve.

'Can we go and see Santa now, Auntie Eve, please?' Phoebe's voice was heavy with impatience.

'Yeah,' said Jacques, with all the enthusiasm of a young boy who had just been presented with a fishing rod at the side of a lake teeming with fish. 'Let's go, Auntie Eve.'

Eve took Phoebe's chilly little hand and warmed it in her own. Somehow, between getting on the train and now, she had managed to lose her fluorescent-pink gloves.

'You know, when I was a little boy, I used to go and see Santa in a cave,' said Jacques. 'Boy, I just love Christmas. Isn't it the best time of year, Phoebe?'

'Yes,' giggled Phoebe.

'He once brought me a bike and the handlebars were covered in soot. Now, doesn't that just prove that it came down the chimney?'

He actually sounds as if he believed that, thought Eve. But she held back on the sarcasm because her god-daughter was enjoying his twaddle.

Phoebe was desperate to travel on the nutter-speed train but the engineers were tweaking it again.

'It won't be ready in time,' said Eve, having a sudden stab of panic. 'It's just madness expecting this park to be open before Christmas. It's the last week in November now.'

'Chillax, *ma cherie*,' said Jacques. 'It will be ready because Jacques Glace has said it will be ready.'

'Captain Jacques, don't you mean,' said Eve under her breath again. She could imagine Alan Carr more in the role of an army captain than she could this clown in front of her, wearing a Dr Who stripey scarf long enough to wrap around the equator.

They walked through the enchanted forest and once again Eve was reminded of her Enid Blyton Enchanted Wood. It was barely mid-morning, yet the snow was falling soft as down on them and was bright-white as if the drops were carrying tiny specks of sparkling light. It was eerie – but nice-eerie. The machines pumping it out were totally camouflaged and the snow really did look as if it was coming from the skies.

'Jesus Christ!' Eve jerked as a full-size grinning snowman appeared from behind a tree and waved at them.

'I thought your visitor would appreciate a few personalities around,' said Jacques, steadying her with his hand. 'So your god-daughter can get a true feel of what a day to Winterworld will be like when it opens.'

So far so good then, thought Eve. Almost killed on a broken train and given a heart attack by a round bloke dressed up in a cotton-wool suit. The even scarier thing was that the snowman didn't look as if he was wearing a costume – he looked too real for comfort.

As they approached the edge of the forest, Eve gave a small, involuntary sneer in the direction of the ridiculous wedding chapel. Effin's men were draping the roof in what looked like a cross between a cotton-wool sheet and thatching.

'Permanent weatherproof snow,' explained Jacques. 'Looks fantastic, doesn't it? It's just come in from Germany.'

'Marvellous,' said Eve, with a smile as fake as the roofing. Phoebe was hopping up and down so much at her side, Eve was forced to ask her if she wanted to go to the loo before they met Santa. She didn't. Or at least if she did, she wasn't admitting to it.

Eve hadn't seen the inside of the grotto yet and hoped she hadn't cocked up by allowing Jacques so much leeway. That stupid illness had kept her eye off the ball too much. But, she supposed, if the grotto was a mess, she had enough time to step in. Just. There wasn't anything she couldn't do. At least in a business sense.

'Ready to meet Santa?' said Jacques, bending down and smiling at Phoebe with his wide mouth and sparkling blue eyes.

'Yes,' said Phoebe.

'Come on then,' said Jacques, and gestured to Phoebe that she should go through the entrance.

Once inside, well, that's where it got weird for Eve. Because no way was the grotto so large inside if you judged it from the outside. The cabin was tantamount to a Tardis.

As if he knew what thoughts were trying to piece themselves together in Eve's mind, Jacques whispered, 'It's a clever bit of *trompe l'œil* and building work. The grotto goes under the false hillside.' And he touched his nose, secret-wise.

'Hello there,' said one of the elves, appearing from their left with a tray full of red-and-white striped candy canes. 'Miss Phoebe, would you like a sweet? I made them myself.'

Phoebe gasped. 'How did he know my name?' she asked Eve with breathless delight.

'Well, he's magic, of course,' butted in Jacques.

'You're at the top of the nice list,' said the elf. 'I recognized you.'

He was a funny little man, thought Eve. Like one of those actors in an American Christmas film, who had obviously been chosen because he really did look like an elf. And his ears didn't look plastic either. Eve half wanted to reach out and touch the left one, which was nearest to her. It had a ghost of a thin purple vein on it. God is in the detail, she thought, which had been a steadfast mantra of hers in the Eve's Events years.

Phoebe took a candy cane. They were all slightly different shapes, giving the impression that they really had been handmade. She didn't unwrap it but placed it in her Hello Kitty bag to take home for her mum.

'Are you coming to see our workshop afterwards and help us make a toy?' asked the elf. He had a name badge on, Eve then noticed. 'Derek'. Derek the elf. She wouldn't have thought that was a suitable name for an elf, but it suited him, strangely enough.

'May I?' asked Phoebe, once again asking permission from Eve.

'Yes, of course.' Eve's eyes were roving all over the inside of the grotto. It really was impressive. There was a window to the right which afforded a 3D view of snowy hills and a blue lake and lots of grazing reindeer. It must be a film screen, thought Eve. She was very impressed. There were presents everywhere from every era – teddies and stylophones, wind-up toys, board games, the Sindy doll that Eve remembered coveting as a child poking out of the top of one of the huge hessian sacks. There was even a faint smell in the air of sweet plastic, which she recalled as being the scent of old toyshops she used to go in. And as they turned a corner, four more elves were wrapping up presents and beautifully so, with thick paper and wide ribbon, and the smell of hot chocolate hit her and made her stomach groan with want.

Phoebe *mmm*-ed. Eve didn't blame her. Then there was a knotty wooden door and at the side of it a smiling elf with 'real' ears and a tiny face, dressed in what could only be described as a green military elf costume. The sort of garb that fairy-folk would wear if they had their own armed forces. *Quel surprise*, thought Eve, looking at the elf's medals pinned on his breast. She might have guessed that if Jacques were involved, there would be uniforms. She half expected the door to open and to see Santa dressed as an Admiral.

'Ready to meet Santa, young lady?' asked the 'guard'.

'Oh yes, yes, please,' said Phoebe, nearly wetting herself with excitement.

'Okay then,' said the guard, and slowly opened the door. Following Phoebe, Eve walked into a room which could have been projected out of her own memory store: a room like the old, oak-panelled library in Higher Hoppleton Hall. A room which could not possibly have been built in the last few weeks because it was old and aged and smelled of the same beeswax polish as the room in her head. And even more odd, the Santa who sat huge and smiling in the old chair with his half-moon glasses on his head and his great white beard hanging down was the same Santa Claus who had restored her faith all those years ago.

Don't be stupid, Eve.

He held his arms out to Phoebe who went rushing towards him and plonked herself on his knee, and Eve could so easily have been watching herself that fateful Christmas because that's exactly what she had done. She came over light-headed and put her hand on the wall to steady herself.

'You okay?' asked Jacques.

'Where did you find him?'

'I didn't,' said Jacques. 'Your Aunt Evelyn did.' He raised his fingers to his lips and said, 'Just watch him at work. He's absolutely brilliant.'

'Where are your gloves?' Santa was saying. Then he pulled a pair of pink gloves bundled together out of his pocket. 'Ah, here they are.'

'You found them,' Eve said to Jacques. 'You might have said.'

'I didn't find anything,' said Jacques, standing with his arms crossed, smiling. 'Santa knows.'

'It's all very well keeping the faith alive in little girls, but I'm not a little girl and you don't have to treat me like one,' growled Eve, as quietly as she could.

'You are a little girl,' said Jacques, turning the full intensity of his warm sea-blue eyes onto her. 'Beneath that hard, stubborn shell, you're a little girl who wants to be cuddled and loved and believe in some magic.'

His voice, like a sharpened dart, pierced her with its tender truth, and though the middle of her yelped with pain, the outside of her stiffened. 'Rubbish,' she sniffed.

'I think I recognize you,' said Santa, raising his black-gloved finger at Eve. His beard looked real and soft. The Father Christmas she remembered asked her to tug at his beard to prove it wasn't a false one. 'You used to like me to bring you Fuzzy Felts, didn't you?'

Eve swallowed. Auntie Susan always had a Fuzzy Felt waiting for her under the Christmas tree at their house. *Oh, don't be silly, Eve,* came a counter-thought. Santa had obviously worked out her age and paired it up with a toy of the times. Everyone liked Fuzzy Felts back then. But, for the sake of Phoebe, who was mesmerized, Eve played the game. Even if she wasn't quite able to keep all the sarcasm out of her voice.

'Yes, I did. How clever of you to remember.'

'I never forget a child, or a toy,' said Santa, smiling at Phoebe, who looked as if she was in seventh heaven. 'And you are a book lady, aren't you?'

Phoebe nodded. She was too excited to speak as Santa leaned over to root around in a huge sack at his side, full of beautifully wrapped presents.

'You can open this now if you like,' said Santa. 'If you promise not to tell anyone.'

'I won't,' gasped Phoebe, ripping off the paper and squealing with delight to discover a *How To Draw Cartoons For Beginners* book with some pencils.

'He's good, isn't he? Go on, admit it,' said Jacques, leaning over Eve's shoulder.

'Yes, he is,' replied Eve. Jacques had surpassed himself with the grotto and Santa was a true find. Eve shivered. In fact this whole grotto was a bit too good. It was stirring things up inside her and she didn't know why. It was evoking memories of being at Auntie Susan's house and eating Christmas dinner one year. And Uncle Jeff had a silly hat on and mustered everyone to the table to play Cluedo and Frustration. And Susan had insisted they stay the night so Violet and Eve had fallen asleep together in her big soft bed. Eve had wished that she could live with them rather than go back to their damp-stinking, poky flat.

Her mobile rang and disturbed her from her mince-pie-scented reverie. It was the printers attempting to butter her up in order to deliver an apology for something they'd done wrong yet again.

'I'll just go outside and take this,' Eve mouthed at Jacques.

'I'll meet you up at the carousel,' said Jacques. 'I'm sure Phoebe would like to ride on one of the horses.'

After Phoebe had said a reluctant goodbye to Santa, she trotted at the side of Jacques, passing Eve at the grotto entrance snarling down the mobile.

'Ooh, that doesn't sound very friendly, does it?' Jacques chuckled. He noticed that Phoebe was hanging behind him and he felt her little eyes boring into his back.

'Everything all right there?' he asked.

'Are those men's jeans?' Phoebe replied. 'They're very nice.'

Jacques creased his eyebrows.

'Er, yes,' he replied. 'Why do you ask?'

'Where do you buy them from?'

'A shop in Meadowhall.'

'Topshop?'

Jacques smiled. 'No, not Topshop.'

'My Auntie Eve says that you wear ladies' clothes.'

Jacques snorted with laughter. 'Does she now?'

'She says you have a lady's uniform hanging up in your wardrobe.'

Jacques' breath caught in his throat and his laughter dried up instantly. 'And what else does your Auntie Eve say about me then?' he asked, trying to sound casual as they walked on.

'She says you collect medals and have one that belongs to her. And that you go to the doctors. Are you ill?'

Jacques' hand rose to rake through his short hair.

'No, Phoebe,' he said gently. 'I'm not ill.' *Not any more*.

He didn't show it as he helped the little girl onto the carousel but he was rocked to the core. The horses whirled around and around in front of him, but he didn't see them. He was too busy piecing things together in his head and sinking to a dark place as he replayed Phoebe's loaded words. Then Eve appeared at his side.

'Why is this place called Santapark and not Winterpark?' she said, pointing upwards at the sign. No prizes for guessing whose idea that had been.

'I'll leave you to it,' said Jacques, walking off, his stride firm and quick.

'What . . . ?' began Eve, but he was gone. And so, she noticed before he turned away, was the light in his eyes.

Chapter 39

'She's worn out, bless her,' said Eve, carrying a solidly asleep Phoebe into Alison's house and transferring her to Rupert's waiting arms.

Eve then unlooped Phoebe's Hello Kitty bag from around her neck and put it on the kitchen table with her book from Santa and the toy wooden carousel which she had helped to glue together in the elves' workshop. Those workshops were going to be an enormous hit, she just knew it, and the elf-people were amazing. She hadn't seen Jacques for the rest of the day though. He was on her mind much more than she intended him to be. What could have made him storm off like that?

'How's it going?' asked Rupert. 'Are you nearly ready to open for business?'

'Amazingly we are,' said Eve. 'Our train keeps going berserk and some idiot has called the park

Santapark instead of Winterpark so that needs changing, but we are just about ready. Oh and I apologize. The café isn't up and running yet so Phoebe just had chips and chicken nuggets for lunch. And some mince-pie ice cream.'

'Sounds yummy,' said Rupert. 'Alison has just made us some salmon, which is why the place stinks of fish. It was vile and I'd kill for chips and chicken nuggets.'

Alison grimaced as Rupert swept his daughter up the staircase.

'I was missing some ingredients and improvised,' she said. 'It wasn't good.'

'Thanks for lending Phoebe to me,' said Eve. 'She was as good as gold.'

'No doubt I'll hear all about it in the morning. I hope she took plenty of photos.'

'I'm not sure if she did or not,' Eve tried to recall. 'She seemed to be enjoying herself too much to want to stop and capture the moment. She's been in a workshop with elves banging hammers and sitting on Santa's knee and looking at snow globes. Phoebe had liked them so much, Eve now knew exactly what to buy her for Christmas.

'How did she get on with the reindeer? That's what she was looking forward to most of all. Did she come up with a name?'

'Noel,' smiled Eve. 'She fed Holly a carrot and got

bullied into parting with lots of polos by the snow ponies as well.'

'Oh it all sounds so lovely,' sighed Alison. 'I can't wait to visit myself. Did she meet the infamous Jacques?' She mouthed a drink at Eve, but Eve shook her head.

'No, I want to get back and look through some accounts. Yes, she met him. He took her to the carousel whilst I was having a ding-dong with the printers. Then he left us.'

Quickly and strangely. Eve wondered what had happened between leaving the grotto and the Carousel to make his mood change so quickly. It was as if a storm-cloud had settled on him.

Eve recalled the conversation she'd had with Phoebe when the carousel stopped. She had been quite disappointed to get off the ride and find that Jacques had gone.

'I liked him. He has really nice trousers,' Phoebe had said.

'Nice trousers?' Eve repeated.

'His jeans,' said Phoebe, leaning in as if to deliver a secret. 'He gets them from Meadowhall. But not Topshop.'

'Oh right,' Eve had replied. What an odd conversation that had been.

'You're doing accounts on a Saturday night?' asked Alison, nudging her out of her reverie.

'Well, they need doing and I've got nothing else on,' shrugged Eve, opening her arms to hug her very rounded friend goodnight.

'Oh Eve,' said Alison to the door when it closed on her friend. You should be going out with a nice man for dinner on Saturday night or going to bed early with him for a cuddle. She shook her head and wished her friend something better waiting around the corner than accounts on a Saturday night.

Chapter 40

First thing Monday morning Jacques called in at the ice-cream parlour with a special delivery box of menus, which had been on urgent order. He took one look at Violet's face and knew she was seconds away from bursting into tears. He also knew that one kind word would tip them over her eyelids, so he chose his next words very carefully.

'Here you go, Violet. Menus. Let's just hope they haven't cocked them up yet again. I think it was the only mistake Evelyn made, picking them to do the job.' He avoided eye contact with her as he lifted the box onto the counter. 'Do you want me to leave these here or put them in the back room for you?'

'They're fine there,' sniffed Violet. 'Sorry, got a bit of a cold today,' she smiled sadly as she lied.

'It's the weather, it just doesn't know what to do with itself,' nodded Jacques. Today was as mild and sunny as a spring day. Yesterday had been full of high winds and the sun had refused to come out from behind the woollen grey clouds.

'Pav about?'

'No, I don't know where he is. Again.'

Violet's head tipped forwards and she sobbed twice then waved frantically at her face in a brave attempt to get herself together. 'Sorry,' she said. 'Oh God.' She quickly grabbed a serviette and blew her nose.

'There's a lot to do, I hope you're not overworking yourself,' he said softly, wanting to close his big arms around her. Wanting to *tell her*.

'Sorry, he said he'd be back soon,' said Violet, trying her best to recover.

'Well, if you could ask him to call round to the Portakabin and see me, I'd be grateful.'

'I will.'

Just as Jacques opened the door, Violet's voice arrested him.

'Do you know where he is, Jacques? Who he's with?'

'No, I'm sorry, I don't,' was all he could say. Even though he knew where Pav was and the woman he was with, he couldn't tell her any of it.

Eve was reading the *Daily Trumpet*, which Jacques brought in with him every morning; the headline didn't make for light entertainment. It carried the story of a young female soldier from the area who was going to be buried tomorrow. She came from Ketherwood, a district made up of a rough, sprawling council estate, and joined the army to better her lot, and for her effort had ended up dead at twenty-one. For once, the piece was written without any typos in it, unless they had totally made a mess of the details – there was no way of knowing if the soldier's name really was Private Sharon Wilkinson from Red Grove. Not unless an apology appeared in the paper in a few days to say she was really Major Davina Pikestaff from Pogley Top and offering apologies to the grieving family. She folded up the newspaper and put it back on Jacques' desk.

Jacques plodded in with his eyebrows low, giving him the appearance of someone in deep thought, or not in the best mood – or both.

'Morning,' said Eve. To her surprise he barely grumbled the word back at her. His movements were very staccato as he threw off another in his big coat collection and grabbed a coffee. He was wearing Armani jeans, she noticed. Not from Topshop. She wondered why on earth Phoebe had thought he would buy his trousers there.

There was none of his customary whistling this morning as he sat at his desk and glued his eyes to the computer screen. He hadn't shaved, Eve saw. She noticed that when he was clean-shaven in the morning, by the end of the day stubble had started to grow. By rough calculations, she reckoned he hadn't shaved all weekend.

'Have you seen Effin this morning?' she asked, as something to say so she could better gauge his mood. This was a very different Jacques from the one she had been accustomed to. She couldn't help but be curious as to the change, especially the timing of it, because she suspected it had something to do with Phoebe.

'No,' he replied, and quite abruptly too. He picked up the newspaper and read the front page.

'Sad, isn't it?' said Eve. 'Hardly a life. Who'd be a soldier?' That's a real soldier, by the way. Not a pretend one that prances around in a uniform in front of the mirror, she added to herself.

Jacques screwed the newspaper up and launched it at the bin.

'She died doing something she loved,' he said, his mouth a grim line. 'How many of us can truly say that?'

'For God's sake. She was only twenty-one years old.'

Jacques came back at her. 'She was a soldier. Only a fool would join the armed forces not knowing that dying on the job was a distinct possibility.'

Oh yes, he'd know all about what real soldiers

thought. But she bit her lip because Jonathan had said the same thing to her more than once. He said that he hoped that when he left her he would come back, but he knew there were no guarantees. It took a brave man – or woman – to do a job like that which carried such a risk. And Jonathan Lighthouse was a brave, wonderful man who was prepared to risk his life for his country's demands. The army was so much more than a job to him: it was his life – and he had been hers.

Jacques yanked open his filing cabinet and pulled out a large black book. As Eve watched him silently, he opened the book, checked something, then closed it again and replaced it back in the cabinet, slamming the drawer shut again. The sound it made was still reverberating in the air when Jacques stood up with such energy that his chair went rolling right across the room behind him. He exited the Portakabin without saying where he was going, and his big presence left a hole in the atmosphere of the room.

Eve hadn't seen that big black book before and wondered what it was. His secret drawing book of uniform designs? She checked through the window that he really had gone, then she quickly snatched the drawer open to take a look. It was labelled 'Wedding Chapel'. On the first page was a note of the only booking and she felt her cheeks warm up with rage so much that she was sure if she looked in a mirror she would be the colour of Violet Beauregarde. Post-blueberry juice. She didn't care what mood he was in, he needed to come back to the Portakabin and explain. The man was impossible.

Eve rang him on his mobile but it went straight through to voicemail. She left a message but was too wound up to sit and wait for Jacques to bother to pick it up and respond to it, so she put on her coat and headed off to find him. None of Effin's men had seen him, though; neither had any of the elf-men and women who were busy unpacking boxes full of wooden toy parts to be hammered together and painted by children in the workshops, nor the elf-actors painting scenery in the tiny thea-tre. He wasn't to be found in his usual haunt – 'Santapark' (that sign really did need to be changed before her brain blew all its fuses), or the grotto or the chapel and nor had Tim, the reindeer and horse keeper, seen him. He wasn't in the snow-globe museum, the shop or the café. She scuttled past the ice-cream parlour but it was obvious he wasn't in there either. Eve was boiling with anger by the time she got back to the Portakabin – only to find him sitting there, putting a jug of water through the coffee machine.

'I've been looking everywhere for you,' she hollered. 'And I rang you.'

'Oh, have you?' was all he said.

'I need a word,' Eve said, her eyebrows matching his now for crossness. 'A big word.'

'What about?'

'I had a look in the wedding-chapel book.'

Jacques' eyes narrowed. They were a cold blue today – glacial ice chips. 'You snooped in my drawer, you mean,' he levelled at her. 'Quite a master at it, aren't you?'

What that meant Eve had no idea, nor did she have the time or disposition to analyse it.

'I didn't "snoop". As far as I was aware, this is *our* park. Not yours.'

'You said we should run separate projects, if I remember correctly. The chapel falls in my remit.'

He was deliberately winding her up now, throwing her own words back at her like some clever barrister. She wondered if he had a wardrobe full of silks and wigs as well for when he fancied another alter ego.

'Why didn't you tell me?' she yelled.

'He didn't want you to know.'

'This,' she gesticulated wildly around the Portakabin, but meant much further beyond, 'is my business too. I have a perfect right to know something like that.'

'Yet,' put in Jacques, 'he wanted you to know when he was ready to tell you. And asked me if I would be complicit in that.'

'Yeah, well,' Eve laughed without humour. She would have to be careful not to let rip about secrets and intrigue. 'It's wrong,' she said. 'You have to cancel it.'

Jacques shook his head in thin amusement. 'Why would I want to do that?'

'It'll be a nightmare, that's why. No one in their right mind would want that to happen. Least of all . . .'

Jacques stood up to his full height of six foot four and looked imperiously down at Eve. 'You haven't a clue, Miss Douglas. You haven't a clue what people want or need because you are too out of touch with everything.'

Eve felt herself bucking inside at his patronizing and blatantly incorrect analysing. 'How dare you,' she said. 'How dare YOU tell me I'M out of touch.' Ha. A fantasist telling her she didn't know what real life was. How funny was that?

She wasn't prepared for his hands landing on her arms, for being twisted around, for being pushed forward and forced to face herself in the long rectangular mirror which hung on the wall.

'That woman whom you see there is as part of the real world as a nun in closed orders on the moon,' said Jacques, an alien, bitter tone in his voice. 'And she will shrink more and more into herself and away from the world with every passing year. Look at her,

Eve. When did that woman in front of you last laugh? When did she think to herself that she was truly enjoying life?'

'Will you get off me.' Eve struggled, but Jacques was a powerfully built man and his hold on her was unbreakable.

'She can't see people in front of her any more because she has no eyes for the present, only the past. And when she does realize she could have had a future, it will be too late. Haven't you learnt anything from your Auntie Evelyn, woman? Do you think she wanted you to follow in her footsteps? Don't you think that watching what was happening to you made her realize all the years she had wasted?'

'I don't need you to analyse me. I am none of your business. What you are intending to do, however, is,' said Eve, still trying to wrest herself from his grip.

'No, it isn't,' said Jacques. 'Stay out of it. You can't stage-manage what other people want when you're such a mess yourself.'

He let her arms go and she still felt where his hands had gripped her.

'A mess? A mess? What do you mean I'm a mess?' She wasn't a mess. Mess-people didn't have jobs or money or ambition – or drive brand-new BMWs. How the fuck could she be a mess? She was less of a mess than anyone she knew. She moved time barriers to organize last-minute events, she couldn't do things like that if she were a *mess*. 'At least I . . .' She stopped herself just in time. He waited for her to finish her sentence, but she remained silent, rubbing at her arms.

'I think your aunt made more mistakes than employing a rubbish printer,' said Jacques, palming his keys from the desk.

'Didn't she just,' Eve called out to his back as he exited with a grim flourish. Ooh, that sounded as if he might be starting to want out. Was she wearing him down? She should have been quite excited about that, so why wasn't she? Why was she stinging from his words and hating him for knowing her more than she knew herself?

Chapter 41

Eve held a carrot whilst Holly nibbled delicately on it. She was a funny thing: small and gentle with beautiful, trusting eyes and almost ladylike in the way she ate. Blizzard and the newly named Noel were a little more confident now and didn't cling on to their mother's shadow as much. Noel was sipping from the trough; Blizzard was lying down asleep, his head turned towards his feet, looking like a ghost version of Bambi.

For two days now a tennis match had been playing in Eve's head. The ball that was being batted to and fro had 'Do I tell her?' written all over it. It fell in the 'Yes' court, then bounced into the 'No' – back and forth. It had given her a headache the previous day and she'd had to go to bed early after taking some tablets.

'Oh Holly, I wish you could talk,' said Eve, getting

an apple out of her coat pocket. But reindeer didn't talk, and neither did candle flames, as she found out often when she asked Jonathan to send her some help, some sign when she needed direction on which path to take. The candle flame just flickered in the air disturbed by her breath, and Holly kept chewing. Flames and reindeer did not give advice: this one was down to her. She regretted that she had ever seen that damned black book.

'I'm dreading this afternoon, I don't mind telling you,' said Eve, after checking behind her to make sure no one was around to overhear her having a one-sided conversation with an animal. 'My granny is a bit difficult, to say the least. I don't want to go.'

Violet's Nan Flockton used to say Pat Ferrell had the eyes of a dead halibut. Nan Flockton, now that was the sort of granny to have: a fun, sharp woman, with a hug always ready in her arms. Neither Violet nor Eve had ever had a hug or a kiss from Pat. Eve felt very disloyal even thinking it, but she didn't love her granny. She didn't like her either, but today she was seventy-five and duty beckoned. At least she would be going with Susan and Violet, so she wouldn't have to suffer the ordeal of sitting in that cold house with an even colder woman. Susan had suggested taking her mother out for something to eat, but Granny Ferrell didn't want to, as her fancy man was taking her out for an expensive posh dinner and she wanted to be very hungry for that.

Eve stroked Holly's nose as she ate the last of the carrot. 'Ah well, best go. See you later, Miss Holly.' Checking again that no one was around, Eve leaned forward and kissed her quickly on the thick fur of her head.

In truth, she would be glad of some company that afternoon – human company. She hadn't seen Jacques since their bust-up in the office. His car hadn't been there yesterday at all so he obviously wasn't in. Such a loud, noisy man left a huge, silence-filled crater when he was absent. Eve found, though she liked to work in silence, that over the past two days the silence had been too silent. She had to get a fix of voices by making an excuse to go over to Santapark just to listen to Effin's four-letter tirades – or rather fourteen-letter tirades – at his builders.

'*Bastads. Newch chi ladd fi yn y pen draw. Dw i ugain mlynedd yn hŷn ers cychwyn y blydi job 'ma.*'

She overheard Arfon translating for Mik.

'Bastards. You'll kill me in the end. I'm twenty years older since starting this bloody job,' Arfon chuckled. 'Oh, don't worry, that's nearly a compliment coming from him. You should hear him when he really starts.'

She smiled to herself as she recalled that incident,

then her mobile rang and she lifted it to her ear. It was her Auntie Susan.

'I'm on my way,' said Eve, slightly stretching the truth. 'See you in a jiffy.' With perfect timing, the train chugged slowly towards her. 'Is it mended?' Eve called. 'Any chance of a lift to the front gate?'

'Totally,' called Thomas.

Eve's hair was almost all blown out of her French plait when the train stopped. It was going more berserk with every journey.

'I car-not understand it,' said Thomas. 'It was fine ten minutes ago. Oh, Effin is going to go bloody men-tal. Again.'

Susan and Violet were waiting outside the front door when Eve's BMW drew up. Violet was standing on the doorstep shivering, despite having her coat, gloves, scarf and hat on, as if the very core of her was frozen. She looked even paler than usual against the black of her clothes.

'Oh, it's lovely and warm in here,' said Susan, climbing into the front seat whilst struggling with a bouquet of flowers. Violet didn't say anything as she got in and closed the back door, carrying a bag of bottles which clanked together.

'We've got her some champagne and some brandy,' said Susan. 'She's into champagne cocktails now, ever since she went on that cruise with what's-his-face.'

Pat Ferrell had met a lonely widower with more brass than sense on a coach trip. He had taken her on a cruise to the Fjords recently and apparently they were spending Christmas in the Bahamas on the *Mermaidia*. He was just one in a very long line of men that Pat Ferrell had – and would – hone in on, chew up and spit out when the novelty wore thin. She would never have discovered her true potential for femme-fatalism if Grandad Ferrell hadn't run off with Nicole from the Miners Arms just after Ruth had been born (a relationship which lasted less than six months, and one of Pat's most treasured memories was telling him to piss off when he came crawling back.) Pat Ferrell made her younger daughter look like Mother Teresa. She should have been living in a web, not in a semi-detached bungalow.

'I've bought her a necklace,' said Eve. 'And matching earrings and bracelet. It's a bit of bling for her cruise. And some flowers as well.'

'What do you buy the woman who has everything, eh?' laughed Susan.

Violet didn't say a word on the twenty-minute journey, but looked out of the window, face still obscured by her scarf and hat, as if she hadn't quite defrosted from waiting on the doorstep for Eve to arrive. They pulled up outside the impossibly neat semi, on an estate of other pristine houses with bleached nets, scrubbed front doors and families of gnomes strategically placed in the garden borders.

'Come on,' Susan geed up her girls. She wasn't looking forward to it either, if the truth be told. Her mother had been a horror-story that made her determined to grow up and be the total opposite sort of parent and woman. Pat Ferrell's house had always been immaculate and showy, but when Susan was growing up there was never any food in the cupboards or clean clothes in the wardrobe. As a result, Susan's cupboards had always been stuffed enough to face a four-month siege, and she washed and ironed every two days at least. Ruth hadn't rebelled against the pattern, however.

Susan knocked on the door, then walked in. 'It's only us,' she said. 'Mum?'

'In here,' said Pat Ferrell, in the faux-elocution-lessons voice she had worked on over the years.

Susan felt a familiar knot in her stomach as she remembered growing up in this house and all the different men's shoes by the door. Unpleasant memories always came rushing at her whenever she stepped foot in 14 Riffington Road.

'Happy Birthday,' Susan said, pushing open the lounge door to find her mother sitting in the big, plush red armchair with the gold-tasselled trim. It looked like a throne. She leaned over and gave her mother a kiss on the cheek, something that only ever happened on birthdays and Christmases, and always given from daughter to mother. Eve and Violet followed suit, touching Pat's stiffly proffered cheek with a brief, dry kiss and handed over their presents, resting the two bouquets on a nearby console table. Pat, fit as she was, didn't offer to get up and make them a drink. Anyone visiting Susan's house would have been sitting with a three-course meal five minutes after being admitted.

'Shall I make some coffee?' asked Susan.

'If you like,' said Pat, slitting open the first card with her fingernail.

'Are you sure you don't want us to take you for something to eat, Mum?'

'No, I said I didn't. Eric and I are going to The Twelve Acres tonight,' she patted her very well-preserved flat stomach. 'I don't want to look bloated in my new dress from Pellyfields.'

Pellyfields was the poshest shop for miles. It cost fifty pounds just to window-shop. Eve had bought a number of suits and dresses there for work, even though she had always been happiest at home in her jeans – as Jonathan was. She had once bought him a shirt from there. Soft grey, the same colour as his eyes.

'What's your new dress like, Gran?' Eve asked.

'Navy and very classy,' said Pat, primping the back of her newly permed, short blonde curls. 'Frank Usher.'

'Very nice,' said Eve, watching Pat skim read the

long poem on the front of the card and turn to the inside quickly, before putting it on the chair arm and opening the second and doing the same.

'I'll put your cards up for you, shall I?' said Eve, picking them up and standing them next to the large flowery 'I love you, darling' card on the mantelpiece from Eric.

'I expect you'll have more to come with the post,' Eve commented.

'Post's been,' sniffed Pat. 'I wasn't expecting anything.'

'I like your flowers, are they from Eric?' called Susan from the kitchen. 'And shall I put them in a vase for you?'

'Would you?' asked Pat. 'I'm not sure I've got one big enough. I can't stand faffing about fitting flowers in vases.' And whether she meant to or not, she gave the two nearby bouquets a mini sneer.

'I'll go and do it for you,' said Violet. 'And I might as well put these in a vase for you whilst I'm at it and save you the trouble.' And she swept up the flowers and disappeared into the kitchen, watched intently by her grandmother.

'What's up with her?' said Pat to Eve, through a shrivelled moue of a mouth that reminded Eve of a cat's bum.

'Nothing,' said Eve, wondering what Pat was talking about.

'She's got a face like a wet weekend in Grimsby,' Pat sniffed. 'Though she never was the life and soul of the party, was she?'

Eve ignored that unfair remark and asked, 'Have you heard from Mum?'

'Have I heck. She's too busy enjoying herself.' Pat was smiling as she said that and Eve felt a stab of envy by proxy; not for herself, but for her lovely Auntie Susan. She had never heard Granny Ferrell give Susan a scrap of affection or a word of credit, and yet selfish, self-serving Ruth remained the apple of her eye.

Susan brought a tray of mugs through, and a plate of biscuits. Bone china, all very posh and matching.

'New crockery, Mum?' said Susan, setting the tray down on the coffee table.

'Eric bought me a tea service,' said Pat. 'Have I told you we're going on a cruise at Christmas?'

'Yes, Mother,' said Susan. 'Just a few hundred times.'

'He made his money in plastic injection moulding,' said Pat, taking the cup from Susan. 'His factory made cat litter trays and poop scoops. Where there's shit there's brass.'

Well, your accent might be posh, but you certainly aren't, thought Eve. She wondered if Eric knew he was going to get his financial gonads ripped off over the coming months.

'What's up with yond?' Pat pointed over her shoulder to the kitchen. 'She's got a face like a slapped backside.'

'No she hasn't. She's had a bug,' replied Susan, rearing in obvious defence. 'There's something going round.'

That was a lie, thought Eve. As far as she knew Violet was perfectly well. She had looked okay the last time she had seen . . . Halfway through that thought, Eve realized that actually Violet hadn't looked okay the last time she had seen her. In fact, Violet had looked awful and started to tell her what was wrong when the printers had phoned. And Eve had promised to go and find her when the call had finished, but never did.

'She looks a shadow of a shadow of her former self,' said Pat, delicately sipping her coffee.

'Mum, there's no need for that,' snapped Susan.

'I'm not daft,' sniffed Pat. 'She doesn't look under the weather to me. She's been crying – over a man. You can tell a mile off.'

'No she hasn't,' said Eve. *Has she? Is that why she came to see her that day?*

'That's what you get for going with a young one,' said Pat, putting her cup precisely back on her saucer. 'I should know. *He* was four years younger than me.' She never referred to Grandad Ferrell by name. 'Older ones are more grateful.'

'Rubbish.' Susan twisted around to make sure that Violet wasn't overhearing any of this. She steered the conversation away from her daughter. 'Anyway, have you heard from Ruth?'

'I've just told you, no,' said Pat.

'No, you told me. Auntie Susan was in the kitchen,' Eve defended.

'Oh. She'll be enjoying herself.' Pat reached for a shortbread round. She'd had her nails done – long pink talons that looked eagle-like on her bony fingers. 'She never moped over men. She just moved onto the next one and bugger 'em.'

Susan didn't comment, just drank her coffee in silence.

'Anyway, when are you getting married to this butcher bloke?'

'We haven't fixed a date yet,' Susan answered. 'Next year sometime. We might even get married in Eve's wedding chapel.' She winked at her niece and Eve tried to smile back, but she didn't want to think about wedding chapels today. She had thought of nothing else since she and Jacques had stopped speaking.

Violet came back into the room carrying a vase full of red roses, which she set down on the coffee table alongside the tray. Eve watched her and was instantly ashamed that she hadn't seen that there really was something very wrong with her. Violet looked terrible. Her skin was dull, there wasn't even that customary shine to her lovely white-blonde hair and there were dark shadows under her eyes.

'There's twenty roses,' said Pat. 'One for every week we've been together.'

'One for every thousand pounds of his money that she's going to spend,' Susan whispered to Eve.

Violet went back to fetch the second vase of flowers, combined from their two bouquets.

'What do you think about your mother getting married again then?' asked Pat, also watching Violet through her small, bright eyes. They were the eyes of a sparrowhawk who had just viewed a garden full of prey.

'I think it's lovely,' said Violet. 'He's a good man. Kind heart.'

'Nice bank account,' said Pat, spraying shortbread crumbs.

'For some of us that isn't a priority,' said Susan, trying to keep the snap out of her voice.

'Well, it should be. You've heard that song by Shirley Bassey, haven't you? Diamonds don't hurt you or lie to you.' Pat flicked her finger at her daughter. 'Take him for all he's worth, just in case he decides to go for a younger model. Or dies before your name's on the will.'

'For God's sake, Mother.'

'Honestly,' Pat laughed and adjusted the cushions

at her back. 'You three are sad cases, aren't you? You've been on your own taking care of a senile old woman who wasn't even any relation to you. When Jeff died you should have shoved Nanette Flockton in a home, but no – you have to go and martyr yourself.' This she directed at Susan before swivelling her neck around to Violet. 'You are looking like death warmed up. That's what happens when you go for younger men. Younger men want younger women.'

'Violet, I swear I didn't say anything to her,' said Susan, watching her daughter's eyes turn to her and fill with tears.

'You didn't need to,' said Pat. 'It's written all over her face that she's got man trouble. And then we come to this one,' and her dangerous, predatory eyes fixed on Eve. 'Moping like that bloody silly bugger Evelyn. "Oooh, my soldier was lovely and he died and I'm sat here killing time until I can drop off me perch and go to him!"' It wasn't clear if that wicked impression was of Eve or Evelyn, but Eve felt the thump of it in her gut anyway.

'Mum, shut up,' said Susan, standing, but Pat was on a roll and wouldn't be silenced.

'He's dead, be telled,' said Pat, her posh voice plummeting into broad Yorkshire. 'He's gone for good – dead, ash, dust, worm food. What, are you waiting for him to rise like bloody Lazarus? It's pathetic. You're a laughing stock.'

Eve wanted to move, but she couldn't. Susan's angry voice was in the distance, but her grandmother's words were reverberating at a thousand decibels through the very epicentre of her.

'Evelyn Douglas. The woman who discovered life when she was over ninety and lived it for about a fortnight, the stupid old bugger. Sat in her house with Christmas trees and her bloody photographs of a dead man whom she'd only known for a spit. And this one's going to end up like her. Who does she think she and him were – Victoria and Albert? At least my Ruth has a bit of spunk in her.'

'I'll say,' spat Susan. She could have said more, but dignity prevailed.

'My Ruth is off living a life and you're here dying a death. You make me sick. I wish I could swap places with you. All that life going to waste. I'd suck it dry if it were mine. And this one here, dopey Dora, she's going to end up by herself an' all before long. You should start a club.'

Violet's head had dropped, and she was quietly sobbing.

'You're evil, Mother,' said Susan, putting her arm around her daughter. 'I think we'll go before any more is said.'

'Aye, piss off,' laughed Pat Ferrell as Susan pulled Violet, then a stunned Eve, to their feet. 'Look at you all. Zombies. I've seen more life in a dead crow.'

'Have a lovely birthday, Mum,' Susan threw behind her as she pushed her girls towards the door. 'Don't get up.'

'I'd no intention of.'

Susan slammed the door shut and dropped her own head into her hands. 'I know she's my mother but I hate her,' she said. 'God help me if she ever needs twenty-four-hour care. I couldn't do it. I'd have to shoot her.'

'Violet, what's wrong?' asked Eve, putting aside what her grandmother had levelled at her because it was too painful to deal with right now. She turned her attentions to her cousin, who looked totally felled. Violet walked into Eve's arms and her head banged down onto Eve's shoulder.

'She's right, that's the worst of it,' cried Violet. 'I know Pav is seeing someone else.'

'What on earth makes you think that?'

'I know, Eve. He rings her, he sneaks out to see her.'

It was out before Eve even thought about stopping it.

'Don't be daft. He's planned . . .' she said. *Shit*.

Violet's head snapped up.

'What?'

'Nothing.' Oh dear God. One paw of the cat was out of the bag and wouldn't be pushed back in.

'What were you going to say then? You said "he's planned".' Violet jumped back from her cousin.

'I don't know what I was going to say.' Eve cringed at her weak comeback.

'No, you know something and you have to tell me what it is, Eve.'

The cat had now totally clawed the bag to shreds. There was no going back.

Eve watched a huge tear roll down Violet's cheek, and the sight of it stabbed her deep inside. Violet was in real pain.

'Please.' The single word carried a whole heartful of sadness and hurt.

'Oh hell fire.' Eve dropped her head into her hands. 'Pav's planned a secret wedding for you both.'

'What?'

'What?' Susan echoed the word.

'Oh Violet, I shouldn't have said . . .'

But Violet had a spark in her eyes – a hopeful light the colour of spring bluebells. 'Eve, you have to tell me. You have to.'

'He's booked a date for your wedding in the chapel in the park. It was supposed to be a total surprise.'

'Don't look at *me*,' said Susan, as Violet's head turned to her. 'I know nothing about it.'

'When?'

'Saturday. This Saturday. The second of December.'

Susan gasped. 'Mine and your dad's anniversary.'

'Oh my God, my God,' said Violet, starting to

shake and cry, but this time the tears were very different. They were big, salty blobs of relief and she was laughing and hiccupping as she cried. 'So all those phone calls . . . Eve, do you know someone called Serena?'

'Serena Potts? She's one of the wedding organizers. Why?'

Violet didn't answer the question directly but gave her another one.

'Does she have a squeaky voice?'

'Erm, yeah. High-pitched. She sounds very young but she's in her late forties.'

Violet started laughing almost hysterically, then she bounced forward and threw her arms around her mother and Eve with blessed relief. 'I just can't tell you how glad I am we came to see this old bat, because I wouldn't have known all this if we hadn't,' she said. 'Oh Eve, you don't know what you've done for me.'

'I really wanted to tell you before,' said Eve. 'I didn't think you'd be happy with that sort of surprise sprung on you.'

'Happy? Happy?' beamed Violet. 'I don't know how I would have felt, but all I can tell you is that I'm the happiest woman in the world at this moment.' All those fears and insecurities, which were hooked into her shoulders and weighed her down, had been flung off and destroyed. She noticed the look of guilty horror on Eve's face and added quickly, 'I am so glad you told me. I'll have a hairdo.'

'Oh Violet, please don't do anything to make Pav suspect that you know. He's planned everything – and I mean everything, because I've seen the notes. Just don't do anything out of the ordinary. Trust me. And stop smiling like that. He'll know if you turn up at home grinning like a Cheshire cat with a coat hanger stuck in its mouth.'

Her cousin reined in the smile, but it popped out in sparkly form in her big violet eyes. 'I can't tell you how I feel. I've been so miserable. I thought he was leaving me.'

'Well, he's obviously not going to do that,' said Susan. 'I wonder if he was going to invite me.'

'Leave it to Pav,' said Eve. 'Trust him.'

'I'm going to have a stiff drink when I get in, early as it is,' said Susan. 'Fancy a sneaky gin?'

'Thanks, but I'm going to drop you two home and then go back to the office for a while. I've got some work to do before I finish for the day.'

'Don't take any notice of that old witch,' said Susan, getting into the car. 'She likes the sound of her own voice too much.' Although, if she were honest, she wished she could have picked out bits from her mother's tirade and presented them in a kinder way to Eve, because part of what she was saying was right. Everyone – except the woman herself – could see Eve wasting her life like old Evelyn had.

Eve went into the empty, dark Portakabin office and switched on the light. It was unnaturally silent in there too as the coffee machine was switched off and not grumbling in the corner. She replaced the coffee filter and poured a jug of water into the top. The new machine on order had pods but it wouldn't permeate the air with the strong coffee smell like this old one; it wouldn't bubble and hiss and take the edge off the heavy quiet. The last thing Eve wanted at that moment was silence, because silence was a breeding ground for thinking, and she didn't want to think. She didn't want to replay the words her nasty old bugger of a grandmother had fired at her because they were too near the bone not to hurt. And what was worse, they echoed what Jacques had said to her on Monday. It was as if they'd swapped notes. Thank goodness at least what her grandmother had said to Violet had been proved wrong. As Eve poured out some milk into a mug, she felt ashamed that she hadn't realized how upset Violet had been feeling recently.

You haven't a clue, Miss Douglas. You haven't a clue what people want or need because you are too out of touch with everything. His words bounced into her skull to kick her whilst she was down. He was right, she was a mess.

She sipped at her coffee and heard shouting and laughter from outside. The men were working 24/7 on the park to get it ready. Everyone was pulling together so hard but there was always a lot of jollity around, most of it at Effin's comic profanities. She remembered the one and only time she and Jonathan had been to a theme park. She refused to go on the big rides, so Jonathan had joined her on the spinning teacups and pretended to be terrified. They'd hardly had time to do many things: one short holiday, one visit to a theme park . . .

'He's gone for good – dead, ash, dust, worm food. What, are you waiting for him to rise like bloody Lazarus? It's pathetic. You're a laughing stock.'

Is that what people thought about her – that she was some sort of modern-day Miss Haversham?

She felt tears gather behind her eyes and reached for the newspaper on the edge of Jacques' table to divert her thoughts, which was a bad idea. The front page was taken up with a picture of yesterday's funeral of the young female soldier who lived in Ketherwood.

The coffin bore a teardrop wreath of white roses. 'Town Mourns Brave Sharon' was the headline.

Brave Ketherwood girl Private Sharon Wilkinson was buried yesterday three weeks after her twenty-first birthday. Private Wilkinson was serving with the Royal

Army Medical Corps when her patrol came under heavy fire.

Her father John Wilkinson of Red Grove said, 'The whole community couldn't be more upset than it is. She was just coming into blossom. It was an honour to have my girl for twenty-one years.'

Her boyfriend Kevin Hall said, 'She were the best (sic). I was going to ask her to marry me on Christmas Day. We had so much to look forward to. I'm totally gutted.'

War amputee Lieutenant Jean Jackson gave a moving eulogy at Ketherwood church at a service led by the Reverend Stephen Moorside.

Donations in lieu of flowers are to be given to the Yorkshire Fund for Disabled Servicemen.

There was a picture of her boyfriend, a young bald-headed man with a tattoo on his neck of Sharon's name. His head looked at odds with the smart suit he was wearing and the long-stemmed white rose that he was carrying. Eve recognized that lost look in his eyes, which the photographer had captured perfectly. He and Sharon had planned out a whole future which had crumbled instantly. He would have no direction, he would crave oblivion. All the things of life would hold no interest or colour for him. He would feel like he was standing still in the middle of a motorway with cars zooming around him.

She closed the paper hurriedly and tossed it back

on Jacques' desk. Today had been a totally shit day. She scanned through her emails and replied to one from the *Yorkshire Post* about drumming up some publicity. Then the front door burst open and one of the Polish workers tumbled in.

'Is Captain here?'

'No, I don't know where he is. What's the matter?'

'It's be–cause,' said the young Pole.

'Because what?'

'No,' and he started to do a mime. 'Bee-course.' He was stamping on the ground with one foot.

What the chuff?

Now he was gesturing that something was very tall and had a huge nose. Then he started thumping his chest. 'BEEE-COURSE. SEEK.'

'Show me,' said Eve, before she snapped. 'I follow you.'

He seemed to understand her pathetic attempt at pidgin English and charged out of the Portakabin, checking she was behind him. He turned left into the dark enchanted forest just as the train was chuffing up the track.

'It's all mended. Want a lift?' called Thomas. 'Goes as slow as an old snail now.'

'I don't know where I'm supposed to be going,' said Eve.

'Oy, Josef. Want a lift?' said Thomas to the young Pole. 'Where are you off to?'

'BEE-COURSE. SEEK.'

'Get on, then.'

The language divide obviously didn't exist between the Poles and the Welsh.

'Did you understand that?' said Eve in disbelief.

'He said that the big horse is sick.'

'Oh no,' said Eve. Not this. Not Christopher. Not today. Not any day. He was a lovely old fellow.

'Has anyone rung the vet?' asked Eve, getting a blank look from Josef.

'Has anyone rung the vet?' Thomas repeated to him.

'*Nie,*' Josef replied to him.

'How the bloody hell can he understand you and not me? I'm saying the same thing.' huffed Eve. 'And why is this damned train so slow?'

'It's mended,' said Thomas.

'Well unmend it,' grumped Eve. 'This speed is pants.'

As they came to the end of the track, Eve recognized the big-coated figure of Jacques in the near distance, talking down his phone and pacing from side to side. He'd had a shave and a very short haircut, she saw as they got even closer. She felt strangely reassured that he was there. He would take command, as he had when Holly was giving birth. Whatever was wrong with the old horse would be sorted. Then she neared the side of the paddock and saw

Christopher, laid out on his side, panting, legs giving an occasional twitch. A few of the elves were standing by the fence, the old one who walked with a limp was wiping his eyes with an enormous hankie. Tim was on the floor, cradling the big lad's head.

'I think it's his heart,' he said with a voice full of trembles. 'He just keeled over. Is the vet on his way, Captain?'

'On his way,' called Jacques, clicking off his phone. 'All we can do is keep Christopher as comfortable as possible.'

Eve rushed inside the paddock and bent on the ground beside Tim and stroked Christopher's huge white cheek.

Tears were coursing down Tim's face and dropping onto Christopher's mane. 'I gave him a right good brush this morning as well. He loves that.'

Eve felt Jacques towering behind her.

Then Christopher's eyes dropped shut as if the stroking was sending him to sleep and Tim felt an increased weight on his leg. 'Oh no,' he yelled. 'Don't you dare bloody die on me, you little sod.'

But there was no rise and fall in Christopher's flanks any more. Jacques dropped to his haunches and placed his hand on Christopher's jaw where the pulse would be. There was nothing.

'He's gone,' was all he said, and a sad eruption of grief overwhelmed them all. Tim was sobbing, some of the builders were shaking their heads, one of the younger elf-ladies was handing out tissues from her handbag. Eve wasn't even aware that she was crying until she saw the splashes land on Christopher's cheek.

The ponies were protesting, shut away in the stable. One of them sounded as if it was trying to kick the door in.

'Go home, Tim,' said Jacques gently. 'I'll wait for the vet.'

'Can we bury him here?' asked Tim, sounding like a small boy wanting to bury a hamster rather than a grown man with a horse.

Jacques looked to Eve.

'Yes, of course, he belongs here,' said Eve. 'I promise you we'll do that.'

Tim, not caring what anyone thought, bent over and kissed the horse on his head, stroking him, saying goodbye. Then Effin helped him up and walked with him, his comforting hand on Tim's shoulder, and the others drifted away, all except for Jacques and Eve, who was still stroking Christopher's mane.

'You can go home. I'll stay with him till the vet gets here,' said Jacques. 'I'll cover him for tonight and Tim and I will bury him tomorrow.'

Eve nodded and leaned over to give the old horse a kiss too. He smelt of stables and the mud he liked to roll in. He smelt of hay and happy times.

Jacques surprised her by placing his hand on her elbow to help her up.

'Thank you,' she said.

'No worries,' he replied, as if it was an automatic, gallant gesture rather than one he had chosen to make.

They heard a car rumble down the service road.

'That'll be the vet,' said Eve.

'I'll take you back on the train, missus,' called Thomas.

Just as Eve was about to board, Jacques called to her.

'Her name was Catherine. She was a sergeant from Devon and she was shot twelve hours after landing in Afghanistan on her first duty. We were together for nine months.'

'Pardon?' said Eve.

'You know,' he said.

Then the vet braked sharply into the space between them and Eve climbed on the train to take the interminably slow service back to the front gates, wondering what the hell Jacques had been talking about. An ex-girlfriend, obviously, but why was any of that Eve's business?

Her house felt especially cold when she walked into it. Large and cold and weighted with loneliness. She walked in the dark to her office to the patiently burning flame and wondered if Christopher had made it up *there* yet. Did animals go to heaven? She didn't think her Aunt Evelyn would want to go there if she wasn't going to be reunited with Fancy and Kringles. A medium she had once been to told her that spirits often hung around until after the funeral before 'making their way upstairs'. Mind you, that medium had also told her that she'd meet a man in a uniform and live happily ever after. 'He'll have an accident, but don't worry, he'll cope with it,' the daft old cow had said. And because of that, when those men in suits arrived on her doorstep, she couldn't take it in: that Jonathan's accident was a fatal one. Were all mediums fake? They couldn't be, surely? She had watched programmes on the television when mediums had delivered details to their audiences that they couldn't possibly have known. So they had to be communicating with the dead, right? Eve had been to a couple of different mediums after Jonathan died, but they'd told her a load of codswallop. 'He sends his love.' 'He says he doesn't want you to be unhappy.' Nothing specific that would identify him, like 'This guy says he wishes he were biting that bit on your ear that always makes you giggle.' Or 'I have someone here who wants to know if you've finally changed that broken light fitting in the downstairs toilet?'

'Jonathan, I'm begging you to send me a sign,'

said Eve. 'I need it so much. Today's been just pants. I wish you were here.' She picked up his old jumper that she kept on her office chair and raised it to her nose, inhaling the smell which wasn't of him any more, even though she had never washed it. Kevin Hall would be doing the same to a coat or a pillow-case imbued with Sharon Wilkinson's scent, no doubt. He would try and cling on to every last vestige of his darling that remained on the real earth, and would lose a little more of her each day.

Then she knew what Jacques had been talking about just before the vet's car drew up. And she wanted to sink to the ground with shame.

Chapter 42

Eve was surprised that she had managed to sleep a wink, what with all the stuff that was whirring around in her head like an over-stuffed washing machine that threatened to blow the door off. But sleep she did because she came-to with the shrill, annoying alarm piercing a dream that she couldn't remember in detail, only that it was something to do with her grandmother driving a train. Before her lay a day where she had to go into work and face a man who *knew* she had been in his house and seen that uniform hanging up in his wardrobe. And piecing together all the clues, it could only have come from Phoebe. She recalled how he had turned to ice after taking Phoebe to the carousel. God only knows what the little red-haired girl had said to him. There was nothing to do but face it head on and get the apology out of the way. She dressed quickly, threw an instant espresso down her throat, and locked up the house. She both hoped he was and hoped he wasn't in the Portakabin when she arrived at Winterworld.

He was there. Fiddling with the portable heater. There was a full pot of fresh coffee, its warm, cosy smell permeating the office space. He stole a look behind him at Eve, gave her the briefest of nods by way of a greeting, and then returned to attending the calor gas fire.

After taking a long fortifying breath she said, 'I'm sorry.'

'What for?' He didn't look behind him.

'You know,' she said.

She watched him stop what he was doing for a moment, then carry on.

'You'll have the office to yourself this morning. I'm going to help bury Christopher. The vet says it was more than likely his heart that gave up on him.'

'That's very sad,' said Eve, taking off her coat and hanging it up on the peg. 'Maybe we could take in another horse. You know, give an old one a retirement home, rescue one from the knacker's yard, like Aunt Evelyn did.'

His shoulders jerked as if they had been surprised by a laugh, but he still didn't turn around.

'I'm sure Tim would appreciate that suggestion.'

'I've also been thinking,' said Eve, still quietly, still shamed. 'What if we renamed the train 'The

Nutcracker Express' and made it a faster, rickety ride. Not as mad as it was, but a little less boring than the mended version.'

'Sounds good,' Jacques was nodding. Then he straightened his long legs and zipped up his coat. 'Do you want to tell Effin, or shall I?'

'I'll do it,' replied Eve, feeling dreadfully awkward with him now. She wanted to ask him what Phoebe had said – God only knows what childish slant she had put on things; she didn't like to think where the Topshop connection came into it. *Please God, don't let her have heard the bit about him being a cross-dresser.* But whatever her little fox-haired god-daughter had let slip, she had managed to make it crystal clear to him that Eve had been snooping in his wardrobe and really, it didn't get more incriminating than that.

'I'll see you later,' said Jacques. And as he went out, the cold air swirled into the office and caused Eve to shiver right down to her bones.

Auntie Susan lifted her mood half an hour later.

'I've just had a visit from Pav. He came to invite me to the surprise wedding,' she gushed down the phone.

'I hope you acted totally gobsmacked,' said Eve.

'I was like Meryl Streep,' laughed Susan. Eve shuddered. She had seen her auntie acting in the Hoppleton Players' version of *A Christmas Carol*. Meryl Streep she was not. 'I'm off to buy an outfit in Meadowhall when Patrick finishes work. I think Pav must be doing the rounds and telling people today, so be prepared. He was off to Max's and Bel's houses next.'

Max and Bel had been a brick to Violet when she was going through the trauma of splitting up from her last boyfriend. They'd been supportive and understanding and protective – everything that Eve hadn't been because she had been too stuck on Planet Eve, surrounded by Eve's problems and all things Eve. Some friend she was. Especially after all the love and support she'd had from the Flockton side of the family over the years. If it wasn't for them, Eve would have been in care for sure. Considering Jacques hadn't been in her life for very long, he seemed to have got the measure of her too quickly.

'What about Granny Ferrell?' Eve asked her aunt. 'Is she coming?'

'No,' Susan said flatly and definitely. 'She's a loose cannon and after all Violet and Pav have been through, I don't want anything to spoil it for them. And as you know, Eve, your grandmother has a particular skill for spoiling things. I won't let her on this occasion. She can look at the photos afterwards and moan that she wasn't invited, but somehow I don't think she'll be all that bothered, whatever her nasty mouth decides to say.'

Eve agreed. Her grandmother was too good at knowing the wounding point. Everyone would be on tenterhooks if she was at the wedding, and she would enjoy commanding that sort of power. She put the phone down and thought how lovely Pav was to arrange all this behind Violet's back, even if it wasn't a church with a vicar, but a tiny chapel in a theme park and Santa Claus conducting the ceremony.

As she looked through her diary, she wondered if she should go over to the paddock and see how Jacques was getting on burying the old horse. She didn't really want to; she was sick of death – it seemed to be everywhere she looked at the moment – in newspapers, on the news, and the image of Sharon Wilkinson's pretty face was branded on her brain. She tried to settle to work but couldn't. She took two more sips of her coffee, then reached for her coat and set off towards the paddock. She couldn't take the train because Thomas wasn't around. He was glued to that train usually, so Eve presumed he had gone off to the loo or for a quick coffee. She cut through the forest and again felt that strange magical feeling that always trembled down to her bones whenever she watched those old Czechoslovakian fairy tales as a child, like *The Singing Ringing Tree* and *Three Gifts for Cinderella*. As she neared the paddock, she saw the unmistakeable back view of Thomas's overalls and his bare bald head, because he was holding his cap in his hand. All the Welsh and Polish lads were there, gathered outside the fence, even Effin.

Jacques was there, spade in hand, and despite the frost chilling the air, his coat was off and his shirt-sleeves were rolled up. There were silvery lines criss-crossing down his arms, Eve noticed. Old scars.

Thomas nudged the workman at his side who budged over to let 'the missus' through the crowd. Even Holly and her twin boys were at the adjoining fence looking across.

'They're just going to start,' whispered Thomas. 'It's heartbreakin', innit?'

Jacques noticed her and nodded a brief greeting, without smiling. He hadn't smiled at her in days, and she was both surprised and annoyed that it bothered her.

'Christopher wasn't with us for very long,' said Tim with a cough, then his voice froze and he couldn't carry on.

'Christopher might not have been with us for very long, but at least he ended his days with good love and care,' Jacques took over, against a background of sniffing. 'A little love in life goes a long way, and I think Tim will tell you that Christopher really perked up living here with us. Some mornings he was like a spring chicken.'

Eve noticed how everyone was hanging on his every word. There was an emotion that was binding everyone together here and she didn't know what it was, she just felt its power, its warm, all-encompassing power and that each and every one clustered around Christopher's grave had a huge respect for the man now talking.

'But he was a very old boy and any time he had with us was a blessing for him and us both.' There was a chorus of nose-blowing. 'It's all any of us could hope, that we are loved to the last. So goodbye Christopher, old boy. We shall miss you. We wish we could have had you for longer, but we're just glad we had you at all.'

During the mumble of 'goodbye Christophers' Eve slid to the back of the crowd and slipped away before anyone saw the tears flowing down her cheeks. Jacques' words were too cutting, too full of meaning. They were as meaningful to her about Jonathan as they were about Christopher. Sometimes she wished she had never met Jonathan, then she wouldn't have this never-ending pain within now, but then she would have missed the short, sweet, rich firework length of time they had together that lit up her life and altered it for ever. *We wish we could have had you for longer, but we're just glad we had you at all.*

'Eve.' His voice came from behind, his body caught it up. He ran steadily and quickly towards her before stopping at her side. 'Are you all right?'

'Yes,' she said, covering any loss of composure with a bristling tone. 'I just have to get back and get on.'

'I didn't ask you to join us because I didn't think you'd want to be there.'

'I didn't,' she said. 'But I felt I should show my face.'

His arms filled the top of his sleeves. He must work out, she thought. Mind you, if he hadn't had a job for ages, he had plenty of spare time to beef himself up at a gym, said her head. Surprisingly another voice rose up and snapped, 'Oh for God's sake, stop bitching about the man, Eve. Give him some credit.

'I'll be helping on the snagging list today, you don't need me in the Portakabin, do you? You're better at the paperwork than I am anyway; if anything comes up, I'm sure you'll be fine with it.'

'Well yes, of course I'll be fine,' nodded Eve, trying to look brave and efficient and not as if she felt near to crumbling like a packet of Digestives under a steamroller. 'Are you expecting any calls?'

'I know Pav is going to tell you about his wedding today,' said Jacques. 'I'd appreciate it if you didn't say you already knew. Serena will be ringing this afternoon about the final arrangements for the wedding chapel.'

Eve nodded. Her green eyes held his blue ones, but there was no impish sparkle in them.

'Right,' she said.

'You know where I am if you want me,' he said.

'Effin's taking the Santapark sign down this morning, so you'll get your Winterpark one up.'

'Ah, good,' replied Eve.

'I'll get on,' and he turned and ran back to the paddock whilst Eve watched him. He ran in a very masculine way, she decided, confident and assured. He ran as if he had done a lot of it – and seriously. She used to run; Jonathan used to say she was incapable of actually walking anywhere. She had stopped running when he died – one of many things she loved but didn't do any more. She used to run up hills until she reached the top, breathless and exhilarated, and the air felt sweeter in her lungs for the effort.

Pav was waiting for her when she reached the Portakabin. She plastered on a wide smile in greeting and prepared to act her socks off.

'Hello there. Thought you were on a day off. Violet not with you?'

'Er, no,' said Pav. 'Can I see you for a moment, Eve?'

'Come inside,' she said, stripping off her gloves as she opened the door into the cosy warmth of the Portakabin. They would be moving into a completed log cabin at the other end of the park any day now, but she doubted it would ever feel as cosy as this little scrappy place, with the grumpy machine making coffee-Tourette's-type noises.

'Sit down. Can I get you a drink?'

'No, it's fine,' said Pav, moving the chair back from the table to give himself leg room. Eve tried not to smile. Pav always exuded such lovely, warm, friendly vibes. She was so glad he was marrying her beautiful cousin. Only now did she realize how distraught Violet must have been to think she was losing him, and how happy she must have been to know that she wasn't.

'Okay, shoot,' said Eve, trying to keep her grin friendly and professional. Pav stroked his thin line of a black beard nervously.

'I haven't told you,' he said, with an apologetic tone, 'but I have booked the wedding chapel for Violet and myself for Saturday.'

Here goes, said Eve. Please don't make me do an Auntie Susan/Meryl Streep.

'This Saturday? The day after tomorrow?'

'Yes. I know it is short notice, but if I told anyone sooner, the secret might have leaked out.'

'Wow.'

That was worse than anything her Auntie could have come out with so she felt duty bound to add more.

'I don't know what to say. I don't know how to react. I'm presuming she hasn't a clue? No, of course she hasn't or she would have said.'

'No, she doesn't know,' said Pav. 'It is a surprise

for Violet. Today, I went to see Susan and Bel and Max. Now I come to see you. It's just a small wedding. In the chapel here.'

'Here? Why here, Pav?'

He seemed surprised that she asked that. 'Because Violet loves Christmas so much.'

'Does she?'

'Yes, of course,' he smiled. 'She goes crazy for Christmas. She is like a child.'

Does she? Again Eve gulped down the realization that she didn't know that. She knew Violet always enjoyed Christmas – how could she not in Auntie Susan and Uncle Jeff's cosy house, with the real tree and all the paper decorations which they and Nan Flockton used to make throughout the whole of November. But she didn't realize that her cousin loved it enough to be married by the Christmas equivalent of Elvis. It seems she didn't know much about anyone she was supposed to love.

'I don't want you to do anything. Everything is arranged with Jacques. I just want you to turn up and be the guest and sign the register as witness. Please don't tell Violet.'

'I'm really happy for you both,' said Eve with a rush of emotion. 'I think you're so good together.'

'I love her with all my heart,' said Pav. 'Maybe on Saturday she will believe it finally.'

* * *

After Pav had gone, Eve couldn't concentrate. There was something circling her brain like an eagle that was distracting her from filing invoices. The eagle wouldn't go away. The eagle had a whiff of lemon French fancies about it. Eve stopped struggling against it, put on her coat and walked up to the amusement park. The sky was dark and dull, but the bubble of Winterworld was a much more colourful and beautiful place. The snow machines were puffing out flakes which fell softly onto Eve's shoulders as she walked. Hundreds of colourful lanterns were lighting the forest with their soft glow. It reminded her of Narnia. But it wasn't the look of the place which was driving her feet forward, it was the feel of it. Something had touched her as she stood at the side of Christopher's grave with all the people whom her Aunt Evelyn had chosen to work here. They were all united in striving towards the same end – Evelyn's vision. Only she was pulling in a different way. Only she was standing outside the snow globe of Winterworld, looking in through the glass.

I can't believe I'm going to do this, she said to herself as she reached the amusement park.

Effin's men were struggling with the huge iron 'Santa' part of the sign. He was screaming at them as usual.

'*Cocs Cymreig a prics Pwyl – s'dim dianc!*'

'He said, "Welsh cocks and pricks from Poland

– there's no escape!'" translated Arfon for Mik, who then promptly translated it into Polish for his work-mates. Eve noticed that one of the Welsh lads was wearing a pair of Christmas pudding deely-boppers on his head; another had tinsel wrapped around his hard hat. The place was soaked in Christmas and there was no getting away from it.

'Effin, can I have a word?' said Eve, touching his arm.

'You can have more than one, lovely,' replied Effin.

Eve took a big breath.

'Leave the sign as it is, will you?'

'Eh?'

'Winterpark isn't the right name. Santapark is.'

Effin tried not to let his top lip pull back over his teeth.

'It's taken five of them over half an hour to unscrew it.' Then he added a respectful, 'Missus.'

'I know, and I'm sorry. But I've had a change of heart.'

Effin sighed through gritted teeth. ''Course. You're the boss, so if that's what you want . . . Oy,' and he shouted up at the men on the scaffolding. 'Don't bloody take that down, leave it up. Screw it back in. And don't take half as long putting it up as you did taking it down, you lazy bastards.'

There was a chorus of protesting groans in response, which set Effin back into paroxysms.

Eve took a few steps backwards to watch the spectacle of the sign being replaced, and crashed into Jacques. 'Sorry,' she apologized.

'Why did you do that?'

'I didn't see you,' she said.

'I didn't mean bump into me, I meant keep the sign.'

'I don't know,' said Eve, and meant it. 'It just felt right. I don't like that I like it. But if we strip all the Christmas references away from the park, I think we'd be doing the wrong thing. I'll admit it, okay?'

Jacques crossed his arms and she noticed there was a smirk playing at the corner of his mouth. Ordinarily this would have make her hackles rise, but that smirk told her the ice was thawing between them and it was more than she deserved.

'What?' she said.

'Nothing,' he replied. 'It's finding you, isn't it? The Christmas spirit of this place.'

'Don't talk bollocks,' she replied.

'Come in with us, Eve. The water's lovely.'

'How are the honeymoon cabins coming along?' she said with a sniff, changing the subject completely and trying to hide the shake in her voice. 'Do I need to check them? I'm presuming one of them will be used on Saturday night?'

'All finished,' he said. 'Come on, I'll show you.' And he threaded his arm inside hers and walked her forward, almost lifting her in the air as he did so. And though she made huffs of protestation, she didn't resist him physically. She thought she had disliked his ridiculously flirty attentions, but to be stone-walled by him was worse.

The first cabin door they came to was open as one of the interior designers was steaming the curtains.

'They're all more or less the same, give or take little touches. They're just getting this ready for Violet and Pav.' He addressed the lady inside. 'Okay to come in?'

'Yes, sure.'

'Bloody hell,' said Eve stepping through the door-way. 'How have they managed to do all this in such a short time?' The cabin was a snuggery of sofas and carpets. There was a tiny wood-burning stove in a large inglenook fireplace, just the thing for a couple to cuddle up in front of; a short run of kitchen units and a bathroom beyond, with a very roomy bath and shower – obviously meant for more than one and no more than two. An open staircase led to a room with a very bouncy-looking bed taking up most of it.

'Nice, isn't it?' said Jacques. 'The designers are all widows of soldiers and set up in business together.'

The military again, thought Eve. It kept cropping up in one form or another.

'How did Aunt Evelyn find all these people?' said Eve.

'She just did,' shrugged Jacques.

'I'm presuming all the elves she found weren't on active duty in Toytown?'

Jacques laughed. It was the first time in ages she had heard him laugh and it was a ridiculously welcome sound to her ears.

'I think they might have been,' he said, turning his eyes onto her and studying her with a tender intensity, which she found uncomfortable. She turned around and looked at one of the watercolour pictures of a snow scene on the wall.

'Everyone has done such a great job,' she said, preparing to admit more. 'I'm not sure the people I would have set on would have done as well.'

'They're good, aren't they?' he said. 'They've done a perfect job – right from the big rug in front of the fire to the big bouncy bed upstairs.' And she waited for him to make some crack about testing out the big bed upstairs, but he didn't. And she felt herself bristle more that he didn't, than if he had.

'Pav didn't twig that I knew,' said Eve.

'Good,' said Jacques. 'We don't have to hang onto the secret for much longer. They're a lovely couple.'

'Right then, back to the grindstone,' said Eve, clapping her hands together and heading for the door. She didn't notice – but Jacques did – that she walked off in the direction of the Portakabin with a spring in her step.

DECEMBER

Chapter 43

The night before her big day, Violet tried not to bubble over with excitement. Pav cooked tea – her favourite, his spicy polish dumplings – which she usually wolfed down, but she was too full of nervous excitement to have much of an appetite.

'Are you all right?' he asked her, trying to coax her into eating another. 'You never usually leave any.'

'I had a big slice of cake with Eve earlier on,' Violet lied.

Pav did a rubbish act of an exaggerated yawn. It was on par with her mother's acting skills.

'I'm so tired. I think tonight, I will have an early night,' he said. He leaned over and stroked her cheek. 'You look happier these past few days. I have been worried about you, my love.'

'Oh, don't be,' Violet smiled. 'I was panicking

that we wouldn't be able to run both parlours. I got myself into a pickle about it.'

'You should have told me,' he said, and wrapped his big arms around her and squashed her into his strong chest. 'You shouldn't keep things from me.'

Violet wanted to giggle. That was rich.

'I'll have a quick bath and then join you,' she said. 'Warm the bed up for me.'

In the bath, Violet tried to shave her legs, exfoliate and super-condition her hair as quickly as possible. As she went into the bedroom she noticed that the big suitcase, which was usually on top of the wardrobe, wasn't there. And when she opened her underwear drawer, a few of her best knickers had vanished as well. Oh God. He must have packed them a case to go away. She was a little horrified that he had gone through her underwear. Still, she had to keep schtum. Pav had obviously put so much work into the wedding that she couldn't and didn't want to spoil any of it for him.

She went to bed and pretended to fall asleep with his arm looped around her. The last thing she remembered thinking was that she would never drift off, then the alarm clock was waking her up and she felt Pav spring out of bed as if he had an ejector seat hidden in his part of the mattress. He might have been composed up to this point, but he was twittery now.

'Are you okay?' said Violet, rubbing her eyes. 'It usually takes you ages to get up. At least three snoozes.' She wanted to giggle very badly.

'Yes, I'm fine,' he said, disappearing off to the shower. She smiled as she thought about the day to come. That someone loved her enough to surprise her like this was magical. Many people wouldn't have liked not to know that by the end of the day they would be married, but Violet wasn't one of them. She had gone down the traditional, heavily planned route with her last fiancé and this – wonderfully – was about as far away from that as she could get. She had under-estimated how much he wanted her to marry him. She had been stupid to think that true love would be put off by a piddly little barrier of nine years.

'I think I'll have a shower to warm me up,' said Violet, pretending to shiver as Pav walked into the bedroom beautifully naked. He had such a gorgeous body. It wasn't marred at all by the long scar on his chest which the dark hair worked to cover. 'It's a chilly one today.'

This is the last shower I'll have as a 'miss', she said to herself, as the water cascaded down onto her body.

Pav had made her a coffee and some toast, as he always did. He was chewing on it but he didn't look hungry, he looked nervous, and Violet really had to pretend she didn't notice anything. This is the last piece of toast I'll have as a 'miss', she said to herself.

Then Pav's mobile rang. 'Hello,' he said. 'Yes, this is Pav.'

Oh God, more Susan Flockton/Meryl Streep acting, thought Violet.

'Yes, Jacques, of course I can pick this up for you. No problems.' He turned to Violet whilst clicking the phone shut. 'I have to pick up a box of something for Jacques before work.'

'Do you want me to come with you?' Violet asked mischievously.

'No, no, it's fine,' he said hurriedly. 'You go to Winterworld and I will see you very soon.'

'How will you get there if I've got the car?' asked Violet.

'Ah. I'll take the car and I will order a taxi for you. You wait until it arrives.'

'Okay,' said Violet. 'I'll just go and clean my teeth and see you later.'

Upstairs in the bathroom, she brushed her teeth and looked at herself in her Nan's old wall mirror. This is the last time I'll see my face in this mirror as Miss Violet Flockton, she said to herself, and blew a kiss upwards to her nan. She felt so happy, she was in danger of bursting like a balloon, one which would spray the world with tiny little love hearts and snowflakes.

Chapter 44

Eve applied an arc of dark-pink lipstick and pressed her lips together. The day, despite looking very chilly and dull, carried a very thrilling buzz about it. Her cousin was getting married to probably the most considerate, thoughtful man in the world. She doubted even Jonathan would have gone to those measures. Or would he? She had found out recently that she didn't know as much as she thought she did about her Aunt Evelyn, her cousin, even herself. So how much did she really know about a man she had been with for only nine months? On the fringe of her memory teased something she had read about Henry VIII and Jane Seymour at Alison's house, but it wouldn't be pinned down and then vanished.

She had replaced the candle the previous night. The flame was long and steadily burning without any flicker. Violet was getting married to a man, and she was wedded to a candle. It would be funny if it wasn't so ridiculous.

She slipped on her green coat which matched her dress and shoes. A Christmas colour for Christmas lovers, she decided. She had put a cheque in an envelope for the happy couple and hoped they would spend it on something frivolous and flighty. Tonight they were staying in one of the log cabins. Champagne was on ice, bowls of chocolate and fruit arranged for them and at six o'clock precisely, a dinner of lobster and all the trimmings would be delivered.

Eve drove round to pick up her Auntie Susan, who was wearing a red dress and jacket. Big Patrick the butcher had a matching red tie on and a red handkerchief tucked in the top pocket of his grey suit. He held out his arm for Susan to take after she locked the door as she looked less than steady on her new high heels.

'I'm sick with nerves,' said Susan as she got into the car. 'I hope it goes all right.'

Patrick looked upwards at the clouds. 'I wish the weather had been better for her. It's like night-time.'

'The forecast is dry but bloody freezing,' said Susan. 'I don't mind freezing, but I do mind wet. I don't want it to rain for her.'

'I'm sure Pav has fixed the weather too,' chuckled Eve. 'He seems to have done everything else.'

'I wonder what Violet's doing now,' said Susan, her voice all trembly. 'I haven't dared ring. I've tried to play the game and pretend I don't know.'

Eve noticed that Patrick was holding her hand tightly. They looked like teenagers in the back of one of their parents' cars. Love made everyone feel sixteen. Eve wished she could experience that smiling inner tickle of joy again. But she knew she never would. Her life was mapped out – work, work and more work, and watching other people holding hands and getting married in her own chapel.

The service road went down the side of the park, past the paddocks, and met with a car park out of sight behind the grotto. They parked up next to a silver Mercedes. Standing next to that car were Violet's friends Max and Bel and their partners. Eve and Susan waved at them.

'Wotcher,' said Max, when they all got out of the car and came over for hugs. 'This is a bit of an unusual one, isn't it?'

'Says her.' Bel thumbed at Max. 'The master of outlandish weddings.'

'Well, wait until you see my next one,' winked Max.

'Where's Pav?' asked Eve.

'Shitting himself in the chapel by now, probably,' said Bel. 'I thought it was one of the snowmen when

I first saw him; all the colour has drained out of his face. He told us not to follow him in until ten to.'

'It's nearly ten to now. Shall we go in?' said Max. 'I'm bloody frozen.'

'I can't walk far in these heels,' said Susan. 'I knew I should have brought some flatties with me.'

'It's not far, Auntie Susan,' said Eve. 'Just around this corner.'

'Aye, come on, my watch says ten to eleven exactly,' said Patrick, and threaded his arm through hers. 'Shall I carry you in?'

'If you think I'm nursing you whilst you're on traction for months, you can think again,' huffed Susan. 'I'll walk, thank you.'

The small wedding party started to walk towards the chapel. As they turned the corner, a beautiful sight met them – hundreds of red and green coloured lanterns hanging from trees and poles painted in candy-cane stripes, bringing their own magic to the dull December day. And light snowflakes began to fall from a secretly placed snow machine.

'Oh my, isn't this just lovely,' gasped Susan. 'I feel like I'm walking in a Christmas card.' There was more to come.

'Bloody hell,' said Bel, as they set foot into the chapel. Which more or less summed up what everyone else was thinking. The tiny chapel was covered in displays of holly and mistletoe, and large swooping ribbons of red and green. Then one of the elf-people, in full elf regalia, started playing on the organ at the front left of the church. It was a portable instrument, but fake pipes had been adhered to the walls to make it look like a grand church organ. Her feet were nowhere near the forte and piano pedals so there was some sort of wire contraption travelling between them and her shoes to allow her to work them. She was playing 'O Little Town of Bethlehem' note perfect.

'It's like something out of a story book,' said Max, mouth open in wonder as she sat on a pew. 'Can I smell gingerbread or am I hallucinating?'

Just as Susan was about to ask Eve where Pav was, he emerged from the door on the right of the tiny altar. He was wearing a black suit with tails, a high white collar and a green cravat, and there was a sprig of holly and the tiniest red poinsettia in his buttonhole. He was flanked by the mighty figures of Santa with his white beard and red cloak, and Jacques, also in a black coat with tails, cravat and holly sprig. Eve gulped. She had never seen him in anything but big puffy coats and jeans. She didn't like that her eyes were appraising him so much. He waved and everyone except Eve waved back, because she was still trying to absorb the figure of him in a suit so obviously made to his exact meas-urements whilst equating him to the clumsy buffoon she was accustomed to. This man with the straight back and gorgeous threads made George Clooney look like Columbo. She watched him reassuring Pav, checking they had the rings, patting his back. Then he waved over at Eve, beckoning her forward.

'You need to sit with me as the second witness,' he said. 'You're very red, are you okay?'

'Yes, I'm fine,' Eve snapped defensively, taking her seat at the side of him on the pew.

Violet was also sitting down. Two women were giving her a manicure, one was faffing with her hair and another was waiting to put some make-up on her. The taxi which Pav was going to order for her never arrived, funnily enough. Instead, a team of smiling women rang her bell and when she opened it, one of them said, 'Hello. We're here for a Miss Violet Flockton, courtesy of Mr Pawel Novak.' So Violet, with trembling hands, went through the charade of ringing Pav to ask who these women on her doorstep were.

'Ah,' he said. 'I forgot to tell you, Violet. Today we are getting married.'

And even though Violet knew of this in advance, the, 'Wha-at?' she gave by way of an answer, was still one of delighted shock.

'Violet. I will see you in one hour. Then you will

be Mrs Nowak,' he said masterfully, giving her no time for protest as he put the phone down.

'You better come in then,' said Violet to the smiling army waiting outside.

The woman now applying make-up to her face had an instantly recognizable voice – high-pitched and squeaky. She didn't quite have as many pronounced curves as Marilyn Monroe, but she had the same blonde hair and slightly dizzy way about her.

'We don't get many brides who haven't a clue we're coming,' said Serena. 'Are you excited?'

'I am,' trilled Violet, who was getting more giddy by the second.

'I don't think everyone would be,' confided Serena. 'I must admit, we were all a bit nervous about coming here. Maria, who did your left hand, had visions of you calling the police on us.'

Violet chuckled. 'If you'd have asked me a couple of months ago if it was the way I'd visualized getting married, I would have said no, but,' *I thought I'd lost him –* 'I love him. I don't think anyone's ever gone to this sort of trouble for me before.'

She tried not to think about her ex-fiancé, who put her on a pedestal but was driven by the need to control and satisfy his own wants. Dear Pav thought of her first, and what he was doing was driven by love for her.

'Time changes all the things you think are set in stone,' said Serena, working on Violet's eyes. 'Look down for me. I used to be bothered about having a big house and a fancy car, but not any more. They aren't the important things in life – people are. You're a lucky lady, pet. He's a lovely man.'

Serena had told her that her soldier husband had been killed in action in Iraq. He never did get to see his twin girls, born a month after their father's funeral.

Violet knew then, knew without a doubt in her heart, how much Pav must love her, adore her, want to be with her. Serena was right – she was a lucky lady. A lady who wasn't going to resist throwing herself into married life with Pav any more. What on earth was she thinking of saying 'there's no rush' in the first place? The way she felt now, she wanted to take that aisle in one running jump.

'When you find someone like you obviously have, you cling on for as long as you can, and you enjoy every minute,' said Serena. 'Keep both eyes closed now. You're going to have a great day. Pav made sure that he didn't leave any stone unturned.'

'I wonder if he remembered a dre—'

'Now open your eyes.'

Violet opened her eyes to see left-hand Maria standing by the door and draped over her arm was the most beautiful pale-cream gown and a fur-trimmed cape and hood. And the woman who did her right hand was holding up a pair of short cream boots.

'Like I say,' said Serena. 'He didn't leave a stone unturned.'

In the chapel, Santa was checking his watch. 'Fashionably late,' he said with a grin, peering at Eve over his gold half-moon spectacles. Eve dropped her eyes shyly. That Santa could see into her soul, she was sure. He was every tick on a Santa checklist – hair, build, beard, clothes, rosy cheeks complete with tiny thread veins, laugh straight out of a boom box. Children were going to love him. Their Winterworld Santa was the best there could be.

'Wonder how Violet is,' Jacques said.

'No one has dared to ring her,' replied Eve, trying not to think how dashing he looked in that suit. How big and handsome and confident.

'You look very beautiful in that dress, Eve.'

Eve gulped. She must have heard him wrong. He wasn't looking at her, his eyes were forward.

'What did you say?

'You heard.'

He still didn't turn to her. So she had heard him right.

'I'm not, never have been, nor ever will be, beautiful,' snorted Eve.

'Many as your abilities are, I don't think you have quite managed to see yourself through the eyes of others yet, unless I'm very much mistaken.' Then his head swivelled around to her. 'Your eyes are the same colour as your outfit. Green as Christmas trees. However much you might hate that comparison.'

Eve opened her mouth to speak and then found no words followed. She didn't like the alien effect they had on her, making her slightly light-headed and her brain full of fizz. She was grateful that Max shouted, 'She's here.' And the organist began to play the first bars of 'The Wedding March' which slid seamlessly into 'All I Want for Christmas is You'.

Pav stood and turned to see his beaming bride in the perfectly fitted dress. He had borrowed her favourite dress and taken it to Serena, whose colleague took the measurements from it. He had designed the dress himself though. He knew she wouldn't want it to look anything like the last dress she bought for the wedding that never was. All his nerves disappeared when he saw her lovely smile. She was here, she looked happy. He knew he had taken a big gamble. Her ex-fiancé was a total control freak and this could so easily have been seen as similar behaviour: choosing her shoes, her dress, searching through her things in order to pack a case for her.

Violet walked down the very short aisle holding a bouquet of white roses and mistletoe, which one of

Serena's girls had made for her. The fur of her hood was softly framing her pretty pale face. She looked stunning, shining from the inside out.

'Dearly beloved,' began Santa in a smiling boom of a voice, as he opened the ceremony to wed Violet and Pav.

Chapter 45

Violet signed the register under her new name 'Violet Nowak'. It made her feel all warm and tingly inside.

'Smile,' ordered Max, raising her camera. 'Look at your new husband.'

Violet turned her face to Pav's. He was looking down at her with such love and happiness, she wanted to cry.

'I thought you weren't going to ask me again to get married,' she said.

'I didn't,' said Pav. 'I just went ahead and booked it.'

'I'm so glad you did,' said Violet.

'So am I, my love,' and Pav leaned down and kissed her on the lips, and there was a rumble of cheers from the small congregation.

'Boys and girls, I do believe there are some refreshments waiting for you,' said that too-real Santa whom Eve found difficult to get eye contact with. So it was to her horror that she felt his arm fall around her shoulder as the party was filtering out of the tiny wedding log cabin.

'Young lady, can I have a word?' he said.

'Y-yes,' stammered Eve, hoping it was a quick one. He made her feel very childlike again.

'I just wanted to say what a wonderful lady your Aunt Evelyn was,' he said.

'Oh, thank you.' Santa made her feel speechless as well as everything else.

'It was a terrible shame she discovered her niche in life so very late. If only she had years ago, when she was young and beautiful.'

Beautiful? Was Aunt Evelyn beautiful as a young woman? The few photographs Eve had of her aunt didn't show her to be what she would call classically beautiful. Evelyn had a long, thin face as a young woman and clouds of sadness in her eyes. Eve was suddenly intrigued.

'Did you know her when she was younger, S . . . Nicholas?' Christ, she nearly called him Santa then.

'Our paths first crossed many years ago,' he said. He had nice, white, small square teeth, Eve noticed. Santa teeth. She half expected him to say that her aunt had come to see him in his grotto when she was a nipper and asked for a whip and top. 'I hadn't seen her for over thirty years when she got back in touch in March to ask if I'd be interested in taking up the position here. She said she'd never forgotten me.' A sad wistful note accompanied his words.

Eve was about to ask what he did in his previous life but amazingly she stopped herself – because she didn't want to know. She didn't want to hear that he had been an accountant or a vicar or swept roads for the council. It suddenly didn't matter. She wanted to believe that he always had been what he was now. She didn't want to hear that he hadn't been the magical Santa who had restored her faith in the library of Higher Hoppleton Hall.

She took a huge gulp of cold air when she left the cabin and walked out into air filled with fat snow-flakes from the switched-on machines. 'What the frig is going on with you, Eve Douglas?' she gave herself a stiff word. But it was hard not to be mixed up, standing in a crowd of small people dressed in elf costumes, throwing confetti in the shape of green holly leaves and little red berries at a happy couple getting married in a snow-filled, bauble-decorated bubble. A few of the builders had downed tools as well to see the newlyweds and give them the thumbs up. Effin Williams was amongst them, a big sloppy smile on his round-as-the-moon face. Luckily he didn't scream that the newlyweds were useless toss-ers incapable of putting a plug in a socket, as he had done at the electricians yesterday.

Pav led the way to the cabin behind the grotto, which had been built as staff quarters. The guests followed, arm in arm with their partners, all except for Eve and Jacques. She was annoyed with herself for feeling disgruntled that he didn't offer her his arm but chose to walk at the side of Susan and chat to her instead.

The buffet that awaited them was a feast to behold. The caterers had excelled themselves with tiny two-bite sandwiches: turkey and stuffing, pork and apple, Wensleydale and red onion chutney, prawn and curried mayonnaise. There were the diddiest little mince pies with a brandy butter swirl, caramel apple crumbles with custard, mini tubs of Christmas pudding ice cream. Latticed pies, pastries, miniature chocolate rum roulades . . . and long-stemmed glasses of steaming mulled wine to wash it all down with.

Violet was grinning like a loon and fanning her face trying not to cry.

'I can't believe it,' she kept saying over and over again. 'I'm so happy. I never thought I'd be this happy, ever.'

Pav leaned over and kissed the top of her white-blonde hair.

'I am going to make you this happy every day of your life,' he said. 'Starting with tonight. Then we are going to fly to Lapland for three days. It's going to be cold. You need to keep very close to me to stay warm.'

Violet's mouth was wide with delight. 'I have always wanted to go there.'

'I know,' he said. 'I only wish we could stay longer, but the park will be opening soon.'

'It's enough,' said Violet. 'It's more than enough.'

'I have packed your case for you,' said Pav.

'Is there anything you haven't thought of?' grinned Violet.

'No,' said Pav. 'Nothing. Oh yes.' He grinned too. 'I don't think I have remembered your nightdress.'

'So you see, men *can* organize things just as well as women,' said Jacques' voice in Eve's ear. She caught the scent of his breath as he bent – spicy and sweet with mulled wine.

'It appears so,' said Eve, trying to herd her thoughts back into order. The sight of Jacques in that suit was distracting her from her mission to keep him at arm's length until she had exhausted the trail on Major Jack Glasshoughton.

'I'm glad you didn't tell her,' he said.

Eve nodded and tried not to look guilty.

'Violet is a very lucky woman, but then Pav is a lucky man. They're right together.' His sleeve brushed against her arm as she spoke and it sent tingles through her. She didn't like it, and she did. It stirred a hunger within her to be touched again.

'They are,' agreed Jacques. 'Finding someone to love is the greatest pleasure life has to offer. If they love you in return, of course.'

'Of course,' bristled Eve. 'There's no point if it's one-sided.'

'I hope you find your happiness soon too, Eve. I hope life is kind to you and gives you peace.'

'I am happ . . .' She turned to make the point, but he had left her side and was heading over to talk to Pav. Why had he said that? It sounded like a goodbye.

At the end of the party Max offered Susan and Patrick a lift, and as Eve had no desire to rush home, she went back to the Portakabin to check on the post and missed phone messages. She tried not to admit to herself that the buzz of the park was far more attractive than a cold, lonely house full of might-have-beens. Especially today, after such a beautiful demonstration of what love should be: what love should have been like for her.

She hadn't noticed it before, but the office looked rather naked after all the showers of confetti and holly, mistletoe, elves and Santas that she had been exposed to that afternoon. It was a plain little oasis in the middle of a snow-filled, mince-pie-flavoured world. She had intended to do some work. What else was there to do on a Saturday afternoon? But instead she picked up her keys and headed out to Morrisons. There was a man there – 'Robin Pud' – who sold Christmas trees in the car park.

Chapter 46

When Jacques walked into the Portakabin on the Sunday morning he walked straight out again, and checked the door before returning.

'Wow,' he said. 'For a minute there I thought I'd arrived at the wrong theme park.'

'Sarcasm is the lowest form of wit,' said Eve, hooking a bauble onto one of the Christmas tree branches. The tree was only three foot tall – she hadn't gone mad. She almost suggested to Robin Pud that he change the company name to 'Robin' Bastards'. She couldn't believe the price.

'Nice baubles,' said Jacques with a grin, and that old twinkle in his eyes that she hadn't seen for a while. 'Did you buy that tree?'

'No, I made it out of crêpe paper and sticky-back plastic,' she replied. 'Of course I bought it.'

'We've got hundreds of Christmas trees in the

park, and you went out and bought one?' he threw his head back and laughed.

'I was doing some market research,' said Eve. 'We should sell Christmas trees. They cost a bomb. And I still hate Christmas.'

Then she stood back to make sure that her red baubles weren't too close to each other, and Jacques grinned inside and knew that he was about to make the right decision.

'Coffee?' he offered.

'Please,' Eve replied.

Silence reigned as Jacques poured a jug of water into the machine. Eve knew that now was the perfect time to expel the huge elephant in the room. It had been present and growing between them since Jacques had learned she had been snooping in his house. He deserved a very big and belated apology for her behaviour. It was only right and proper that she gave it to him.

'I'm, sorry about the . . . seeing the uniform,' she coughed. Oh God, that was terrible as apologies go.

She raised her eyes to him and found him cross-armed and waiting for more.

'What uniform?' he asked, eyebrows raised. He knew exactly which uniform and wanted to see blood, that was clear. And could she really blame him?

'The lady's uniform. In your wardrobe.' She

cringed as she was saying it. 'It was unforgiveable of me to take your keys when you'd left them in trust to me.'

She dared her eyes upwards and found him still staring at her. His eyes were burning her skin. Eventually, after what felt like hours, he said, 'I think I understand why you felt you needed to . . .'

'Snoop?' she supplied.

'Snoop,' he smiled. 'You don't know much about me. I imagine you were curious. You just put two and two together and made ten. Catherine's parents asked me if I'd like to keep her uniform. It would have been rude of me to refuse their kindness.'

If Eve thought he was going to use this opportunity to give her more details about his life, she would be sadly mistaken.

'I'm sorry,' she said again. 'How long ago did . . . she . . . you know,' Eve picked up a golden bell and polished it on her skirt before adding it to the tree.

'Five years,' he said.

Same as me then, thought Eve.

'Were you . . . engaged?'

'No,' returned Jacques. 'It was nice, going well. We weren't together long enough to know if it would be for ever. In the end, it wasn't.'

'You said it was nine months. That's a good amount of time together, isn't it? ' said Eve. She and Jonathan had been with each for that amount of time and had *known* they were right for each other. Weren't they?

'Every couple is different though, aren't they?' said Jacques, taking the milk out of the mini-fridge. 'Some know they're right together from day one, some take longer, some don't make it.'

'Has there been anyone in your life since?'

'No,' he said flatly.

'You must miss her,' said Eve. 'Soldiers tend to impact rather heavily on the heart.' She presumed it was the same for men with female soldier girlfriends.

Jacques put a cup of coffee down on her desk.

'She was a lovely person and our time together was sweet. But she's gone.' That sounded rather cold, thought Eve. She didn't mean to exhale quite so loudly as a comment on his words.

'Life is a precious commodity and for the living, Miss Douglas,' he went on. 'It is a privilege not a right, and as such should be treated like a peach – tasted, savoured and drained of its every drop of juice. Not my words, but those of a wonderful lady.'

'Catherine?'

'Your Aunt Evelyn,' said Jacques, perching on the edge of his desk. Eve noted he hadn't made himself a drink.

'She never said as much to me,' sniffed Eve.

'She said them by leaving Winterworld to you.'

'Half of Winterworld,' said Eve. 'The other half she left to a stranger who purports to know more about my aunt than I ever did.' It came out more arrogant than she intended, but before she could retract her words, Jacques amazed her by nodding in agreement. 'Yes, you're right, Eve. But not for much longer.'

What the heck does that mean? Are you just one big lump of cryptic messages and mystery, she wanted to fling at him.

'What do you mean?'

'I mean that I agree with you.'

He opened his drawer and picked up a file.

'I just came for this. It's Sunday, Eve. Give yourself a break. Go and read the newspapers and drink coffee. This place is running itself because Evelyn planned it that way, so you don't need to be tied to that desk, day in, day out, evenings, weekends. You look tired.'

He had left the Portakabin by the time she had found her voice to answer him.

She studied herself in the mirror on the wall. She looked exhausted, not just tired. She was unrecognizable from the woman who was laughing in the photos on her office wall at home. But she didn't go back to Darklands to read papers and relax. Instead she sat in the office, going over paperwork she didn't need to go over, and when she was sufficiently bored of that, walked over to see Holly. She couldn't catch the train because it was grounded as the lads worked on making the track more higgledy-piggledy. Everyone was working so long and hard. She'd never seen anyone put as many hours in as Effin – no wonder he was always so bad tempered, she thought. He must have been totally knackered. She waved to Thomas.

'Morning, missus,' he said. 'Great idea calling it The Nutcracker Express, on account of it being nuts and a cracker of a train.'

'I'm glad you like it, Thomas,' she returned. It was a very silly Christmassy name for the train but Christmas was the heart and soul of this park, and if that's what her crazy Christmas-mad Aunt Evelyn wanted as her last wish, who was she to try and stop it?

Nearby, Effin was talking into his phone and Eve wondered if he had been exchanged for a doppel-ganger.

'*Ie cariad, ddoi adre cyn bo hir a wnai pigo'r siopa fyny ar y ffordd. Caru ti,*' he was saying, in the same quiet, affectionate tone of voice that Eve used when talking secretly to Holly.

'Who is he talking to? His bank manager?' she chuckled.

'Angharad, his wife,' whispered Thomas. 'A woman of gigantic proportions and the face of a sea-lion that ran into a wall. But he adores her. He's just telling her now that he'll be home very soon and will bring the shopping with him.' Then he added with a wickedly exaggerated impression, 'And now he's saying, "I love you".' And he puckered up his lips and made kissy noises. 'Like a lamb with Angharad, he is. Buys her roses, chocolates and those big padded cards. Like *Love Story*, they are. He's never looked at another woman since he met Angharad at Sunday School.'

That was a shocker. Effin was someone else she'd got wrong it seemed.

'Are you married, Thomas?' asked Eve.

'It was many moons ago,' said Thomas. 'Terrible woman. Then I met my princess Eunice,' and he pulled his wallet out of his pocket and showed Eve the passport-sized photo of a woman's smiley face. A very ordinary-looking woman with plump cheeks and brown curly hair, and yet Thomas was sighing at the photo as if he was seeing Penelope Cruz. 'She showed me what I was missing all those years. Oh yes, life is very sweet with my Eunice.'

Was the whole flaming world in love? thought Eve as she half stomped through the wood. Everyone except her.

As Holly ambled over to her, sensing a carrot treat,

Eve looked over at the snow pony enclosure. Life was going on without Christopher as if he had never been there. Soon there would be a new Shire Horse joining them: Snowball, a fifteen-year-old mare found in a shocking state in a stable. The old girl was going to have a treat after all she had suffered. Life would begin again for her.

Eve felt the pain of tears prodding at the back of her eyes. This damned place was changing her and she didn't want to be changed. She didn't want to buy Christmas trees and look at Jacques' suit with dilated pupils. She wanted to stay in her old comfortable world with its familiar memories and old loyalties. A world where Christmas was a means to filling her bank account and reindeer were nothing more than a commodity. A world where she knew where she was and what she had to do. She was scared of acknowledging that Jacques Glace's merest touch had made her nerve ends sigh. She didn't want to admit that she was lonely, starved of affection, needed someone to touch her, hold her, love her. But as Holly took the last of the carrot from her hand, and Eve stroked the soft fur of her head, she wondered if it ever would be possible to go back.

Chapter 47

Mr Mead opened the email and studied it. He even cleaned his glasses to make sure he was reading it properly.

'Goodness,' he said, buzzing through for Barbara, who came scuttling through seconds later.

'Will you look at this?' he said. 'I always thought that Mr Glace was a mysterious sort of fellow, but this has come rather from left field.'

Barbara patted her ample bosom. 'Goodness indeed,' she echoed. 'I better ring him, hadn't I, and make an appointment.'

'I think you better had,' said Mr Mead, peering at the words again. And he thought at his age that he'd seen everything.

Chapter 48

Effin's men worked through the night to finish the changes to the railway track. It would become even more of a wild ride in the summer when the park was closed down for a couple of months for more building work to take place, but it would be bone-shaking enough for the first few months of opening. Effin was his usual encouraging self, shouting at the men.

'*Wnai roi'r sac i bob un ohonoch chi a cyflogi'r ceirw a'r ceffyle – 'newn nhw job can gwaith gwell na chi, y wancyrs twp.*'

'That doesn't sound good,' said Eve to a very tired-looking worker as she passed him on the way to open up the Portakabin.

'Oh, it's his usual diatribe,' came the weary answer. 'He says he's going to sack us all and employ the reindeer and a horse who will do the job a hundred times better than us stupid wankers. If you'll excuse my language, missus.'

Eve smiled. She wasn't sure she could live without her fix of Effin's Welsh Tourette's when the park opened.

In the cabin there was an envelope underneath the tree, wrapped in Christmas paper. It was the size of a single A4 sheet. There was a Santa-shaped label on it and the writing read:

To Eve. Not to be opened before December 16th. J.

December 16th? Twelve days' time – the grand opening day. She was tempted to take a peek and tried to peel back a corner of the paper just at the moment when Jacques made his appearance.

'No looking,' he said.

'I wasn't,' fibbed Eve. 'What is it?'

'A gift,' said Jacques.

'I gathered that.'

'You'll find out on December sixteenth, won't you?'

Only twelve days until the gates opened to the general public and an old lady's dream was realized. It only seemed like yesterday that she had been sitting in Mr Mead's office learning that her batty old aunt had left her a theme park – to be shared with the international man of mystery himself. That yesterday had been devoid of reindeer and horses, tiny people, and the man who called himself Santa, who *knew* that she liked Fuzzy Felts. That yesterday, when held up against this one full of swearing Welshmen and patient Poles, soft furry animals and a team-spirit that could have been sold for a million pounds if someone knew how to bottle it, was a much greyer, colder place.

'It's looking good, isn't it?' said Jacques. 'I see from the office diary you've managed to get the nationals interested.'

'Yes, photoshoots have been arranged for the day after tomorrow,' said Eve. 'So if you—'

'I won't be around,' said Jacques before she could go on.

'Oh.'

'You don't need me,' said Jacques. 'You've got it all covered.'

'Well, I have, of course,' agreed Eve, who didn't doubt her abilities to escort the press around the park, 'but I thought you'd want to be there too.'

'Nope,' he replied. 'I ticked the no publicity box.' He pulled all the files out of his bottom drawer and plonked them on the table. 'The permanent log-cabin office will be ready to move into in the next couple of days.'

'It's ready now,' Eve cut in. 'I'd planned to start moving over there today because Effin is itching to move this Portakabin off-site.'

Jacques nodded. 'See? You have it all up here, don't you?' and he tapped his temple with his finger.

'I like to think so,' said Eve.

'I might as well pack as much as I can into boxes and get them taken up to the new office then. Once the press see the pictures of Violet's wedding, I'd be prepared for a flurry of bookings for the chapel if I were you. You may need this.' He handed over the big black book.

'I thought you were handling the chapel,' said Eve.

'I'm taking a bit of a break,' replied Jacques. 'I know you won't mind. Ships steer much better with one captain.'

'Well they do but—'

'This is the Santa's grotto file. The architect has drawn up some tentative plans you'll need to look at as it features an extension at the side. There are more snow globes arriving before the weekend. Oh, and here is an idea about a 'snow-globe experience' in Santapark. It's a virtual ride. People will think they're being shaken and turned upside down—'

'Whoa, hang on,' put in Eve. 'How long will you be away for?'

'I don't know,' shrugged Jacques. 'Maybe I'll be a sleeping partner.'

A sleeping partner. Eve's every wish come true. Herself in sole charge of the running of Winterworld. No Jacques bloody Glace to alter and 'improve' her plans. It was just too delicious to think about. No sparring with him, no one to erect unsuitable Santa signs whilst she was fighting off adult versions of childish diseases. On paper that would be bliss. 'Well, that of course is up to you,' said Eve.

'Yes it is,' said Jacques. He looked at the Christmas tree beautifully decorated now with carefully chosen tinsel, and he smiled.

Oh yes, the office was going to be quiet at last. No one singing Christmas carols all the time, no one booming down the telephone and stomping everywhere with big boots on and taking up half the office with his enormous coats.

'You aren't going off immediately though, are you?' asked Eve, watching as he continued to empty the drawers of his desk. 'You're not leaving me to oversee the grand opening by myself?'

'You don't need me for that. You arrange events – you're the best at it.'

'Well, I know I'm capable but—'

'The new office will be yours and yours alone. I'll make sure you have everything from me that you need before I go.'

'Oh okay, if that's the way you want it,' said Eve, trying to be brave. Trying to remember that this was what she had wanted from the beginning.

'I do.'

She was finally going to be the 'Captain' rather

than 'missus'. No one was going to mistake her for Jacques' PA or chief tea-maker. She was going to be steering the Winterworld ship completely, utterly and fabulously solo. And yet watching Jacques begin to pack up the office, she couldn't help thinking that there was something very wrong with this picture.

Chapter 49

Effin's men lifted the Portakabin off-site the next morning, and Eve watched it being loaded onto the back of a truck with mixed feelings. Aunt Evelyn had worked from there and Nobby Scuttle had sweated in there. The coffee machine had spat in there and Jacques Glace had sung and been noisy in there. Now he wasn't in the park because he was 'taking a break' and she was finally at the helm of Winterworld as its sole driver.

Eve felt like a newlywed as she stood outside the pristine cabin office. At best she should have been carried over the threshold, at worst there should have been a ribbon to cut. But there was just her and a door, which she opened to reveal a lovely rustic space. She wanted to dance around it. She wanted to shout 'It's mine, all mine!' and put her arms around it all.

Eve sat on her chair trying not to imagine it was a throne. A throne fit for a captain. She celebrated by having the first coffee out of the swanky new machine that wouldn't answer back or spit, just obediently pumped water through a pod. It even came complete with milk and a layer of crema on the top.

'Oh, this is the life,' said Eve, taking her diary out of her desk and checking her jobs for the day. There was a crockery order to chase, and more toys were needed in Santa's workshop, and one of the tills at the entrance kiosk wasn't working properly. It was all grist to the mill for Eve though. She picked up the phone and made the first call. She needed a PA, too. Someone who would call her 'Captain' behind her back. Eve laughed to herself. The PA would sit at Jacques' old desk; it would be a great job for a school-leaver. A nice, quiet girl, who didn't disturb her with big boots and hummed tunes and a whisper as loud as a foghorn.

By half-past eleven, Eve decided she didn't like the new coffee machine. It didn't pervade the office with a rich roast smell and it was so *quiet*. It was a shiny, characterless piece of metal that delivered a perfect drink that was as boring as the silence which it was apparently famous for. She couldn't hear any workmen in this corner of the park either, no Effin shrieking at his men how incompetent they were. It was all very plush and fabulous and state of the art . . .

and boring. There was no Jacques annoyingly tapping his Spiderman pen on the desk as he concentrated, or his ridiculous *Daily Trumpet* to borrow and read the latest apology. Apparently more people bought the paper for the retractions than they did for the news. There were even Facebook pages to share them with the rest of the world.

The little Christmas tree now stood in the corner with Jacques' present underneath it. A couple of baubles must have fallen off in transit and the build-ers had put them back in the wrong place. Eve walked over and re-hung them, adjusting the tinsel and stabbing herself on a needle in the process. Again she picked up the envelope and wondered what it was. She was more than tempted to open it, but instead put it back. There wasn't long to wait until the 16th. She could manage to hold out until then.

Mr Mead rang just after lunch asking for Jacques.

'He's not around at the moment,' said Eve. 'Can I help?'

'No,' replied the old solicitor. 'I'm afraid you can't in this instance.'

'Can I pass on a message?'

'If you could just ask him to ring me please,' replied Mr Mead. 'If I'm not around, would he either leave a message for myself or Mrs Cawthorne.'

Eve recognized the name. She dealt with property.

She had acted as solicitor when she and Jonathan bought their house. What was Jacques up to?

Eve decided to take a little drive to Outer Hoodley, and discovered a man erecting a 'For Sale' sign outside Jacques' cottage.

Chapter 50

Eve sat in the car and hurriedly stabbed the number of the estate agent into her phone.

Eventually a young woman's voice answered. She only sounded about twelve.

'Hello Watson and . . . er, Wilson and Hughes estate agents. First day nerves, sorry about that. Tiffany speaking, how may I help you?'

'Hi,' began Eve, brightly and casually. 'You have a cottage in Outer Hoodley for sale. I haven't seen it advertised before, has it been up long?'

'Er, let me just check.' There followed a few clicky keyboard noises. 'No, it's only been on the market since yesterday.'

'Ah, that's why I haven't seen it before,' Eve forced a smile into her voice. 'Is . . . er . . . is it a definite sale? I mean the owner isn't going to pull the house off the market?'

By her own admission that sounded a bit weird.

'That's what happened to me last time,' Eve added quickly. 'You get a bit cautious.'

'Can you just bear with me?' said Tiffany. Eve had visions of her telling her co-workers that she had a right twat on the phone, and them miming at her to put the phone down and slowly back away. But Tiffany surprised her.

'It's definitely on the market. The owner's looking for a quick sale, hence the price, because he's going to live abroad.'

'Going abroad?' echoed Eve. Why, where, and when?

'Do you want to know the price?' asked Tiffany, anxiety flagging up in her voice now.

'No, thank you, it's fine, I've changed my mind,' said Eve, quickly clicking off her phone. Going abroad, the estate agent said. It was all too fast and smelt of intrigue. He was doing a runner for some reason – and people didn't do runners for good reasons.

She sped back to the office, breaking the speed limit and hoping a covert camera didn't pick her up. Her head was spinning. She needed to find out once and for all what and who the mysterious Jacques Glace was. She was going to ring Mr Mead back and make him tell her everything he knew about the man, however small the detail. Then her phone rumbled in her pocket and the screen showed that it was Violet.

'Hi there, how are you?' Eve injected some fake jollity into her voice.

'Eve, my signal is pretty weak, can you hear me okay?' Violet sounded a little breathless.

'Yes, you're quite quiet but I can hear you.'

'Listen, we bought a *Daily Trumpet* to read on the plane but we didn't get round to it.'

'You rang me to tell me that?'

'Listen. Are you near a computer? I've just read it in the Ice Hotel bar and I've taken a picture of one of the pages. You need to view it on a big screen.'

Eve's eyebrows dipped in puzzlement. 'What is it?'

'It's urgent, that's what it is. Let me send it before I lose my signal.'

'Okay. Is everyth—' but Violet had gone. Eve waited for the text, refreshing the screen impatiently over and over again. Eventually it arrived, and Eve opened up the attachment but it was too small to read. She could only make out that it was one of the bloody *Trumpet*'s apologies. She didn't know where this was going but she forwarded it to her email and then opened the file and zoomed in.

> The Daily Trumpet *would like to apologize to the family of Sharon Wilkinson for the erroneous reporting of her funeral recently.*

Oh God, said Eve to herself. Of all the stories to cock up. Though why Violet had forwarded it on during her honeymoon was anyone's guess.

The commanding officer who read the eulogy was not, as reported, Lieutenant Jean Jackson, but Lieutenant Colonel Jean-Jacques Glace, holder of the Military Cross medal for gallantry and founder of the Yorkshire Fund for Disabled Soldiers . . .

Eve was reading the words but they weren't being absorbed. *Jean-Jacques Glace.* Where had that name cropped up before?

She googled the name. Amongst the references to Glace Bay and French language entries, she found the entries relating to the army officer Jean-Jacques Glace. The army officer who saved the lives of three of his men, shielding them from Iraqi gunmen and losing his right leg below the knee in the process. Jean-Jacques Glace, a brilliant soldier who had quickly risen through the ranks only to be invalided out of the army aged thirty-six, twenty months ago. There was a single picture when she pressed 'Images', a grainy newspaper head-and-shoulders portrait of a soldier in a helmet and 'camo' uniform. There was no mistaking those eyes though, bright and shiny and blue.

Eve caught sight of that parcel under the tree and

no force in hell would have stopped her fingers pull-ing off the wrapping now. It contained a single sheet of paper – a letter. She stared at the words, trying to absorb the enormity of what they said. Then she unlooped her bag from her chair and drove into town, fingers clamped onto the steering wheel to keep her shaking hands steady.

Chapter 51

'I need to see Mr Mead. Urgently,' said Eve, breath-lessly, because she'd had to park quite a long walk away from the solicitor's office and ran all the way from there.

'He's in a meeting,' said Barbara. 'I can get him to phone—'

'No,' said Eve adamantly. 'I have to see him. Today. I am not leaving here without speaking to him.'

Barbara shrugged. The young lady was in for a long wait then.

'Well, there's some coffee over there, but I have to warn you that he will be quite a while.'

As if it had heard mention of itself, the old coffee machine – which could have been the sister of the old one in the Portakabin – belched.

'I'll sit here until he can see me,' said Eve, lifting

up a magazine from the table in the corner. She read it from cover to cover, read every word of another two, went to the loo twice, had five cups of coffee and was on a twelfth game of 'Word Mole' on her Blackberry, when Barbara popped her head around the door.

'He can see you for five minutes if that's enough,' she said.

'It'll be enough,' replied Eve, getting to her feet and stretching her back. And if it wasn't, well, there was no way that Mr Mead was going to get her out of his office until she was satisfied with the information given.

Eve walked into the office, not knowing if the slightly fusty smell was the building or the man himself. He looked as if he could be a user of mothballs.

'I'm sorry you've had a long wait,' he apologized, 'but without an appointment, I'm afraid—'

'It's okay, I know,' Eve cut him off. 'But I need to talk to you urgently, Mr Mead. About this for a start,' and she foraged in her bag and put Jacques' present down on his desk.

'Oh. I rather had the impression that you shouldn't have seen this yet,' said Mr Mead, his huge shaggy eyebrows hooding his eyes.

'There was a note saying not to open it until the sixteenth, but I disobeyed it.'

'Ah.'

'When certain information came to light about Jacques Glace. Or should I say Lieutenant Colonel Jean-Jacques Glace.'

'Ah,' said the old man again, his expression even more pained this time.

'You have to tell me, Mr Mead. You have to tell me what's going on now.'

'The Lieutenant Colonel was most specific that his rank and background weren't to be mentioned,' said Mr Mead.

'Why?' said Eve. 'I don't get it. Why?'

Mr Mead took off his glasses and rubbed his eyes. 'You should really ask him . . .'

'His house is up for sale, he won't answer his mobile, he's going abroad apparently and' – she stabbed the papers with her finger – 'he's signed over his half of the park to me.'

'That is correct,' said Mr Mead.

'Is he a secret billionaire that he can afford to do that?'

'Not at all,' replied Mr Mead. 'Just a very honourable man who thought that maybe your aunt had been a little reckless in leaving such a fortune to him after a relatively short acquaintance.'

'He was a hospital visitor, wasn't he? That's how he met Aunt Evelyn?'

'No,' said Mr Mead. 'It was your aunt who was

doing the hospital visiting. That's how she met a lot of the people who now work in the park. From what I understand, Evelyn was there for him when he was having trouble adjusting to the loss of his limb and subsequently his military career.' And he coughed, fearing he had breached a confidence.

'Aunt Evelyn was visiting *him*?' Boy, she really had got all this the wrong way round.

'She wasn't well herself, of course, just having had that stroke, but hospital visiting perked her up no end. And, her acquaintance with the Lieutenant Colonel led to her building Winterworld.'

'Thank you for telling me, Mr Mead,' said Eve. 'Just one more thing.' She picked up Jacques' hand-written intention to assign the deeds to her and tore it in half. 'If Aunt Evelyn wanted the *Captain* to have half the park, then I'm not going to go against her wishes.'

Chapter 52

It was very late when Jacques got home and parked his car in the hamlet car park. He squinted because it looked like Eve's BMW in the bay across. Then she got out, dressed in a thin coat, hands tucked under her arms and voice shivering as much as her body.

'Where the hell have you been? Have you any idea how much waiting around I've done today. And I hope there are no CCTV cameras because I had to have a wee in a bush over there.'

He had one of his ridiculously big coats on and a daft hat with a pom pom.

'Eve. Why are you here?'

'I opened your present.'

'You shouldn't have.'

'Can we talk inside? I'm so cold, I'm turning blue.'

He gestured that she walk forward. 'You know, of course, which house I live in.'

Eve's cheeks attempted to blush at that but her blood vessels had all hibernated.

Mrs Cerberus's curtains gave a tiny twitch, but satisfied that Jacques was accompanying the stranger-to-these-parts woman, she returned to her sofa and the TV. Jacques opened the door to a warm kitchen; a slow-cooker was flavouring the air with the smell of beef stew. Eve's stomach keened as the scent of it hit her nostrils. It sounded like someone had kicked a wolf at full-moon.

'Coffee?' he asked.

'Yes please,' said Eve.

'Take a seat,' Jacques invited, gesturing towards the sofa in the lounge. Everything except that sofa and the coffee table was packed up in boxes.

'You're going abroad, I hear,' she said, as he busied himself with getting cups out and boiling the kettle.

'You've done your homework. Yes, I've booked a flight.'

'When?'

'I fly out in the morning.'

'Where?'

'Australia.'

'Couldn't you get any further away?'

He smiled. 'I have friends out there. I've never visited them. I thought it was about time I did.'

'You didn't even stay here long enough to unpack, and now you've packed up again and are leaving. '

'I've been used to moving around a lot.'

'What about Winterworld?'

'It's all yours.'

'Why?' She gulped down the rise of emotion in her throat.

He walked into the lounge with two cups of coffee and almost filled the doorway.

'As you said,' he replied, setting the cups down on the coffee table, 'I have no right to your family's fortune. Or this.' He reached over behind Eve to lift something off the shelf and gave it to her. Stanley's medal.

'My aunt gave it to you,' said Eve. 'You'd appreciate it more than I would.' And she handed it back. 'I won't take it. Please.'

His hands stayed down at his side, so she put it on the chair arm. 'I won't be leaving with it. And I ripped up your letter of intent.'

'The legal papers are being prepared anyway,' said Jacques. 'It's yours.'

Eve looked at him, really looked at him, and tried to imagine him in a uniform, leading men. It wasn't that difficult really. Despite the stupid woolly hats and SpongeBob SquarePants sock, he was a natural leader of men and that had been clear from the off.

'Why didn't you tell me? Why did you let me believe that you were a . . . a . . .'

'Gold digger? A cross-dressing gold-digger at that,'

he supplied, and then smiled to himself as he sat down and picked up his mug, drawing warmth from it. 'Mischief at first, I think. You were so incredibly snotty. I suppose I had faith in my ability to both win you over and teach you a lesson.'

'Why didn't you tell me you were a soldier?'

'I'm not a soldier any more, Eve. It had no bearing on things. I'd rather be judged on what people find me to be now than have them pity me because I'm a disabled ex-soldier.'

'You weren't just a soldier though, you were a wonderfully brave one. You lost a leg defending your men. I didn't have a clue – you don't even limp.' She remembered how he had run through the enchanted forest as sure-footed as a goat.

'Prosthetics have come on in leaps and bounds in the last few years. We amputees no longer need to resort to a wooden leg and a parrot.' He smiled at her – his big open twinkly-eyed smile. 'It was painful to wear at the beginning until they got the fit right. I've thrown a few legs across the room in anger, I can tell you. It takes time to learn to walk in a different way from how you've been accustomed to for the whole of your life.'

'I'm so sorry,' said Eve. 'I thought you were either deranged or a practised con man who went around taking life savings away from old ladies.' She put her cup down because she felt in danger of dropping it.

'I couldn't have been more wrong about everything, could I?'

'And you've got so much right too,' said Jacques. 'Delivering baby reindeer, rescuing horses, bringing Evelyn's dream to life. You could run Winterworld blindfolded.'

'Why are you really leaving me?' said Eve, surprising herself even with that question.

Jacques smiled at her. 'Because you bought a Christmas tree.'

Eve wiped a perfidious tear from her eye before he saw it. 'I don't know what you mean.'

'You'll be all right,' he said. 'Christmas is making progress with you. It's all your Aunt Evelyn wanted, to see you join the real world again. When you bought that Christmas tree, I knew you'd be fine. You're starting to need people again, to enjoy them in your life. You're looking forward more and more instead of backwards. Your heart is opening up, Eve Douglas, and you're letting Christmas into it.'

'I thought it was you who visited Aunt Evelyn in hospital,' Eve blurted out, the rein on her emotions getting harder to hold. 'Not the other way around.'

'I was in a bad state when Evelyn came into my life. I didn't care about any medal I'd won. I couldn't see any future – disabled and out of the army, my head was a mess. Then this funny little old lady

dragged me out of my own head kicking and screaming, gabbling on about how much she loved
Christmas and asking me to help her design a theme
park. I thought she was barking.'

'She was,' laughed Eve.

'And she told me all about her niece who was as
disabled as I was and as trapped inside herself. She
wanted to help you much more than she did me, but
she knew all the words had been said to you and
none of them had worked.'

Eve's face fell into her hands and she sobbed. Then
she felt warm strong arms close around her and her
face being pushed into Jacques' shoulder, and she
smelt his foresty aftershave.

'And she did it,' he continued. 'She helped me –
and you're nearly there.'

'Don't leave, Jacques. It won't be the same. I was
climbing the walls in the new office today after two
hours. The new coffee machine is too swanky and
perfect and there's no noise.'

'You'll get used to those little changes,' said
Jacques. He raised her head with his finger and
looked into her eyes.

'The colour of Christmas trees,' he said. 'You're
going to be fine.'

She felt his face near hers, she closed her eyes
anticipating his lips falling onto hers, but they merely
grazed against her cheek.

'I'll see you to your car,' he said, his arms releasing her. 'I think you'll sleep well tonight.'

Jacques waited until she had driven out of sight before returning to the cottage. He would miss her so much. He was only happy that he had done his duty by Evelyn and set her on the road to recovery with their spats and fights and one-upmanship. Jonathan would have been a lucky man had he lived, but he hadn't. And life was for the living. No one who truly loved another would want them to waste their precious life grieving. They would want them to live and love for them both.

He closed his eyes and saw the scene of him lying in his hospital bed, bitter and frustrated. He'd rather have died on duty than be a disabled man with no hope left in his life. The bomb had crippled his head more than his body.

He remembered the first time he heard her voice. 'Hello, I'm Evelyn Douglas. And you are Lieutenant Colonel Jean-Jacques Glace.' She had pronounced it 'Jeen'. 'Is it all right to call you Jacques? My sister-in-law is called Jean and I could never stand the sight of her.'

And despite himself he had laughed, and she had sat down on the chair at the side of the bed and talked until he listened.

And weeks later Evelyn Douglas had placed her

hand on his and said, 'You'll never know how much you've changed my life, Jacques. You make me think that anything is possible. When I first met you, you were such a grump. But you've come through so much. You make me feel ashamed that I had all that life and wasted it, when you have fought so hard to keep hold of yours. But no more. I'm going to try and make up for lost time. I won't make up for all of it, but I can set some balls rolling downhill.'

'Good for you, Evelyn,' he said, thinking she was going to go off and book a cruise.

'You're right, Jacques. Life is for the living. I just wish I could make my niece believe that. I wish you'd fall in love with her,' Evelyn had said with a heavy sigh. 'Oh, she might play the big career woman, but I know that girl's heart and it's lonely and crying for someone to love it. Make her fall in love with you, Jacques.'

'Life isn't a romance book, Evelyn,' Jacques had said kindly. 'You can't write your own happy ending. It's in bigger hands than ours.'

'You'd be good together,' Evelyn had nodded, ignoring him. 'She's not an easy woman, but she's worth the effort to get to know. I'm going to sort it that you spend some time together. I'm going to leave you both half of my Christmas theme park. You'll have to work together.'

'Yes, you do that,' he had chuckled. If only he had known she wasn't joking.

Then he found himself joint owner of Winterworld.

He had played the game for a while, in accordance with Evelyn's wishes, because it was clear from the off that if he didn't, Winterworld would have become a different place to the one Evelyn wanted. But he had always intended to sign his share back over, just as soon as things were on course. It wouldn't have been right to accept that sort of inheritance from an old lady he had known for such a short time.

He didn't bargain on falling stupidly in love with the stubborn, snotty, über-confident, super-efficient, megalomaniac of a niece of hers though. And he couldn't be around her because she needed time, lots of it, to recover. Because she was moving into the here and now, and that meant she would finally start to grieve for Jonathan – and be able to let him go.

Chapter 53

Eve tried to sleep but she couldn't. Her head was a mess, a jumble of old prejudices and new enlightenments. Facts were easier to compartmentalize and deal with than the feelings bombarding her heart. Because those feelings were wrong, so wrong, disrespectful to Jonathan's memory, but at the same time they were so strong, so undeniably and magically strong.

Eve made herself a cup of instant chocolate and carried it into the chilly office where the cheerful candle burned brightly in the window. The sight of it churned her gut and she slumped in the chair at the desk and let the tears roll down her face.

'Oh Jonathan,' she said, her voice choked with emotion. 'I don't know what to do. I feel myself changing and I know if I do, that I'll be moving away from you. And I can't do that. Because we made a vow to each other and I know you're with me and I couldn't ever hurt you. I couldn't let you go.'

She pressed at her chest knowing that the big coat-wearing, daft-hat-and-gloves buffoon Jacques Glace had been denied access to the door there, so he had climbed in through the window.

Then a rather extraordinary thing happened. The room suddenly grew warm, as if a giant fire had been turned on behind every wall, floor and ceiling. And through the haze of her tears, Eve saw the candle flame expand, grow brighter and higher than should have been possible. She wiped her eyes, just in time to see the flame disappear, as if someone had wet their fingers and extinguished it – just like that. The candle was smoking, the end of the tip a faint orange, which faded before her eyes to black. And the room grew as quickly chilly as it had become hot.

Chapter 54

Everyone agreed that Phoebe May Tinker's childish squeals of delight summed up the noises they all wanted to make: from the elf-people to the caterers, Mr and Mrs Nowak and the Polish and Welsh workers, now out of their hard hats and work gear and in jeans, holding the hands of their babies who had come to see Santa along with everyone else who was queuing at the gates – and those queues went a long way back.

It was funny to see Effin out of his fluorescent-yellow jacket. He had a shirt and tie on, and he was linking arms with one of the biggest, ugliest women Eve had ever seen. He was pointing things out to her and she was nodding and listening to him, and it was more than evident how proud he was of his contribution.

'Well, I don't know how you did it, but you did,'

said Violet, coming up behind Eve and putting a hand on her shoulder.

'*We* did it,' corrected Eve. 'It was a joint effort. Everyone had a part to play.'

'You look lovely,' said Violet, lifting a shank of her cousin's loose dark hair before letting it fall. 'You shouldn't ever tie it back again. It makes you look years younger like this.'

But Violet knew it wasn't just the hair that was doing that. Since the candle had gone out, she had felt Eve move back into the world with them again. She had watched her face soften over the days, seen a brightness return to her eyes.

'Is that invitation still on to spend Christmas with you lot?' asked Eve on a whim.

Violet smiled. 'Eve, you would make us all very happy if you did. Mum's freezer is bursting at the seams with food. Patrick has got her the world's biggest turkey. It's like an emu.' She linked her arm through Eve's and squeezed her. 'That's just the best news I've had in ages; Mum is going to be so made up. We'll buy you a Fuzzy Felt. You can't change your mind, you know. You've just entered a verbal contract.'

'Good. Hold me to it,' said Eve. She didn't want to be alone this Christmas. She wanted to be with her family, eating around Auntie Susan's big table, clinking glasses, laughing at corny Christmas cracker jokes. She wanted to make some fresh memories of lovely Christmases and stamp out all the unpleasant ones of years past. The decision to spend Christmas with her family might have been a hastily decided one but boy, it felt so right and brought a lovely thrill of anticipation with it. It was as if she had moved into that giant snow globe at last. She was no longer peering in from the outside. Christmas was all around her and she was part of it – and it was part of her.

And in the first week of the new year, Darklands was going up for sale, she decided. It was too big a house for herself to rattle around in with old, cold memories. The house deserved to be full of life and light and children – it was the final act of letting go.

'Have you heard from Jacques?' Violet asked softly.

'No,' said Eve. Violet saw her gulp a ball of emotion down as she said it. 'I'm not sure I'll ever hear from him again.'

'I thought he might have turned up. Hot-tailed it back from Australia. I know it was a mad thought, but it's no madder than what else has happened in the past three months.'

Eve didn't say that she had hoped for the same. She so wanted him to be here and see his creation, because this Winterworld wasn't the one she had envisaged. If shingles hadn't driven her to bed, she would have ridden rough-shod over so many of

Aunt Evelyn's plans. Holly wouldn't be here and consequently Noel and Blizzard, or the Schneekugelmuseum. There would be no people dressed as snowmen or as many elves, and she had recruited more in the past week – an elf brass band who were presently gearing up to play to the visitors. This Winterworld was the glittery, Christmassy nightmare she would have fought every step of the way to prevent happening – and what a mistake that would have been. Jacques Glace had been loyal to Aunt Evelyn in a way she wouldn't have been. And because of him, she could feel her aunt's approval floating down with every snowflake from those giant German snow machines. He, more than anyone, deserved to see the smiles of everyone who walked in through the gates.

She wanted to email him, say 'Come home, Jacques. Because this is your home and your Christmas family are missing you, dear Captain. I am missing you and your daft flirtations and your SpongeBob SquarePants phone sock on your desk.' But he deserved better than her. She had never met – nor was she likely to meet again – anyone who was as brave and honourable. And she, as he once so delicately put it, was a mess.

Eve hadn't contacted any celebrities to open up the park – there was only one person who could cut the huge red and green ribbon and let the crowds in

– Santa. He was in position on his motorized sleigh, ready to ride to the front gate. He looked amazing and even more real than usual. Next year they would have reindeer pulling that sleigh.

'Are we all ready?' said Eve. She raised the glass of mulled wine which she had in her hand. 'A toast to the good ship Winterworld and all of us who sail in her. And to you, darling Aunt Evelyn. You've given so many of us so much, I only wish you were here to see your dream come true. And a toast to you, dear Captain Jacques – wherever you are.' *Come back to us. Please.*

Glasses were raised and touched together. The elf band leader counted in his musicians and they followed Santa's sleigh to the gate playing 'Winter Wonderland'. Fat flakes of snow drifted down on their heads from the machines and the atmosphere couldn't have been more filled with Christmas if it had tried. Not the Christmases that Eve remembered, though, but Christmases she had read about, seen on films: mince-pie scented, cosy fireplace-warmed, snow-filled, happy, contented Christmas. The sort of Christmases she would have from now on.

'Welcome,' said Santa's booming voice. 'Welcome to Winterworld, my friends.'

And the masses poured in, gasping at the snow, the lights, the elves, the snowmen, the cabins, the lovely enchanted forest, and the train waiting to shake their bones. The soldiers and their families were first in, the children running here and there, not knowing which direction to go in first.

'I want to go to the ice-cream parlour.'

'I want to go on the train.'

'Santapark.'

'Reindeer, before the crowds.'

Eve felt a tug at her sleeve. Phoebe was pulling her down so she could whisper in her ear. 'Oh Auntie Eve, it's perfect.'

And it so very nearly was. The only thing missing was Jacques, and if he had come through the gates, Eve thought her heart might leap out of her chest to greet him. But he didn't.

Chapter 55

Six Months Later

'*Job a hanner bois. Dw i'n browd o chi gyd.*'

'Oh 'eck, Effin's off on one again,' Eve chuckled, hearing the little Welshman's voice blasting at his workmen. The park hadn't been the same since they had finished work in December. Thank goodness lots of new plans had been approved and Effin and his men were now back here working.

'Actually he's saying, "That's a job well done, lads. I'm proud of you",' smiled the young pretty blonde who was walking at her side: Thomas the Tank's step-daughter, Myfanwy. She had been Eve's PA now for four months and was a total godsend. The log cabin office was a much jollier place with her in it – and Gabriel. The cat's home hadn't been able to sell him and so Eve bought him from them. He sat in the corner with the baubles on his antlers and for a reason that Eve could never fathom, he made her smile every time she saw him.

'Get lost,' grinned Eve. 'You can't talk Welsh. You lied to me.'

'Honest,' said Myfanwy. 'I'd get him to the first-aid cabin if I were you. By the way, can I nip over and get an ice cream?'

'There's a shocker,' said Eve. 'Go on, I'll wait.'

Myfanwy crossed to the ice-cream parlour, now run by the new manager Janet, as Violet and Pav had returned to Carousel. Still, Eve saw a lot of Mr and Mrs Nowak and her Auntie Susan, who had married Patrick on Valentine's Day. It was so nice to see those she loved happy and being looked after. Violet and Pav had decided to have a baby – they were just waiting for her to 'catch on'.

'It can't be long,' Violet confided. 'We're at it like rabbits,' which made Eve crack up with laughter because Violet wasn't one for crude talk. Still, her lavender eyes looked as if they had a 1000-watt light-bulb behind them these days.

Eve watched Myfanwy studying the flavours in the cabinet. She always spent ages looking, only to pick the 'Reindeer Nose', which had big cherries in it. She took even more time to decide when Janet's big handsome son Robbie was working there. He had a look of a young Jacques Glace about him – albeit one smaller and younger with brown eyes, instead of blue ones, full of mischief.

Eve hadn't heard from Jacques since the night when Jonathan's flame died. He had gone off to Australia and she had ploughed all her energies into making the park as successful as could be. But six months down the line, as proud as she was of her achievements, it wasn't enough. A part of Jonathan would be with her always, and with the passing of time, she had remembered how much he had loved life, that he would want her to live and laugh – and love. He had blossomed young, Evelyn had blossomed old. Neither of them would have wanted their Eve not to have her time to flower.

There was a lot of shrieking going on at the other end of the park, which was closed for two months whilst the builders worked flat out. The train tracks were being extended, the increasingly popular wedding chapel was being enlarged, and two more honeymoon log cabins were being built. A children's roller coaster and the Snow Globe experience were being erected in Santapark, and a craft market and more toilets. Holly had a new companion – a young female reindeer called Ivy – and there was a small sanctuary for snowy owls who couldn't, for one reason or another, be released back into the wild. One of them – Stephen – was a real character, very tame, and delighted crowds of children with the tricks he could do. He and his handler gave two shows a day and Stephen never tired of showing off. Jacques would have loved the owls, she thought. She could imagine him literally charming them out of the trees. Her thoughts often strayed to him. She hoped he was happy.

'He's gorge, isn't he – Robbie?' said Myfanwy, returning with her cherry-studded ice cream. 'I reckon he's on the verge of asking me out.'

'Oh definitely,' said Eve. 'His pupils dilate to the size of dustbin lids when he sees you.'

'I know,' said Myfanwy with a confident casual sniff as she licked her ice cream.

'Lot of shouting going on over there,' said Eve, as another round of noise hit the air. 'Shall we go and have a look what's going before we head over to the gift shop?'

They walked through the enchanted forest, something which Eve never tired of doing. She still got that magical prickle under her skin whenever she was in there.

'Morning, missus,' called an engineer who was servicing the snow machines from up a tree.

'Morning,' sighed Eve. She never did become 'Captain' in the end. She was stuck with 'missus' and probably always would be.

'Who's that?' said Myfanwy, pointing in front of her.

'Can't see that far,' said Eve.

'Great big tall bloke with a cowboy hat on. Hang on, it's one of those Australian things with all the corks dangling off it. All the builders are crowded round him.'

Eve's heart stopped in her chest for a beat. *No, it couldn't possibly be.* Her pace accelerated so much that Myfanwy couldn't keep up.

'Hey missus, look who it is,' called one of the Welsh lads. And the big tall man turned around – and it was him in yet another silly hat. He grinned and his blue, blue eyes sparkled against his antipodean tan.

Eve felt her heart thump against her chest wall as if it was making a bid for freedom, though her legs suddenly glued themselves to the spot. She couldn't move, even her breathing seemed to stop.

'Well, there you are,' he said in an exaggerated Aussie accent. 'Long time, no see, Sheila.'

'You're telling me,' she managed on the little remaining breath she had inside.

She had mentally rehearsed what she would do if she ever saw him again. She saw herself running up to him, throwing herself around his neck and raining kisses on his cheek, but now he was actually here in the flesh, all she could do was stand there and not breathe.

'I came back to see my girl,' he said, then added, 'Holly.'

'Ah,' said Eve.

'It's the antlers. I love a woman with antlers.'

'I'll try and grow some.' Her mouth wanted to grin, so she let it.

'You could do anything you set your heart on, Eve Douglas.'

Jacques made 'see you later boys' noises at the builders, then he held out his big hand towards Eve. 'Take a walk with me, *missus*.'

She moved slowly towards him, his hand curled around her own and together they fell into a slow stride.

'A postcard would have been nice,' she said, as they headed for the heart of the enchanted forest.

'Absence makes the heart grow fonder,' said Jacques, his grin equally as wide as hers had grown.

'Out of sight, out of mind,' parried Eve.

'Never thought of that one,' chuckled Jacques. 'Have I been out of your mind then?'

'No.'

Jacques stopped. 'No? Is that all I get? I don't know. I come back to marry you and that's the extent of your declaration of affection for me.' And he carried on walking, tugging Eve forward when her legs stopped moving.

'You're unbelievable,' said Eve. 'I never thought I'd see you again.'

'I told you I would marry you on our very first

meeting. An officer and a gentleman never breaks his word, you should have known that.'

'Well, I didn't.' Her tears began to fall, happy tears full of relief.

'Ah, you're sounding snotty again. I thought I'd come and book your wedding chapel. I've seen on the internet that it's been a big hit. I saw the grand opening on YouTube too – it looked fantastic.'

'Yes, it was perfect. Well, it would have been but something was missing.'

'Me?'

'A hotdog kiosk.'

Jacques threw back his head and laughed. The sound filled the forest. My God, how she had missed that ridiculously loud, annoying, rich-as-a-Christmas-cake boom of a laugh.

He was leading her towards a circular bench which had been fitted around one of the tree trunks. There was a brass plaque on it which read, 'In memory of Christopher, the biggest, best and most beautiful snow pony in the world.'

'Anyway it's 'our' wedding chapel. You might have made a letter of intent, Jacques, but I never accepted it. That would be going against Aunt Evelyn's wishes, so any profits due to you have been banked separately. Don't buy a penthouse yet, though. This is one big, expensive place to run. We're opening up a Christmas tree farm this

November, which should up our income. We've planted acres more. And we're extending Santapark.'

Jacques sat down. 'I hear you don't charge entrance fees for families of the military still.'

'No,' said Eve, sitting beside him.

'Any plans to end that?'

'No.'

He smiled a smile that reached right up to his blue eyes. 'Do you say no to everything?'

'No.' Eve's eyes began to twinkle too, like the little lamps hung between the trees.

Jacques put his hand on her cheek. It felt so soft. *She* looked soft. Her hair was loose and long around her shoulders and his fingers strayed to it. He had thought of this moment so many times, wondered how long he should leave it before returning. Gambling that she would miss him, think of him, have space in her heart for him at last.

'Dear Eve,' he said. 'You look beautiful with your Christmas tree eyes. Should I ever leave you again?'

'No,' she said, her mouth a smiling arc that wanted his placed upon it. *Now.*

'If I tried to kiss you, would you push me off?'

'No.'

'Do I need mistletoe in order to do that?'

'No,' she replied, and watched his mouth slowly and tantalizingly descend upon hers. As their lips touched, she felt him shift into the place in her heart which was ready and open for him with Jonathan's blessing. His kiss was like the best Christmases ahead of her, waiting for her to enjoy, all come at once.

Sometimes our light goes out but is blown into flame by another human being. Each of us owes deepest thanks to those who have rekindled this light.

Albert Schweitzer

Acknowledgements

As always a massive thank-you to the team at Simon & Schuster for their support, affection, kindness – and patience: Suzanne Baboneau, Ian Chapman, Nigel Stoneman, Maxine Hitchcock, Clare Hey, S-J, Ally, Dawn, Rumana, Georgina . . . everyone there. And to my darling agent Lizzy Kremer. It's always a bonus when you feel the people you work with are your friends too.

Thanks to my little son George for all the coffees whilst I was working – and to my big son Terence for setting up all the gadgets. What would I do without either of you?

Diolch o gallon i Owen Williams who has been an 'effin' godsend. I'm sorry I made you translate so much filth, Owen – especially as I rather enjoyed doing so.

Thanks to Yummy Yorkshire (www.yummy yorkshire.co.uk) for the ice-cream flavours inspiration.

The current size of my bottom is your fault.

Thanks to dashing Major Dan Jarvis MP for being both an officer and a gentleman and helping me with the military detail.

Thanks to my *Come Dine With Me* friend 'Party Paul' Hoyle – for being a top bloke, and Dennis Higgs for telling me all about dear Ben the lion who really did patrol his premises, like a nice frozen sheep's head on a warm day, go driving in the van with him and play football with a box in the yard. People can say what they like about Barnsley, but we know how to stop burglars.

And to Andrew Stenton at Billingley Christmas Tree Farm in Billingley S72 0JF (enquiries@ billingleychristmastrees.co.uk) for helping me with Christmas tree and reindeer details and letting me pet 'Comet', 'Cupid' and their lovely baby. Sometimes research is just too good.

CBS○drama

Whether you love the glamour of Dallas, the feisty exploits of Bad Girls, the courtroom drama of Boston Legal or the forensic challenges of the world's most watched drama CSI: Crime Scene Investigation, CBS Drama is bursting with colourful characters, compelling cliff-hangers, love stories, break-ups and happy endings.

Autumn's line-up includes Patricia Arquette in supernatural series Medium, big hair and bitch fights in Dallas and new Happy Hour strand daily from 6pm with a doublemeasure from everyone's favourite Boston bar Cheers.

Also at CBS Drama you're just one 'like' closer to your on screen heroes. Regular exclusive celebrity interviews and behind the scenes news is hosted on Facebook and Twitter page. Recent contributors include Dallas' Bobby Ewing (Patrick Duffy) CSI's Catherine Willows (Marg Helgenberger) and Cheers' Sam Malone (Ted Danson).

www.cbsdrama.co.uk

facebook.com/cbsdrama

twitter.com/cbsdrama